OUR GHC

JAMES CHAMBERS	CAROL GYZANDER
ALLAN BURD	MEGHAN ARCURI
CAROLINE FLARITY	MARC L. ABBOTT
TREVOR FIRETOG	ALP BECK
APRIL GREY	PATRICK FREIVALD
STEVEN VAN PATTEN	ROBERT P. OTTONE
JONATHAN LEES	LOU RERA
JOHN P. COLLINS	AMY GRECH
TEEL JAMES GLENN	ROBERT MASTERSON
GORDON LINZNER	OLIVER BAER
RANDEE DAWN	RICK POLDARK

EVEN IN THE GRAVE

—————— EDITED BY ——————

JAMES CHAMBERS and CAROL GYZANDER

NEOPARADOXA

PENNSVILLE, NJ

PUBLISHED BY
NeoParadoxa
a division of eSpec Books LLC
Danielle McPhail,
Publisher
PO Box 242,
Pennsville, New Jersey 08070
www.especbooks.com

ISBN: 978-1-956463-03-3
ISBN (ebook): 978-1-956463-02-6

Copy Editor: Greg Schauer, John L. French
Interior Design: Danielle McPhail

Cover Art and Design: Lynne Hansen, LynneHansenArt.com
Interior Art: Jason Whitley
Interior Icon @glassseeker, www.fotolia.com

"Moshigawa's Homecoming" originally appeared in *Rod Serling's Twilight Zone Magazine*, November 1981.
"Taps" first appeared in *Never Fear - The Apocalypse: The End is Near*, 13Thirty Books, 2015.
An earlier version of "The Source of Fr. Santiago de Guerra de Vargas' Monstrous Crimes" appeared in *The World of Myth Magazine* (no. 88, September 2020 and no. 89, October 2020). www.theworldofmyth.com

CONTENTS

"In death - no! even in the grave all is not lost."

-Edgar Allan Poe

INTRODUCTION

Ghost stories grow from the deepest roots of horror fiction.

Perhaps the earliest form of scary stories, they sprang from the minds of people trying to make sense of frightening experiences: death, the dark, the missing, the unexplained, and other mysteries. These universal experiences fostered ideas about ghosts and spirits in every culture in the world throughout history. From disembodied voices whispering on the wind outside the light of a campfire to spirits who decided if crops succeeded or failed; from Jacob Marley's ghost clanking his chains to Patrick Swayze's spectral pottery class; from psychic mediums and spiritualists to the contemporary gold rush of ghost hunters and paranormal investigators, ghosts — or at least the idea of them — have literally haunted us for all of human history.

Why shouldn't they? They explain the unexplainable. They provide reassurance that, perhaps, existence does not cease with death. They offer hope for the living to reconcile with injustices or unfinished business from the past. Whether you believe ghosts exist or not, they embody fundamental notions and questions about the nature of the human spirit. Too often, though, the answers are inconclusive or unsatisfactory.

Have you ever seen a ghost?

In some circles, that's the perfect cocktail party ice-breaker. As a writer of horror stories, I've been asked that more than a few times, and I've heard many others answer it. That's what it comes down to in the end. If you've seen a ghost, you're more likely to believe in them regardless of what mundane rationale might explain your experience as a quirk of shadows, light, and air. If you've never seen a ghost, chances are you're open-minded but dubious at best and a full-on skeptic at worst. Those ghost chaser shows haven't proven a thing in decades on the air. No one really believes in ghosts on the basis of a photograph alone, especially ones of mere blobs of light more suggestive of passing dust motes than apparitions. Belief seems to require a personal, tactile experience. Seeing a disembodied face while standing in a sudden cold spot. Hearing voices where none should be. Finding items in your home a touch out of place with no obvious explanation for the movement. Feeling an invisible presence over your shoulder. Very few people experience these things in a ghostly sense, and not all who do attribute them to ghosts. Yet many of us readers love ghost stories whether or not we believe in the reality.

Tales of specters, phantoms, and haints run a constant thread through horror fiction, one that branches heartily out to classic literature and to pretty much every other genre and sub-genre in some form or another. We know well the stories of restless spirits who only move on when their bones receive a proper burial, the departed who linger until the one who wronged them in life receives their comeuppance. We all know stories of angry ghosts, who seek revenge on the living, or hungry ghosts beseeching the living to sustain them. We all know those ghost stories that defy convention or usher us into the spectral world in unexpected ways. Fritz Leiber's classic story, "Smoke Ghost," brought ghosts out of graveyards and creaky old mansions and brought them into the heart of urban life. Toni Morrison's novel, *Beloved*, brought ghosts into the horrifying world of slavery. Films classics, such as *Ghostbusters*, put ghosts squarely in the pop culture arena, and there they remain today.

The ghost story is a deceptively adaptable type of tale. Writers and readers love to discover new ways to stretch its boundaries, reinvent it, place it into new and surprising settings, and create new ideas about ghostly manifestations. They love experiencing this old favorite in new designs. Ghost stories have come a long way from table-tapping seances and ectoplasmic projections. Yet the ideas those tropes represent — our desire to communicate with the dead, to see a manifestation of the afterlife in the living world — remain.

For *Even in the Grave*, Carol Gyzander and I asked authors to give us their vision of a ghost story. We placed no requirements on time, place, type of ghost, or any other story element except for one ironclad rule: the story had to include an *actual* ghost. No Scooby-Doo endings where we unmask old man Withers running around in a glow-in-the-dark ghost face to scare people off the old carnival grounds. Without exception, the stories in this book are ghost stories. Beyond that, they are each author's personal and inventive way of approaching this classic sub-genre and exploring themes of life and death, past and present, and where the boundaries and intersections between them lie. They take place in different times and locations, feature different types of ghosts, and range from humorous to melancholy to darkly frightening.

They and their authors remind us again why we love ghost stories.

James Chambers
February 2022
Northport, NY

Ghosts have intrigued me since Casper the Friendly Ghost was one of my buddies when I was a kid. I was an only child of only children. With no siblings, aunts, uncles, or cousins around, I spent a lot of time with my nose in books and comics, and developed a vivid imagination — why *couldn't* he come to play with me and be my friend?

As a student at Bryn Mawr College a decade later, I majored in anthropology, the study of a people's culture. Religion is one aspect of culture that shows a group's sense of cosmology and the role of individuals in their world. Ghost stories, while less formal than religion, also help to explore what happens after we are gone — both for those who have departed and the ones who remain.

I had the occasion to experience this myself when my grandmother, Alva, passed away. She was the one who taught me how to play cards, met my wacky humor with her own, and encouraged me to break out of my shyness. I was devastated by her loss. Alva appeared to me as a ghost, sitting at the kitchen table and dealing out a hand of gin rummy. Seeing her engaged in our favorite pastime was comforting and made me realize she still loved me even though she was gone. And that I wasn't alone.

My family also has a story about my other grandmother, Mother Evelyn. She had been in a nursing home with Alzheimer's but would frequently try to escape, saying she must get to the train so she could get home. One of my distant relatives dreamed he was visiting our *great*-grandmother, who had already passed away. They had a delightful visit until she heard a train whistle and said it was time for him to leave because Evelyn was coming. He woke up from the dream in the middle of the night—at the exact time that Mother Evelyn passed away. So, she was reunited with her family and wasn't alone, either.

Stories like these come out of the "real" world. Now imagine what happened when James Chambers and I sparked the creative minds of our local author friends and asked them to *create* a tale involving ghosts. Turn it up to eleven!

The result is this wonderful group of ghost stories. They span different locations and time periods, look at friendly as well as hostile ghosts, warm and encourage your heart—and some may stop it dead and cold.

Gather your courage and read on!

Carol Gyzander
February 2022
Bergen County, NJ

THE FINAL EXPERIMENT OF EUGENE APPLETON

ALLAN BURD

I thought I'd seen everything.

Then Eugene Appleton walked into my office.

A slight man with neatly combed, genuine silver hair, he wore a casual, button-down shirt neatly tucked into cuffed khakis, and rubber sole shoes. His pale complexion indicated he spent a disproportional amount of his time indoors. Nevertheless, he looked good for his age, which I approximated in the mid-fifties. A real professorial type, who I pegged as anything other than a college professor. I stared at his hands — clean fingernails, though not manicured, no callouses — and added post-graduate education to my assessment, figuring somewhere along the way he had earned a doctorate degree in something.

"You're Douglas Bowden, the bounty hunter?" He asked it as a question but meant it as a polite opener. He already knew the answer. My picture was all over the ads I ran. Broad shoulders, bulky frame, bushy hair, resting scowl face... you could say I had the look. No one who came to see me ever had to ask my name.

I flipped the lid off my cup of hot coffee and took a sip. "I prefer apprehension specialist. What can I do for you?"

"Apprehension specialist... I like that. Perfect, in fact, as I would like to hire you to help me apprehend something."

He had a brazen gleam in his eye when he said it. I didn't like brazen. "Some*thing*. Not some*one*? I'm in the people business, Mister...?"

"Appleton. Dr. Eugene Appleton."

I got the doctor part right. He extended his hand across my desk. I set my coffee down, rose out of my chair, and shook hands. "Nice to meet you, Dr. Appleton."

He looked at the wall behind me, which held mounted animal heads: an elephant and leopard, both from Africa, a buffalo, a rhino, and a lion. "You like to hunt?"

"I did. All I hunt now are fugitives."

"Big game. All of the big five. Very impressive."

I pulled up my sleeve and showed him the long scar on my forearm. "The lion almost got me. The bastard covered the hundred yards between us in under five seconds. My first kill almost killed me. One more second, and my head would've been in his den."

He chuckled. "Yet that didn't stop you from going on to kill the next four. You are a man who lives life unafraid."

The man had me chest-puffing, but I stayed humble. "It was a good life lesson, taught me to do better research ahead of time. This scar is a constant reminder to always be prepared." I leaned against my messy desk. "Which brings me to ask… what's this *thing* you need my help in apprehending? Because I don't hunt animals anymore, and I don't reclaim property. I'm not a repo man, and I'm most definitely not a burglar."

"Oh, it's neither of those things," he said. "This is something… unique."

"Well, I never take a case without knowing the specifics, so you might as well spill whatever water you're holding. Before you tell me, though—and I'll be right up front about it—I won't do anything illegal, nor will I take a job I deem unethical."

His expression didn't change. "It's neither amoral nor illegal. Though I can't tell you what it is without you immediately dismissing me. It's best if I show you."

I was about to dismiss him anyway, making our brief acquaintance even briefer, when he pulled out a check with my name on it for $10,000.

"That's incredibly generous, but no amount of money is going to make me do something I don't want to do."

"This is just for tonight. The show. Immediately afterward, I'll give you the tell." He handed me his address along with a legal contract. "You'll either accept the job or you won't. But I think you will. Just be mindful, I'm not looking to hire you just for your obvious skills. I'm also hiring you for your discretion. Pick me up at midnight. I'll show you what you need to know to make an informed decision. Then, even if you decline, as long as you've signed that non-disclosure agreement, the money is yours. However, if you accept, I'll give you ten times that amount on completion of the task."

After he left the office, I Googled him. The first thing that came up was his picture on the cover of multiple science magazines. One of the covers named him Scientist of the Year for 2036. Dr. Appleton was a Doctor of Physics, a renowned quantum physicist, to be precise. A year ago, an unfortunate car accident cost him his wife. Tough break. One that seemed to remove him from the spotlight.

I reviewed the legal document, a non-disclosure agreement to ensure my silence. It was standard stuff, and as a matter of principle, I never talked about my cases anyway unless required to do so by the law. Whenever a client asked me to sign an NDA, it usually meant more business with them down the road. I used my lucky pen and had my secretary deposit the check.

That night, I went to his place in my pickup truck, and I went heavy—a Glock 26 around my ankle and a Taurus PT-111 tucked in the waistband under my shirt—just in case there was more to this guy and the situation than met the eye. Two hours later, I reached the address and made a right through wrought-iron gates onto a black-topped road which led up a mile-long hill to a brick-laced Victorian mansion with a well-manicured front lawn, including some stylish topiary. Appleton wasn't just rich; he was *rich* rich.

He came out of his house wearing the same outfit he had on in my office and hoisted himself into the passenger seat. In his hands he held two pairs of high-end goggles with an overkill of tech. There was a touch screen on the frames along with a digitized readout that currently displayed triple zeroes beneath a flattened sine-wave line.

"Where are we going?" I asked.

"A place just outside of town. I'll direct you along the way."

When I got to the bottom of the hill and passed back through the gates, he instructed me to make a left. A few minutes later, we hit a main road, and he pointed straight ahead.

"I'm not big on surprises," I said.

"This one may change your mind. Tell me, Mr. Bowden, do you believe in the afterlife?" he asked.

His face was partially covered by shadow. I couldn't get a good read on him.

"For real?"

"Yes."

His cadence told me he was serious. "Fine. I'll play along. I do not."

"So no to ghosts, spirits, phantoms?"

"I don't put much stock in the paranormal. I'm a down-to-earth kind of guy."

After a long pause, he said, "I going to show you something... unusual. Something that conventional science doesn't explain. I trust you'll keep an open mind. Make a left here."

I pulled onto a tertiary road. Whatever else Appleton may have been, he was a man of science. Nothing about him screamed whack job. I looked over at him. "I'll deal with whatever it is just fine. Ghosts?"

"An entity that can't be seen by normal means."

"Is that what the goggles are for?"

"They allow their wearer to view into a narrow band on the electromagnetic spectrum in a way that's never been done before."

"Like night-vision goggles."

"Exactly... though these prototypes are far more advanced than that."

He pointed, and I made another left. Almost immediately, I noted the hundreds of rows of tombstones off the side of the road. "Seriously... you weren't being facetious with the ghost analogy. Pretty cliché, though."

"My claim to fame as a scientist is that I discovered a way to communicate at faster than light speeds, something previously thought impossible. Since my wife died, I shifted my focus to the possibility of communicating with those who passed. I broke one physical barrier thought unbreakable. Why not another? When one wishes to talk with the dead, you go to where the dead are. In doing so, I stumbled across something that fits the description of a ghost."

"Your wife? Is this where she's buried?"

A somberness compressed his expression. "No. She's buried with her parents a few hours from here. This is the closest cemetery to my house. A logical place where I could easily test my equipment. They don't lock the gate at night. You can drive right in."

I did, and he directed me to a section toward the back. We weaved along the narrow, paved paths, parked the car, then got out.

He handed me the goggles. "We have to walk from here. Put these on. They're preset to the correct frequency."

He put his on. I followed suit. Everything looked exactly the same except for a faint violet grid that overlaid the view. There wasn't any magnification. They didn't even have the green tint you had with night vision. Except for the barely visual grid, it felt like I had strapped on a pair of oversized swimming goggles. Appleton pointed up a slight incline, and we started walking.

"Everything looks the same," I said.

"The moon is bright, which obscures the initial glow. You'll see it plain as day once we're closer."

Halfway up the slope, I saw it: a faint pale radiance, as if someone had set off a dull magnesium flare. I lifted the goggles, and the glow disappeared. I slid them back on, and there it was again. Curiosity increased my pace. Appleton grabbed my arm to slow me down.

"No need to rush," he whispered.

I nodded and slowed. Once we went over the incline, the light took shape: a washed-out humanoid silhouette with no more substance than a shadow, undecipherable as male or female, not even necessarily human, completely undiscernible. Its back was to us. Its body cycled with spiky oscillating protrusions, which made the thing appear as an out-of-focus blur. In the top half of the lenses, the sine wave stuttered with uncertainty.

Instinctively, I reached for the gun in my waistband. Once again, Appleton grabbed my arm and stopped me. "That won't do anything. The bullets will pass right through it."

We moved closer. The entity didn't seem to notice us, or it knew we were here and simply didn't care. About thirty feet from it, I got a closer look. A thick back hunched over a grave as spindly extended limbs phased through the ground as if reaching for whatever lay beneath.

"You see," whispered Appleton. "It cannot make physical contact with our world."

"It certainly looks like it's trying," I whispered back. "And it's directly over a grave."

"For reasons unknown, it has an affinity, or perhaps a need, for human remains. I would like to discover why."

Curiosity overtook me again. I picked a pebble off the ground and tossed it at the entity. The pebble arced through the air and went right through it, landing on the ground at its feet. The entity stirred and swiftly spun toward us. Its blank oval head formed a black maw where a mouth would be as if an abyss had emerged from within it. Above the dark patch, hidden folds opened and flickered scarlet, like two blood-colored eyes. Its limbs pulled out of the ground revealing long finger-like tendrils that darkened from fluffy white to smoky charcoal. Then, with an unexpected burst of speed, it charged at me, maw widening as if releasing a silent scream, tendrils lashing out with terrifying intent.

I immediately thought of the lion. It was on me before I could react, yet the entity passed through me, sending a panicked chill through my spine. I stumbled back, fell on my butt, and instinctively grabbed the Glock from my ankle holster. Then I quickly got back to my feet and spun, scouting the area in search of my target, which was gone. All I saw was Appleton, hiding behind a granite tombstone.

"Put that away before you accidentally shoot someone. Namely me. It's gone," he said.

I was heaving breaths. My eyes darted about to make sure. Finally, I realized Appleton's assessment was correct and holstered my weapon.

Appleton came out of hiding and took off his goggles. For the moment, I kept mine on.

"How did you know?" I asked.

"Because every time I've disturbed it, that's what it's done. It won't be back until tomorrow." Appleton smirked. "So, what is your opinion now?"

I looked around again, reconfirming the entity was gone, then took off the goggles. I caught my breath, glared at the advanced optical device in my hand, and thought it over. "You programmed these, right? None of this actually happened. You planted a suggestion in my mind, then when we got here and reached a certain location, the goggles presented the visual you primed me to see."

"I could have done all that, and your skepticism is well-founded. However—assuming you researched me after I left your office—you would know I'm a principled man of science. What you saw, however bizarre, however unbelievable, was as real as you and me."

I've been around people long enough to tell when someone is lying. Every instinct I had told me Appleton wasn't. I shook my head. "Fuck me." We started walking back to the car. "You're really going to tell me that was a ghost, an honest-to-god ghost?"

"Are you familiar with quantum entanglement?"

I shook my head.

Appleton continued. "It's a phenomenon in physics. The physical laws we see every day, how objects move and react to other objects, all work differently at the quantum level. Picture two distinctively separate particles. By all accounts, they appear to have no connection to one another. However, in truth, they are connected, entangled on a quantum level by an invisible force that's too undetectable to see. So, what you do to one directly affects the other, no matter how far apart they are. Imagine spinning a tennis ball here, and a tennis ball in China spins with it, without ever having been touched."

"That makes no sense," I said.

"Einstein called it spooky action at a distance. It's the phenomenon I used to develop technology that allows for faster than light communications. Now, imagine the body and the soul are actually two separate objects similarly entangled. Because atomic particles also act like waves, I theorized if I could find the right quantum frequency on the deceased, then, perhaps, I could make contact with their souls. A few months back, I stumbled upon that... *thing*. I've been back at least four nights a week ever since, observing its movements. Every time I've tried to communicate with it, it reacted to me the same way it reacted to you. But it always comes back the following night. It doesn't always appear in the same place, but when it moves, it tends to linger awhile, as if it has a connection to the grave it hovers above."

"This is crazy."

"No... this is groundbreaking. Having seen it, Mr. Bowden, will you help me apprehend it?"

As nice as the money was, suddenly, dollars became a secondary concern. I had to know what it was. I had to see this through. "I will," I answered.

Appleton patted my shoulder and waved a finger on his other hand in the air. "Together, we will catch the biggest game of all."

The following evening, I showed up at his place an hour earlier so he could instruct me on how we'd be apprehending something that neither of us was able to touch. He unfurled a tightly knit high-tech net. It had a rectangular shape, and each twine was interlaced with thin filaments of fiber-optic wiring that filled the gaps. The much thicker perimeter featured conductive coils, numerous grips, and two digitized touch-screen control panels.

"This net bridges the gap between our frequencies. The outer portion resonates normally, while at the push of a button" — he tapped the display and a sizeable circular section on the inside glowed with a faint violet light — "the inner portion resonates out of phase with our perception of existence and into the frequency range where the entity exists."

"Seems pretty simple," I said.

"Simplicity is the soul of modern elegance," said Eugene, proud of his genius.

"Have you tested it?"

"Only on myself." Appleton dragged the net toward him then pushed his arm through the inner section, which no longer seemed to exist, as if there were a large round tear in the net's center. Then he tapped a button, causing the violet glow to disappear, and he grabbed the part of the net that was immaterial just a second ago.

I shook my head in disbelief. "You could give Houdini a run for his money. Or orchestrate one hell of a jailbreak."

"Only if the bars were solely made with neutral atoms and infused with treated ionic wire."

"Just what I was thinking," I muttered.

He instructed me on how to operate the net on my end. It all seemed easy enough, and if for any reason the net failed, all that would happen is the ghost, if that's what it was, would get free. And even if that happened, I'd still earn my full payment because faulty equipment on Appleton's part didn't nullify our deal. We loaded all the gear into Appleton's van, along with the goggles, and went on our way.

We reached the cemetery around 1:00 a.m. The weather was clear with a slight breeze. The crescent moon was bright enough to light our way. We donned our goggles, grabbed the net, and walked toward the graves where we saw the entity last night. There it was, in the same position, seemingly digging into the same grave. Its back was toward us, its oval head down.

We each grabbed one side of the net, spread about thirty feet apart, and cautiously approached. We tiptoed, careful not to disturb it prematurely and alert it to our presence. Appleton powered up the net, then without hesitation, just as it turned toward us, we threw the net over the spirit. It slumped under the unexpected weight, and before it could regain its balance, we twisted the net beneath it, sweeping it up so the net completely encircled the entity, making sure it couldn't disappear through the ground.

Its bottom limbs kicked out with a ferocity that billowed the glow. Its tendrils elongated and repeatedly jammed outward, forming lengthy spikes that threatened to tear the immaterial fabric. Its eyes roiled with scarlet rage that conjured thoughts of Hell. Its inky circular mouth formed shadowy teeth that caromed outward and snapped at the lattices. We struggled to hold on as if there were a great white shark entrapped in our fishing net.

"There's no way we can drag him out of here like this," I said.

Appleton's fingers started to bleed from the friction. If we ever did this again, I'd make sure we wore gloves.

"I prepared for this," said Appleton. He pressed a second button on the display, and the violet incandescence pulsed blue and cascaded through the fibers like a shockwave. The ghost's mouth inverted, its dark red eyes dimmed, and its essence paled, curled, and went still. The tension on the restraints relaxed as if all we held now was a weightless fluffy cumulus cloud.

"What did you do?"

Appleton wiped the sweat from his brow. "I disrupted its frequency. I wasn't even sure that would work, but it seems to have done the trick."

"Is it dead? I mean more dead. Dead again," I rambled. I didn't know what I was talking about or even if it was possible to kill a ghost.

"It's stunned. But I don't know for how long. We should move quickly."

The net felt as light as when we brought it. Appleton handed me his end, pointed to the shock button should it awaken, and I carried it solo back to the van while Appleton bandaged his hands. I gently placed the ghost in the back of the van then I remained in the rear with it while Appleton drove us back to his mansion. Thankfully I didn't have to press the button a second time.

Once home, we hustled it into Appleton's lab and placed it into a containment chamber Appleton had specially designed, literally by positioning the inner portion of the net within the chamber and de-activating it, so the ghost slipped free before the chamber's energy field locked it inside. A red button lit up, indicating do not open. The inner layer of the twofold glass glowed with incandescent violet, which meant both we and the ghost would only be able to touch the side of the glass we were on. The entity remained still, floating within the chamber like a harmless thicket of cotton.

"Mission accomplished," I boasted.

"Now I can learn about it, try to communicate with it, discover of what energy or matter it is made, ascertain its purpose."

I noticed a microscope on his workbench next to a rack of unused slides. Adjacent to that was a series of surgical blades along with some tweezers and two small scrapers. Each tool had on it a miniature version of the control display that was built into the net. I had no doubt that at the touch of a button, every instrument on that table would come alight with a telling violet glow.

He noticed where my eyes went. "A skin cell sample from it would be fascinating," he said.

He was right, but I didn't share his enthusiasm for lab work, and the entity looked like it was still inert. "I believe my work here is done," I said.

"It is. You were an enormous help. I will wire the funds into your account first thing in the morning. And remember, discretion is of the utmost importance. One day, hopefully soon, I will release my findings to the entire world."

I removed the goggles, reflecting how weird it was that without them, the chamber appeared empty. I extended my arm to hand them back.

"No, you keep them. I insist. If, as I suspect, this entity is not unique, I will be employing your services again."

Those words were like music to my ears. The catch was fascinating, and it was the easiest 100K I'd ever made. And the publicity, once I was allowed to tell the story, would make me the most renowned apprehension specialist in the world.

I put the goggles on again to glean one last look at the entity, which floated there like an innocuous clump of mashed potatoes. Nevertheless, I had to admit, more so than any other game I've bagged, that thing, a being of unknown origin which no one would see coming, was going to give me nightmares. I was glad he let me keep the goggles.

"I wonder how it's going to react when it wakes up."

Appleton chuckled. "I'm certain it and I will get to know each other quite well."

I showed myself to the door, absorbing the brisk night air and what we had accomplished this evening. We had captured something that no one else ever had before, perhaps undeniable proof that there was truly more to life and death in this universe than met the eye. Knowing that, I decided to keep the goggles on, at least until I got home. As I got in my pickup, I had no doubt that when Eugene Appleton was ready to reveal his findings to the world, the world would never be the same.

I shifted into drive and slowly descended down the hill, my mind drifting from thoughts of the unknown to thoughts of a bright future.

As I reached the large wrought-iron gates that promised exit and entry to Appleton's property, a glimmer, not from the moon, reflected in my rearview mirror. I adjusted the angle and saw a hoary silhouette floating toward the mansion across the dark backdrop of night.

I slammed my brakes and hurriedly glanced out the passenger window, seeing five more entities approaching with it. I glanced out the window on my side and saw three more pale shapes drifting toward the mansion. I faced forward, and coming straight at me was a swirl of charcoal and snow with blazing scarlet eyes. Blackened talons extended from its already lengthy limbs as it passed through the hood of my vehicle. Its head churned inside out, revealing circular rows of inky fangs like a boring drill bit about to cut a hole through me right after its talons sliced me to bits.

An instant later, it passed through me.

A biting chill echoed through my otherwise unharmed bones.

Then it phased out the back of the vehicle.

Shaking, I turned around and watched it soar up the hill, an angry fog with a specific purpose.

I jammed the car into reverse, hit the gas pedal, and spun the wheel, executing a quick one-eighty onto the lawn. Then I thrust the gear into drive and sped back up the hill, watching at least twenty more entities descend upon the house, their swirling, opalesque presences whooshing through the roof and the walls.

The curves of the road prevented me from driving too fast. Every second felt like a minute too long as I swerved repeatedly to get back to the front entrance. Once there, I rammed the pickup into park and leapt out. Two ghosts exited the wall near me and drifted upward. A third right behind them stopped right in front of me, pausing my stride. Its eyes burned a citrine orange glow. Its tendrils surrounded me like an octopus with dozens of limbs.

I swung my arm through it, remembering that just as I couldn't touch it, it couldn't touch me.

I reached the front door, grateful I hadn't thought to lock it, and pushed my way through. Two more ethereal entities swooped toward me. Despite their horrifying teeth and orbs that resembled rotten burning cherries, I ran through them, knowing that physically all they really amounted to was a pair of nightmarish mirages. Once I reached the lab, I smashed through the door in time to see the last of the entities flee through the ceiling.

Violet sparks sizzled like discarded fireworks from the now-empty containment chamber. I stepped further into the room, seeing spatters of blood on the cabinets and on the floor, along with the tools that previously lay on the workbench and other tools I hadn't known were there. My next steps allowed me to see the cause.

Eugene Appleton, a true visionary, genius, and pioneer who ventured far beyond the known boundaries of the laws of physics, lay lifeless on the floor. One of his eyes was popped out and hanging by the stem. The top of his head was missing, his brain neatly above it as if it gently spilled out the top of his skull. The view below his head was equally severe. His chest was ripped open, a sternal retractor that vibrated with violet energy still in place, leaving his lungs on full display. His heart was cut away at the arteries and leaned on its side against the open cavity. Rib shears that vibrated with the same glow lay next to his body, along with his liver and a single kidney. And next to Appleton's brutally murdered, dissected mass of sinew and bone, was a message scrawled with his blood.

"If you study us, we will study you."

Eugene's final experiment had worked. He had indeed successfully communicated with the dead.

I AM HELEN ANNE GUNTHE

Caroline Flarity

I thought I knew love when I met my husband Frank, God rest his soul, but then my baby son curled his tiny fingers around my hand, his nails like perfect crescent moons. A mother's love is all-encompassing and never fades or dies.

Before his father left to fight the Germans in the first war, young Arthur followed him around the house, imitating his every gesture. Frank carved Arthur a wooden razor and tried not to smile as the boy carefully moved the maple chip across his hairless cheek.

Almost a year after Frank departed, there was a hollow knocking at the door. The telegram said that Frank died of pneumonia. *It is my painful duty to inform you…*

Soon after, a letter arrived from my husband's trench mate. He wrote that they had to stand in the pits for days. These pits filled with rainwater until the skin on their legs peeled away, allowing dirt and disease to seep into their bodies. He wanted me to know that my husband stood for as long as he could, and that the last words he said before collapsing were our names.

I sat my son down at the kitchen table and read him the letter. We huddled together, his cheek pressed against mine. Our tears seeped into the paper clenched in my hands and stained my fingers blue with ink.

"You're my little man now, Arthur," I said. "You're all I have left."

As a child, my son dreamed of armies of stick people. Many nights I heard the creaking of his mattress as he thrashed about in bed. I rushed to his side and held down his flailing limbs until he woke.

"I can't stop," he'd say between gulping sobs. "I'm marching with them, and if I stop, they'll all fall."

The second war came, and then Arthur, too, left home, even more handsome than his father in uniform. He was a soldier in the first battalion to liberate the prisoners from the German camps. When the war ended, he came home and crouched beside my bed, allowing me to shower his face with kisses despite my sour breath. I pretended not to notice his clenched fists and that his eyes had lost their softness. It was a bitter, wet winter, and I was very ill.

"You make your old mother proud," I'd say when the words would come. More often than not, the phlegm and blood in my throat choked them back, and Arthur would look away.

Before I was confined to my sickbed, Arthur's muffled cries again broke the silence in the hours before dawn. Once more, I rushed to his bed and concentrated my waning strength on holding down his twisting limbs. He was stronger than me now. I had to scream his name to wake him. He shot straight up in bed and fixed his eyes on mine, his body tight as an archer's bent bow.

"They couldn't get the food down," he said. "I saw it in their throats as they tried to swallow."

"You are a hero, Arthur! You saved them. Oh, my darling. It's over now, and everything will be just as it was."

"No, it won't, Mother. It will never be the same."

His hands were callused now and deeply lined, stained with dirt and gunpowder that never washed away. They gripped my arms and forced me back. My face burned with the shock of it.

"We gave them our rations, the dried meats. We didn't know what we were doing. They started choking. It was too rich, too dry!"

He started going into town again and met a woman he soon married. As I lay in bed, my lungs slowly rotting, his young bride hovered in the background. She was a shifty-eyed sort and not much of a looker. The first time I saw her was on their wedding night. They both smelled like cigarettes and whiskey, and she wore a yellow wedding dress that revealed her impurity.

"Hiya, Mrs. Gunthe," she said, my son's hand in hers.

I watched in horror as her crimson-smeared mouth opened to reveal a gap-toothed, nicotine-stained smile. I turned my head into my pillow and willed it to be a dream.

Wherever Arthur was, she lingered nearby like a funhouse shadow. The little harlot could barely keep her hands to herself, always marking him as her territory. As if she could ever comprehend the bond that Arthur and I shared. I carried him inside my body, gave him life at my breast.

I referred to her as Eleanor the Whore. Poor Arthur lost his sense of humor in the war and left my bedroom whenever I did. I suppose it was too much to bear at times, the sound of my wheezing laughter and how the blood sometimes sprayed from my throat.

One night I dreamed of my dead husband, Frank. He was young again and beautiful.

"Come now, my darling," he said and offered me his arm.

"Where are we going?"

"Home," he said.

"But what about Arthur? I can't leave him alone with that woman. He needs me now, and I need him."

He reached for me, his eyes smiling and patient, and it took all my strength to shrink back from his touch. A hollow knocking filled my ears, and my husband's face wavered like a heat mirage. I pointed an ink-stained finger at him.

"You should have stood longer! Arthur and I were all alone. We only have each other now, and I will never leave him!"

I fell away from him until he was just a pinpoint of light in the distance. The next morning the pain was gone, and I was free. After suffering the confines of my bed so long, I rushed through my house, eager to explore every room that held the echoes of my husband's laughter and the footprints of my baby boy.

"Arthur, Arthur, I can walk! Arthur, I can run, and there's no more pain."

But there was no answer. I retreated to my bedroom for my slippers, and that's when I saw it. Something ghastly lay in my bed. Blood-red eyes bulged out of its head. Its lips were cracked and covered with congealed black scabs. Its swollen face was an explosion of webbed purple veins inside gray skin that hung in folds of flesh as thin as rice paper.

I fled to Arthur's room and hid beneath his bed, tucked between the bedpost and the wall, where the dust collects. I waited there, watching the rising sun hit the wooden floorboards countless times.

I knew with a certainty that could never be questioned that I must not ever again lay eyes on the thing that sank into the center of my bed, transforming the mattress into a pus-filled boil of stink and rot. Instead, I focused on how excited Arthur would be to see me well again. There was nothing to do but wait for him to come home.

Time passed, and my house was torn down and built up again, getting uglier with each transformation. Eventually, it was abandoned in ruins. The earth swallowed it up until all that remained was thick with weeds and bramble alongside a black serpent of a road. Despite my constant prayers, Arthur never returned. Then, at last, I could take no more, and my heart shattered and fell away, leaving only a tiny shard that held the memory of Arthur.

The pieces of my fallen heart collected under me and caught fire. The flames burned with a trembling rage and bursts of grief so intense that they propelled me upwards, high above the trees, tunneling through the clouds into the darkening sky. I floated there and dreamed only of Arthur's face, his tiny moon-shaped fingernails, wondering how he could ever find me in the fog of clouds.

Far in the distance lay a black cloud, impenetrable despite the rays of the setting sun. It made no sound but instead emanated a *lack of noise* that nonetheless had great resonance, like the sound of air moving aside as knuckles fall hard against wood. From within the cloud came a simple truth.

Arthur cannot find you here, but you can look for him down there.

I looked down at the earth and the knowledge that Arthur was somewhere below flooded through me. The remaining sliver of my heart swelled with joy. I looked up at the dark cloud and drifted closer to it, sensing movement inside, a simmering. Then, for the first time in what seemed like eternity, I heard the voice of my son.

Mommy? Mommy, I can't stop, or they'll all fall.

I moved like a bolt of lightning, following his voice down to the towns and snaking roads, soaring across rooftops, hope heaving through me. I swooped down a chimney into a strange house and crawled across a floor toward the sound of my son's voice. I climbed atop a small bed and reached out to settle the flailing limbs of a sleeping boy crying out for his mother. A boy who was not Arthur at all. Arthur was not freckled and pink like a piglet splattered with mud!

I returned to the sky, circling the perimeters of the dark cloud, now blacker than the moonless night. The wind died before it. Billowing columns of ash collapsed and expanded, opening holes in the cloud that emanated a low pulse. I listened.

Now when I hear the calling and fly down to find not my son, but yet another imposter, I want to kill them, crush them, and rip them apart. I sit on their chests and scream into their faces, yet they do not hear me.

You are not my son. Where is my son? You sniveling little bastard, you motherless sewer rat, tell me where he is, or I will suck and smash the breath out of you and keep pushing until your puny chest caves in and your ribs crack open and tear into your guts.

There are some that hear the scraping of my nails as I drag myself across their bedroom floorboards. When I pounce on their chests, their faces freeze into grimacing masks of fear, their breath escapes in thin whistles. As loud as I scream, they do not hear, but they feel. Yes. They feel their frozen limbs sink under my menacing weight.

As I straddle them, smother them, my gray hair cascades down my back like the proud mane of a predator. I push with all my strength, but I cannot penetrate the light that surrounds them. There is no choice but to shoot through the roof and fly into the night sky, higher still until the lights of the cities are obscured by the mist.

Mommy, Mommy, where are you?

I hear Arthur's voice even as the cloud feeds me. I can fly higher now and dive down with the speed of a hawk, dropping its claws for the kill. The dark cloud promises that I will soon slash through their light and shred them into pieces so small that they'll rise like hot ashes in the air.

The dark cloud churns and boils. It wants to consume me, and I want to go to it, join with it, surrender to it.

There is no light in here, it says. *There is nothing to stop you from tearing and pulling, choking and ripping.*

I understand what the cloud wants in return for the power it promises. It wants the little piece left of my heart, my memory of Arthur. In exchange, I can destroy the vile impostors in their beds. No past with

Arthur, no future with Arthur. Time does not exist in the cloud, only the constant present, the annihilation of the Light.

Moving closer, I see the blackness rolling into itself, a swirling promise of hunger satiated with pure and perfect hate. And closer still, I surrender my son, screaming. If Arthur could hear my cry, he'd cover his ears against the roar of grief louder than the thunder. As the light is extinguished, Arthur's sweet face leaves me forever.

The cloud lies.

AUTHOR'S NOTE: *This tale was inspired by the infamous Old Hag Syndrome, a form of sleep paralysis usually reported by men who claim that an evil hag sits on their chests and tries to smother them in their beds. I wondered, who is the "old hag"? This is her story.*

WHAT'S YOUR SECRET?

TREVOR FIRETOG

The host has a classic style—buttoned suit, long black tie, and slicked-back hair. Even though the show is black-and-white, you can somehow tell his suit is blue. He's seen with a lit cigarette between his fingers but rarely ever takes a drag.

The show always starts the same. The host, Carey Holland, stands in front of the camera. It's framed in a tight close-up on his face, nothing but darkness behind him.

"Hello, my name is Carey Holland, and I have a secret to tell you. Behind these curtains, we are hiding a special guest. However, this guest has a secret of their own. Over the course of this evening, we will find out exactly what they're hiding. I just told you my secret, what's yours?"

The audience claps as he steps back. The camera pulls out as the lights illuminate the set, revealing the game show's name in big light-up letters over the host's desk. To his right, a panel of three celebrity judges sits behind a long table.

This show's format is simple, possibly overly so. Sitting together on one side of a plain set, each of the panelists takes a thirty-second turn questioning and then guessing the contestant's secret.

Many other game shows of the same style use up to four contestants throughout the night. However, in this episode of *What's Your Secret?* there is only one contestant.

It is always the same person.

Every single night.

Same guest, same panelists, same questions. However, if you watch closely enough, you can see the slight differences.

Carey Holland usually holds his cigarette with his right hand, but one time he perched it between the fingers of his left hand. Once, during his opening speech, he gave a slight pause as if fumbling over his own words. A few nights ago, one of the celebrity panelists, Gerry Jones, sneezed while Holland introduced them.

After Carey Holland's introductions, they bring out the guest from behind a red velvet curtain. Like Carey's suit, the color seems obvious, even in this black-and-white broadcast.

She takes her place on a wooden stool next to the host's desk. Her blonde hair sits shoulder length, and she squints at the stage lights. There is an S-shaped scar on her chin. She's young, maybe in her twenties. The 1950's style of clothing makes her look much older.

Carey Holland doesn't introduce her. Never says her name. Instead, Carey explains the rules. She has to respond *yes* or *no* and nothing in between. Other programs like this display the person's secret or occupation on the screen for the audience right before the questions start. This show doesn't do that. The audience knows nothing more than the panelists.

Carey Holland starts by offering a hint.

"This young lady's secret concerns some place where she spent some time. Mr. Jones, we'll start with you."

Gerry Jones always goes first.

—Some place where she spent some time…

Pause for audience laughter.

—Is it a resort of some kind?

—No.

—Well, it's not prison, is it?

More audience laughter. The girl laughs as well.

—No.

When she says no, she shakes her head, blonde hair swaying.

—An institution of some kind?

More laughter. Sounds canned, like they're playing the same track over and over.

—No.

—That's a relief. Now is this the kind of place you went to of your own accord?

—Yes.

Jones pauses here to rub his forehead. Once he dabbed the sweat away with a handkerchief, but tonight he simply rubs a palm over his forehead.

—Was this for research or any kind of experiment?

—No.

—Were you at this—

The buzzer sounds.

"Go ahead and finish your question, Mr. Jones," Carey Holland says.

—Were you at this place by yourself?

—No.

This show reminds me of the ones I used to watch with my mother. We'd sit on the couch for hours, watching reruns whenever I was home sick from school. Sweet moments from beautiful days that have long passed. I wish those days never had to end.

The shows, however, were never like this.

Next panelist is Rita Lewis. She doesn't make much progress during her allotted time. Instead, she prefers to make jabs at her colleagues and get the audience laughing.

It goes on like this for a while. Every now and again, Holland takes a commercial break. The advertisements are for products that no longer exist.

Get richer looking, better tasting, more appetizing results in everything you bake or fry. Get Golden Fluffo.

Right before the broadcast fades back into static, the third panelist, Walter Boyle, quizzes her. He's the oldest of the three, and wears thick, plastic-framed glasses. His accent is British, and he has an odd habit of giving a short, throaty chuckle after every one of his questions.

—Did you have fun at this place?

—No.

—Is this the kind of place where I should go?

—No.

—Was this a building of some kind?

—No.

—So, this place is found in nature?

—Yes.

The picture flickers, static dances across the screen.

Every night they air one more question than the previous night.

I've never seen any of these people before. Carey Holland, Gerry Jones, Rita Lewis, and Walter Boyle don't exist. You can't find anything about them online.

The girl doesn't look familiar at all.

—Is this the kind of place where I should go?
—No.
—So, this place is found in nature?
—Yes.
—It's not a building of some kind?
—No.
—Oh, well, that puts me at a bit of a loss for the moment. I was sure I was on the right track.
Buzzer.

"Well, that's just fine, Walter," Carey Holland cuts in. "Because we're going to circle back and begin again with Gerry. Gerry, your time begins now."

I have never seen this girl before. I know nothing about her, and I have to make assumptions based on what little I do know. It's impossible to tell how she dresses or wears her hair outside of this show because one can assume she received this wardrobe before the broadcast.

If she has an accent, I can't tell from the one-word answers she's giving.

The S-shaped scar on her chin defines an otherwise plain-faced girl. It's the kind of scar a lover might trace their finger along.

"Gerry, your time begins now."
—So, you were at this place with someone, but did you go there alone?
—No.
—Did you go with a friend?
—No.
—A parent or family member?
—No.
—Someone you just met?
—No.

—Was it a lover?

A mixture of woos and laughter from the audience.

—Yes.

If I'm not watching TV, the television set turns on by itself. If I leave it unplugged, I still hear their voices, coming very faintly through the speakers. If I yank the plug out while the broadcast is playing, the TV powers down, but an image of the game show stays on the screen for a while, lingering like a ghost.

Sometimes, if I'm not home, the game show starts playing on my phone. If I log into YouTube, every single video is of this game show.

The game show *What's Your Secret?* does not exist.

Rita's turn to question her.

—So, was it a date of some kind?

—Yes.

—Are you sure we're allowed to ask more questions about it? We need to be TV-appropriate.

Audience laughter.

—Yes.

—Was it live entertainment? Like a play or a concert or something like that?

—No.

—How about a party? Do kids party in the woods?

More laughter.

—No.

—Was it an activity of some kind?

—Yes.

A long, silent stare from Rita. The audience cheers.

—Are you *sure* we can talk about it on prime-time television? Remember, this is a family show.

—Yes.

Why should I know her? She's from the '50s. They haven't even mentioned her name. There's no way I would know who she is. If she's even still alive today, she must be older than my grandma.

Back to Walter.
—An activity of some kind, huh? Was it a sport?
She looks to Carey for confirmation because, of course, he's in on her secret.
"Some could consider it a sport, but for the sake of this show, let's go ahead and say no."
—Okay, so not exactly a sport, but still a strenuous activity.
—Yes.
—Wasn't a question, my dear, but I'm still glad you answered.
Laughter.
—Did this take place on a boat?
—No.
—What about in the water at all?
—No.
—Okay, well, how about mountain climbing?
—Um...
"I'm going to jump in and speak for our lovely guest here. The answer is no." Carey Holland says.

That scar could be from a bike-riding incident when she was just a little girl. She and her friends were riding along the road when she hit a patch of sand. She lost control of the bike and landed on the glittering remains of a broken bottle. She probably screamed and cried and bled for hours while her friends looked on helplessly, all afraid to tell an adult because she wasn't supposed to have friends over.

I've seen this show every night for the past eleven years. Every single night. If I try to spend the night out camping or in a hotel, I still hear it playing on the TV in the next room or echoing somewhere deep in a forest. No one else sees the show. I've made other people sit and watch it with me, but they're only staring at static. Everyone thinks I've gone insane. I keep a notepad of all the differences, anything that might help me figure out why they haunt me.

I got married two years ago. Haven't told my wife about this, and I'm afraid to. I set up a TV in the shed. I call it my *mancave*, and she never questions me when I go in there every night.

It's pointless to avoid the show, you see. It'll always find me. Best thing to do is embrace it. The show only runs for a little over twenty minutes so far. There are still another ten minutes left. The way it's going, I'll probably finish the show in another five years.

I need to embrace it.

I admit I know the girl on this show.

Gerry's turn.
—So, could this be considered camping?
—Yes.
—You went camping with your boyfriend?
—Yes.
—And is it safe to say that something happened on that camping trip?
—Yes.
—Something not good? Or maybe something quite sad?
—Yes.
—Which one?
She looks at Carey Holland. He nods.
—Yes.
The audience laughs.
—Did you not come back from camping?
She's smiling now. So is Carey Holland.
—Yes.
—Yes, you didn't?
—Yes.
—Are you dead?
—Yes.
Buzzer sounds.

You can construct any narrative you want, the way I have. You can lie to yourself, as I have done. You can gouge out your eyes or slide needles into your ears to burst your eardrums, so you'll never make it to the end of this show, as I have contemplated doing.

If I do that, I'm scared the show will play on repeat inside my own head. The voices of Carey Holland and the celebrity panelists will echo in my skull until the show reaches its conclusion.

The cast of the show likes it when we watch. I'm sure I'm not the only one who's seen this show. It has played for many people, although the guests and questions may be different.

This is my episode.

It's just a show. They're trapped in a TV, and luckily for you and me, we're able to watch it from the comfort of our own beds or couches. We're warm, under our blankets. We can get up and go make popcorn or crack open a beer. You and I are alive. The people in the show, Carey Holland, the panelists, the girl, even the laughing audience have all died.

It's best you and I remain where we are.

"Ladies and gentleman, I want to jump in here and say that we're getting close to uncovering the rest of this young lady's secret, so I'm going to forfeit the remainder of the round and have her tell you."

The camera cuts to a close-up of her face. Her doe eyes reflect the studio lights.

"Well, myself and my boyfriend had planned a romantic weekend in the woods, on a camping trip. It was his idea, but I was always excited to try camping for the first time."

She pauses here to giggle. She's smiling and hesitating, almost afraid to continue as if she might fall into a giggling fit.

"Please, go on," Carey Holland says. The audience cheers their support.

"He got drunk, and we were in a fight, and he hit me."

"Oh, no, that's too bad." Carey Holland says with a smile.

"When he realized what he'd done, he tried choking me." She speaks calmly, almost cheerfully. As if this has been rehearsed. "But it didn't work because he was too drunk and kept falling over. I tried running away, so he picked up a rock. There was a flash of white, and the last thing I heard was him saying how sorry he was, and when I looked up, he was clutching the rock. He raised it above his head and…"

She pauses here, giggling more.

"Now, I understand you have a souvenir of the incident? Is that right?" Carey Holland says.

She smiles at him, nods, then turns around and lifts her blonde hair. Beneath is a wet crater in her skull. The studio lights give it a bright sheen. It looks bumpy, like spoiled hamburger. Fresh blood pools on her shoulders.

"Oh, well, would you look at that," Carey Holland says.

The audience laughs.

She lets her hair fall back down and then glances into the camera.

We zoom out, showing the rest of the set, along with Carey Holland and all the panelists looking directly into the camera.

There should be ten minutes left. There should be more questions, more laughter, more giggles from her.

They're only looking at the camera, staring at me.

That's how they spend the next ten minutes, silently watching me.

Every single night after that, the show doesn't play again, or at least doesn't play the way it used to. Now they spend the entire thirty minutes staring directly at the camera.

There are still breaks for advertisements of long-forgotten products. Those products were real at one time, that much I know to be true.

Try Wilkens Coffee – It's Just Wonderful!

When the show returns, it flickers back to the whole cast watching me. They know I'm here; they know I'm shaking.

Maybe they want me to admit it. To come clean. I've tried apologizing to her. I've tried getting on my knees and praying to the TV, letting her know how sorry I am. How I've changed. How I don't deserve this.

Every night is still the same, and I'm not sure what it will take to end this nightmare. I've tried everything. There's one more thing left to try, but it's the end of all things. Not just this nightly game show, but every joy I've ever felt or what's left to feel. I'm afraid my life won't end, but I'll wake up somewhere in a black-and-white world, maybe trapped inside a 1950's game show.

So, there it is. I've told you my secret.

What's yours?

HOUSE OF CRACKS

April Grey

I paid the taxi driver and, ignoring the pain in my shoulder, retrieved my backpack and wheeled bag, struggling with my one good hand.

Just beyond the side-street pavement of the building loomed a huge garden. My mouth gaped, and I wondered how such a garden could exist in midtown Manhattan. Skyscrapers defined the City that Never Sleeps. Yet, only a few blocks away from Central Park, a frozen winter oasis glittered.

January wind blew hard off the river, and I stamped my feet while my good hand struggled with my backpack, feeling for the scrap of paper with the name and number of the person holding onto the keys for my sublet. The sound of rustling leaves dragged my gaze to the garden. A dust devil swirled the leaves up in a cone on the eclectic brick and stone pathway. It had to be at most twenty degrees Fahrenheit today, even colder with the wind chill. The garden ran along the length of the back of the building and was as wide as it was deep. Remnants of the last snowfall nestled in shadowed nooks around the thick roots of the willow tree and the stone steps meandering around the garden past the tree.

Someone sat on a stone bench in there — I made her out through the metal bars in spite of the glaring, winter sunlight. I blinked, and the person vanished. Maybe just my imagination, a side effect of my medication, or she'd moved behind the huge willow overshadowing the bench.

A gust of wind tried to rip the paper from my hand.

Shaking my head, I pressed the buzzer and waited.

I studied the red brick tenement before me. It was covered with ivy on the garden side, and the lobby and back apartments with their fire escapes had garden views. Looking up, I counted five stories. I hoped there was an elevator, despite the cheap price—amazingly cheap even for Craig's List sublets. The front of the building facing the avenue was outside my line of sight.

"Sergeant Rosa Leone?" from the speaker came a broken, tinny voice.

"Yes," I managed from frozen, trembling lips.

The buzzer hummed. I pinned the door open with my bad shoulder and pulled my luggage through. After a second door, I reached the lobby.

From duct tape on the elevator door dangled a sign, handprinted with green crayon on the back of an envelope: *Out of order.*

A deep groan escaped my lips. There were no ground-floor apartments. So, the apartment I had sublet, 4B, was actually on the fifth floor, not the fourth.

What other surprises now?

Slipping the backpack onto my shoulder and grasping my heavy wheeled bag with my right hand, I trudged up a narrow staircase in search of apartment 3C, where I could pick up my keys. Since my injury, I'd let myself go—what I could normally have run, I now huffed and puffed, cursing my useless left arm and clinging to the right wall. If I lost my balance and tumbled backward, I could easily break my neck. The thought made me cling harder.

An assorted medley of scents: disinfectant, boiled cabbage, and mold lurked in the stairwell. Cracks ran up and down the walls, in spite of what looked like a fresh plastering job.

I put down my wheeled bag and slipped off my backpack when I reached the right landing.

"There you are," a frail voice quavered.

I abandoned my bags to search out the source.

In a dark doorway, a woman of about my age bent over a walker. Her hair was a natural red, but freckles covered her dark skin. I assumed that she had rheumatoid arthritis, though I wasn't a doctor; nothing else made sense that a youthful woman should be so stricken. She wore mismatched sweaters and black sweatpants. A striped, blue blanket wrapped around her bony shoulders. Fumes of Bengay wintergreen ointment stung my eyes.

I gasped, "Elevator's out."

With an eye on my bad arm, she nodded with the inscrutability of a smelly Yoda. "It's out about four days a week. You're just lucky you didn't get stuck in it. Though I dare say, you've dealt with worse?"

I swallowed my anger. Not her fault, and judging from the walker, she couldn't take the stairs and so was trapped here. As much as I hated my infirmity, there were others worse off—now ghosts, or those who left bigger chunks of themselves on the desert sand than I had. Pete, with his guts dangling, Judy dragging herself to help him though she lacked feet. *Go away!* I silently implored them.

Her knotted hand presented me with an envelope, dragging me back to reality. "Mr. DeCastro is in the Dominican Republic with his cousins. He won't be back 'til after Easter. He left you his keys."

"One more flight up?" My legs trembled.

"You have any questions, you can ask me." Her blanket slid off one shoulder. "To save time—heat is off during the day and comes on right when people come home. Oil costs money, so we don't waste heat here. Pipes are rusty, so just let the water run a bit before you use it." With a pained lurch, she shrugged the blanket back on. "Garbage room and laundry are in the basement, as is Mr. Strunk, our super, but you best leave him alone. He doesn't take to being bothered."

"Isn't that his job?"

Her face twisted into a rictus mask. "Don't rightly know." As she closed her door, I thought I heard a chuckle.

Rather than struggle with my backpack to get it over my dead arm, I made two trips for the final flight.

A dim skylight over the stairwell spat out a sliver of light for the top floor. I walked to the back of the hallway to find my apartment. My determined jiggling of the key in the lock persuaded the door to open with a groan.

I jumped at a loud bang from the back of the rooms.

"Who's there?" I stepped inside, leaving the front door ajar as an escape route. "It's okay, Mr. DeCastro sublet his apartment to me. My name is Leone… Rosa."

A breeze swept the hair off my face. Another slam. Had he left a window open? I shivered; it was colder in the room than outside.

I edged my way in, fingers itching for a pistol. Like everywhere else, cracks ran along the walls and ceilings. In the tiny galley kitchen, I noted that the tiles on the floor were cracked, but none missing.

Another slam.

Crab walking down the shadowed hallway away from the entry-way, I yanked open a door leading to a clean but dingy bathroom. Hardly enemy territory. I forced myself to breathe.

Bam! The door to the bedroom closed and then slowly creaked open again. I glimpsed the bed through the open doorway. Another gust and the door slammed again.

The door latch obviously wasn't securing it against the gusts of air, but I had my knit scarf. Once draped over the inner and outer door handles, it formed a good cushion. Again, the door slammed, but noiselessly and then shimmied open with a creak.

A double bed sat in the corner of the room, neatly made with a heavy quilt and extra blanket, both in shades of gray, folded at the foot of the bed. There was a closet with space cleared out for me. With little room left, a bureau and wooden chair were crammed in between the door and the bed.

I inspected the window where a draft lurched in between the rotted sill and lower rail—a wadded newspaper the length of the window frame on the floor. It fit the crack perfectly.

No more breeze. The door quieted its antics.

Still, it was cold. I touched the radiator, lukewarm.

The beauty of the windswept, crystalline garden distracted me. A spot of black crept into my vision. Down along the fire escape, it flowed gracefully with a flash of two pale green eyes set in glossy, well-kept fur.

Someone's cat was on the prowl.

Though I was tempted to open the window, lure it in and find its owner, it seemed to know what it was doing—stalking a plump gray mourning dove the next flight down. It leapt, and the dove headed off, landing in the limbs of the large willow tree with the bench.

I imagined the bird giving the cat "the bird."

The midday sun fled, hidden behind a towering apartment building on the opposite side of the street. Another gust of wind howled, this time creaking the ceiling, threatening to rip the roof off. The front door, which I had left ajar, slammed shut. No one there, just the wind.

Chilled to the marrow, I clicked the bathroom's fluorescent light and turned on both taps. The smell of mildew battled disinfectant. The tiles on the shower were cracked and tinted orange. Water tumbled out of the spigots.

Blood. Pinned on the ground by something heavy and oily, maybe part of our vehicle's engine? Sand gritting my teeth, covered in stickiness, my own and my friends'. The fire in my shoulder flamed white hot; I suffocated on acrid smoke from our burning Humvee, my chest rising and falling uselessly like a fish out of water. Judy dragging her body, a trail of red from where her ankles dumped her life. She called his name. Flies lit on his shiny purple innards, ready to feast.... Judy needed tourniquets to survive, but I was —

The pipes rumbled and strained. The water ran clear again, having voided the bloody rust from its pipes, and I was back in the present, running a bath.

Just as my body relaxed in the soothing warmth, the water ran cold. I should have taken the hint from being told they shut off the heat during the day. Shivering in the cold bathroom air, I wrapped myself in a towel and hurried to the bedroom to bury myself under the blanket before my body lost its heat.

An unsettling thought—bedbugs! Everything else was wrong with this building, so why not some nasty pests waiting to feast on me? I held tight to my towel, heat drifting away into the freezing room as I peeled back the bottom sheet. I knew all about vermin from my deployment. If it could sting or bite, I'd already met it. And hopefully whacked it with my boot.

Would the lack of heat discourage them, or maybe I'd be seen as the second coming and their savior by showing up as they were about to turn blue. Then they'd drive a line of bites down my body, which would quickly turn into burning, itchy welts. I sniffed the mattress for the distinct raspberry odor of bedbugs.

No telltale scent. I then searched for little red dots. None.

I stripped the mattress anyway and put on fresh sheets I'd brought with me. Extra blankets were neatly folded in the top of the closet.

Yet again, frozen to the core, I slipped into the arctic-cold sheets and shook as I hugged the blankets around me. I thawed and drifted into sleep.

The abrupt trilling of my cell phone startled me out of a blood-splattered dream.

I shifted my good arm from the igloo of blankets and located my phone in the pile of clothing by the bed.

"You were supposed to call when you got to New York." Mom's voice still held a New Jersey twang in spite of living the past thirty years in Nowhere-You-Ever-Heard-Of, Ohio.

"Sorry, Mom."

"Honestly, I was worried sick."

"Uh-huh." I brought the phone back to join the warmth.

"Larry dropped by." I heard her light a cigarette in the background and her 'ah' as she inhaled.

Well, of course, he did. The two were thick as thieves.

"There's an opening for a June wedding at St. Barts. But he needs to snag it now," she continued.

"Can this wait?"

"I just said he'd have to snag it now."

"Then tell him, 'No, not now, not ever.'"

"Rosie." The whine of a mother's anguish for her despoiled child lilted her voice. I'd joined the army to find myself and lose Larry. Both epic fails. Now Larry wanted to protect me, to prove to me that my shattered body was no impediment to his love. "You're lucky he'll still have you."

I clicked off and, with great satisfaction, clicked the ringer off as well. I tossed it far under the bed.

Tears warmed my face. Not because I wanted my high school sweetheart—I didn't. But I was a coward, should have said no to the ring instead of giving him false hope when I signed up for service.

The red, angry mass where my left breast used to be pulsed.

I cried because I didn't want anyone.

Look up "venerable" in the dictionary and behold a picture of the Art Students Academy in New York City. Located in a Beaux Arts building in midtown Manhattan, walking distance from my tenement, my mouth went dry approaching it on the morning of my first class.

Backpack securely on and with a firm grasp of the ornate iron railing guiding me up the marble steps, I entered the one hundred and thirty-year-old institution feeling like Dorothy and the Emerald City.

Old marble floors, ornate high ceilings; walking there was walking back to the time of the old masters or at least the salons of Paris.

I hit the registrars for my student ID and then the on-site art store for supplies. Loins figuratively girded, I punched the button for the third floor.

These elevators, though old, worked.

I stood outside the door assigned to my art therapy class. The door was wooden, with an ancient brass handle. My heart racing, I feared a panic attack.

I could have stayed in Ohio and slowly gone mad, added to the suicide rate of veterans.

I turned the handle and pushed in.

"Hey. Awesome, we finally got a decent model. Ol' Abe's got his junk knocking about his knees!" hooted a shaven-headed man with an aluminum leg. He was opening a locker, one of the many lining one side of the room. A platform squatted in the center of the room; ancient wooden desks with chairs and easels all scattered around it.

"Shut it, Kelly. You know you aren't allowed to make personal comments about models. Anyway, if you weren't half blind you'd know," said a man in his thirties to the left of me. I got a fleeting impression of a strawberry-scarred face before I looked down.

"Know what?" Kelly said, in a tone daring a beat down.

I didn't look up. I just listened to the roaring in my ears. I took a place at the table and began the laborious process of getting out of my backpack and winter coat.

"She's one of us," Scarface purred, ready to win the debate. "Look at her left arm."

My face flamed, and I tossed a look around me. Red, red every-where. On the easels, the paintings, splashed on the floor. If I hadn't been sitting, I would have fainted. I heard the bombs going off again, felt the desert sun against my face.

"Okay, Bob. You're right." Kelly became conciliatory. "I'm an asshole, grade one. Welcome to the class. It's just most of us are in pretty bad shape."

I pulled out my art supplies.

Bob, the man with a half-face of strawberry-red, webbed scars, knelt next to me.

Red, red everywhere. The sun a red ball. The Humvee engulfed in crimson hell. Greasy black smoke. Judy calling to her lover, Pete, so many shades of red dangling from his stomach….

"Hey." He put a damp paper towel in my hand. "You look in rough shape."

"I apologized, don't put this on me," said A-hole Kelly with a guilty whine.

Splattered on the sand, soaking my uniform, bloody me.

"Miss… miss?" Bob, a thousand miles away, snapped his fingers in front of my face.

"What's up." An old geezer, balding with a long white ponytail, walked into the center of the room to the elevated wooden platform. "Where's all the students?" He pulled off his green floral kimono. Our model, Abe.

A man with a claw for his right hand spoke up. "After Gunderson died, a lot of us lost the sac for it."

I blinked and looked around. A half-dozen men were in the room, mostly staring at me, some polite enough to get on with pulling out brushes and paper.

The sound of clapping hands. "Students, let's get on with it. This semester we will continue exploring the monochromatic scale through the color red." I darted a look at the source of the clipped British voice coming from the door.

Her dyed-black hair, worn short in gelled spikes à la punk rockers; the deep wrinkles on her face, a black tee-shirt and jeans, all blotched with scarlet, increased my impression that here was one of the original denizens of CBGB. Ruby- and diamond-encrusted skull earrings dangled from her ear lobes. "With our examination of red and all its various hues, we will discover the meaning and healing power of red light. We shall create values and tint our red to pink and explore what will happen when we shade. We will mute our colors, locate neutral tones, learn patterns and textures, and differentiate warm versus cool."

Bob put down a bowl of water next to my pad of paper. Looking up, I kept a straight face. Yes, Abe's junk was old and withered but not exactly knocking his knees yet.

"You must be Rosa Leone." The teacher gave me a frosty smile. "Welcome to the class. Remember, there are no mistakes here, only learning and healing."

A smudge of beet red marred her cheek. It caught me, and I nearly zoned out, back into the desert. Swallowing, I said, "Thank you, Ms. Tremayne. I'm sure I'll learn a lot."

Bob grinned and gave a thumbs-up behind her back.

My body ached by the time the session ended. Vermillion, Pyrrol, Cadmium, and Venetian, so many reds… my brain hurt, but they were just pigment, binder, and water, not blood.

After the class, I packed up quickly and ran. Bob still managed to catch up to me. It was dark out but well-lit on these midtown avenues.

"How about a drink?" The scarring caused his smile to go squint, still, a nice smile.

"Can't." I tried to see where the next bus stop was although I didn't need a bus. I didn't want him following me home like a stray dog.

"Coffee then?"

I faced him. "It's very nice of you."

"Look, I see the engagement ring. It's beautiful, and I respect it. I just thought you could use a friend."

"Thanks, maybe another time. That's my bus."

"It goes to Washington Heights, are you sure?"

"Bye." I waved to him and jumped on. After a block, I apologized to the bus driver. He let me off at the next stop.

I picked up Chinese food from a place little more than a hole in the wall. Then I bought a pint of vodka and stopped at the bodega across the street for some OJ.

Fuck the meds. I wanted a drink. I had forgotten I was still wearing the ring. Yet it did serve as an excuse to not be hit on. Except by Bob.

Mom, Larry, and now Bob. Why won't people leave me alone?

I awoke to a throbbing head and metallic taste in my mouth. I could see my breath. The windows rattled in their frames. Snow came down in gentle little flakes, chasing one another down and down.

No class today, which was a good thing as then I would have missed it due to a one-two punch of mixing my meds with alcohol. Since it was after nine a.m., the cheapo landlord had the heat off until the end of the workday.

Fuck no to that.

I dressed as quickly as my dead shoulder allowed, with as many layers as I could, and headed to the basement.

Hallelujah, a working elevator. I checked that my cell phone was on me so I could call 911 should that situation change.

The basement was warm, not just warm, toasty hot. Along a network of whitewashed corridors, the aroma of chili fries led my nose to a door covered by pinups of girly pictures cut from magazines.

First, I knocked, and then with no response, I banged. "I can smell your breakfast, so don't pretend you aren't there."

The door swung open. Our super, Strunk, an obese teen in all his oily hair, greasy face, and wife-beater tee-shirted glory, waddled back to his armchair, its stuffing attempting to escape from the cracked surface of pleather. He sat down with an 'oof' in front of a dusty TV playing a talk show on low and picked up his Hot Pocket, which had been sitting on a chipped plate. My mistake, but it really did smell like chili fries. Next to the TV was an old microwave perched on a mini-fridge. All the comforts of home.

His eyes wandered to the TV and glazed over as he stuffed the food in his mouth, puffing out his cheeks like a chipmunk.

"Strunk?" I had a hard time imagining this grease-coated boy had the will or temperament to keep a building running. Which explained a lot about the condition of said building.

Hands now free from the Hot Pocket, he felt around some papers on the floor by his feet.

He handed me a card—NYC Heat Complaints and the number 311 emblazoned on it.

"You want me to call, to complain?"

He dragged his empty hazel eyes from the set to center on me. And nodded before riveting them back onto the TV.

"Okay." Sometimes a person can be so passive and pathetic, you don't even want to kick their butt. Maybe I could move a chair down to the basement and join him for the warmth and the sparkling conversation?

The elevator was still working. Miracles! As I got out on my floor, my nose was assaulted by the smell of Bengay and the sight of my erstwhile concierge. "I tol' you not to bother him." My friend in 3B had also taken advantage of a working elevator and was waiting by my door.

Here was someone I could complain to. "We have a right to heat and hot water. And how did you know I'd go there?"

"I got nothing to do but watch the front sidewalk. Usually, you're out and about by now." She pointed to the card in my hand. "Don't call. Greeley, the landlord, don't take kindly to snitches."

"Snitches?" My voice went shrill. "I have a sublet. I paid for it. A habitable sublet, with you know, heat?"

"Look around you, girl. There's no money for repairs. There's a problem with the foundation. You call 311, and the inspector sees those cracks in the walls. He takes one look at this place, and we'll all be homeless. The rent is cheap here, but it's New York City." She drawled out the New in New York City and rolled her eyes. "This our home, but they'll condemn this building and put up another high rise with co-ops for the rich so fast your head will spin."

My jaw hung open with dismay. I walked past her to open my door.

She continued, speaking to my back. "We paint the walls, but the cracks come back. Don't call. If you do, I'll tell Greeley you're the one who did."

Door half open, I asked, "So what?"

"Back when I was a girl..." Her whole body seemed to spasm. "Bad things can happen."

I stared, my one good hand going into a fist. "Are you threatening me?"

Her eyes welled up. "We have a roof over our heads. Just be grateful."

I went in to call.

I was back in the desert. Bob joined us, face half-erased and dripping Alazar Crimson from class, as I flopped around pinned by machinery trying to breathe, unable to scream.

I lifted my head from the pillow. Sounds overcame the roaring in my ears—the front door of my apartment creaking, and a hissing. Then a whiff of gas.

Not sure if it was real, I poked my head out from my bedroom. There in the hallway, in faint light from the streetlamps below, I saw a monstrous figure. It took a moment to realize that the deformity was due to the person being encased in a yellow hazmat suit. They held a pump spray can in their hand, and a vague smell—some sort of poison or tranquilizer.

I closed my bedroom door and pushed the chair against it. I didn't have much time and lacked the strength to move any major pieces of furniture.

The fire escape offered my only hope.

I pulled a sweater over my flannel pjs. Footsteps ground outside my bedroom door. The time to be quiet over, I forced the lock on the window's safety gate, and it screeched in protest.

The chair propped up to keep the door closed would only last so long. Finally, the gate opened, and I scrabbled at the lock on the top of the window. It clicked, and I used all my right-side strength. My muscles screamed in protest before the window budged an inch.

The bedroom door exploded inward just as I managed to get the window open wide enough to accept me.

The wind howled, ten times worse than the moaning in my ears, and I threw myself over the windowsill onto the ice and snow-covered iron.

A yellow plastic-covered hand emerged from the window to brush my leg. I held in a scream and shimmied over to where the fire escape steps led down towards the garden.

Light from streetlamps twinkled over swirling snow.

I slipped over the edge. Losing my cold-benumbed grip, I continued to slide down the steps toward the thirty-foot drop below. At the last possible moment, my good arm latched onto the railing. I cried out in pain.

Above me, the yellow-robed figure emerged from the window. Whoever it was, was crazy. I was crazy, too, believing coming out here would save me.

The air cut like a knife through my lungs as I pulled myself round the corner of the fire escape. The lights were off in the apartment below me, and I belly crawled around to the next set of steps. I felt the tremors of the fire escape as the yellow monster followed.

Bruising my frozen legs and feet, I skidded down another flight on my backside.

I made it to the second floor without falling off the escape. The rungs led to the garden directly below me. I crawled out into space, my one good arm all to keep me from falling the final ten feet. My fingers gave out, and I fell anyway, down into the dark.

The snow on a huge shrub broke my fall. Over my chattering teeth and the banshee howl of the wind, I heard the monster still on the fire escape just feet above me.

I slipped off the shrub to land on the snow-covered ground.

It was behind me, and I tried to get to my feet, only to slip and fall again.

Come to me. A figure built of shadows beckoned from near the willow tree. Next to her, two dark forms, wearing fatigues, outlined by the weak streetlight. I shook my head. Was it finally time to join my comrades? Is that why they were always there, bordering my awareness, waiting?

Sobbing, I got my feet under me and up the stone steps toward the tree. I heard the yellow monster land in the garden behind me.

The three shades moved behind the willow, and together they pushed. Though the wind screamed, I didn't feel the cold anymore. I was ready to complete the journey that started in the desert months before.

A crack, sounding like a thousand boughs breaking, just as I reached the willow. With a freight-train rumble, the enormous tree fell, so close to my side that it covered me in dirt and glittering ice shards. I dropped to my knees.

My body burned from the snow. Staring down below the roots, once horizontal, now erect, I faced the white bones of a decomposed body. The roots had lifted up the stone steps where a body had been entombed.

The wind died. One shadowed form stepped to where the tree trunk crushed my yellow-clad pursuer. She laughed and gave a thumbs-up to my fallen friends. *Thanks,* her words echoed. What was left of Judy and Pete gave a sharp salute, and all three faded into the darkness.

In the back of an ambulance, wrapped in a thick blanket, I dozed. The vehicle's lights flashed out over the snow-draped garden as snow gently fell. Yellow police tape blocked off the entrance. A tarp was draped over the figure in yellow, at least the part not crushed by the tree.

An Asian police officer entered the back of the ambulance and got my name, age, and address. He then asked in a voice jaded by god only knew what, "Can you tell us anything?"

I tossed my head toward the garden. "That sack of shit in yellow chased me onto the fire escape."

"And your relationship?"

Behind the policeman, I saw the woman who I thought of as the concierge with Strunk. "You should ask them. They were in on it."

He hightailed it over to them. I eased back on the bed. A body bag moved past me into a different ambulance.

The next thing I knew, I was in a hospital bed in an emergency room. A white-haired, wizened female by my side introduced herself as Detective Haines.

"Did you get them?" I asked through chattering teeth.

She looked up from her cell phone and, in a voice that could have been reading her grocery list, said, "The super, Antony Strunk, is a high-functioning autistic. He's harmless, and very upset; his mother has picked him up, with his social worker's blessing. Poor kid, totally freaked." Haines gave a longing glance down at her cell, where a text message beeped. She continued.

"The woman, Clara Dawes, claims that the man who chased you is Frank Greeley, the owner of the building. She had let him know that you were going to report the building for heat violations. She says she didn't know that he was going to gas you. Just bug spray, it looks like maybe he was only trying to scare you. The body…" She took another peek at the phone. "Ms. Dawes thinks it might be a tenant organizer who disappeared back when Ms. Dawes was just a child."

"Okay." I didn't know what to say. I didn't know if I'd let this scare me away or what. Then I thought about giving up my art classes, going back home, tail between my legs. The too-eager fiancé, the wedding meticulously planned by my mom. Shit, the teacher was going to let us use green next week. "How soon do I get out of here?"

The detective stood up and headed out between the drapes. "Doctors just want to observe you. I gotta go. By the way, you were pretty lucky there. The wind knocking over that tree." She looked like a German Shepherd who'd had its squeaky toy taken away.

Within the hour, I was released from the hospital and back to my new home. Cold and lacking a super, it was still mine. I didn't know what would come next, but hell, I'd paid for my sublet, and I was there to stay.

Time to face facts — I'd call Larry in the morning and let him know I wouldn't be returning to Ohio. I hadn't loved him in years, and it wasn't fair to keep him dangling.

Now I knew my lost buddies had my back, and even though I couldn't take care of them when they needed me, they were all right.

I closed my eyes and saw my friends no longer broken. The way Judy's eyes lit up when Pete laughed at her awful puns. I remembered the last time we had a laugh together and how good it felt to have friends.

I doubted if Bob would believe any of this. Yet it was time to get that drink and make a new friend.

BLIND SPOT

Steven Van Patten

I took my stepfather's eye when I was ten years old. It was not intentional. The bathroom was small, and the door had been ajar, so it didn't occur to me that someone else was inside. Even though I had been yelled at for doing it many times, I enjoyed kicking doors open, like in the cop shows. I didn't know he was on the other side of the door, leaning into the medicine cabinet mirror. He was trimming his bushy eyebrows. Prior to that day, I often made cruel little kid jokes in my head about those eyebrows. I don't remember the jokes now. I do remember the blood. His scream, followed by Mother's. Then, the sudden resolve that came over them as we hustled ourselves to the car. More blood and the realization that I probably wasn't going to school that day. A suspicion confirmed as I sat in the emergency room watching *The Price Is Right*. I never saw a game show and went to school on the same day.

Before the accident, he had tried to reach me. He had taken me to baseball games, even though I was clearly more of a bookworm and a movie lover. Of course, that was back when you could afford to go to a baseball game; when domestic beer wasn't fifteen dollars. But still, it had been a nice gesture, one of many that I probably took for granted. There had been other little niceties, comic books, candy, even boxing lessons and encouragement when I found myself getting bullied by Richard Blake. All of that stopped dead when he finally got back home from the hospital. All of it.

Being ten, there were some things I was not aware of. I knew he had lost his job, but I didn't know that the reason my stepfather had been grooming his two caterpillar shadows with my mother's manicure scissors was that he had an interview that morning. Oh my, look at that. I do remember at least one of the jokes.

Unemployed and partially blind, he sank into a deep depression. I only know that now. At the time, I identified it as a "bad mood." It took me a few days to build up the nerve to speak, but I did apologize. That pause between the words passing my lips and him finally saying, "It wasn't your fault," felt like an eternity. On top of that, it was insincere. Of course, it was my fault. No one else had been there humming the theme from *Miami Vice* and kicking the door in on him. That was me. All me.

Their marriage fell apart, but it died slowly, like a severely injured animal might linger on with seeping, infected wounds and labored breathing. In the end, my mother got it in her head that she couldn't take care of a child and a half-blind man who had given up on himself. The drinking didn't help. Vodka. That was his drink of choice. During the last days, he'd sit across from me at breakfast, drinking Absolut with grapefruit juice while I uncomfortably swallowed down scrambled eggs and grits before running off to school.

Then one day, he was gone. Many of the things he'd brought when he first moved in were still present, including various pieces of silverware, books, and old Motown albums. Also still with us was his body odor, that pungent mix of cheap cologne and alcohol forcing itself out of someone's system. The smell had permeated the sofa and my mother's linens. But most of his clothes and the ponderous collection of porno magazines that I'd stumbled upon once when I was bored and alone in the house, these things he took with him. Occasionally, I would overhear my mother having a phone conversation with him. Even as I grew into a teenager, it never occurred to me what the real motivation behind those conversations was. As an adult, I now know those keeping-in-touch and checking-in calls are the desperate lifelines that people throw to one another, especially when they wake up in the cold light of day filled with regret.

It didn't occur to me that my mother loved him, but she must have. She never took another husband, and only a boyfriend or two until I moved out. Those guys always seemed to be on some kind of temporary financial upswing when they met my mother. Once their good fortune dried up, so did my mother's interest. Until adulthood, it never occurred to me that even though she did care for my stepfather, she could not defeat her own shallowness. At the end of the day, money and love were two things that needed to be equally present for you to matter to her. If you couldn't provide the first, then you weren't worthy of the latter, soft feelings be damned.

I never completely abandoned her. How could I after I destroyed her second husband? But try as we might, while we may love, we don't like each other very much. Of course, that doesn't stop her from calling me when she needs money. I send it, knowing that there's a fifty percent chance that her "emergency" is contrived and she's spending the "loan" on something frivolous. I don't care. If the money means I don't have to physically be there, it's fine.

Everyone rebels against their parents, right? I'm no exception. With nothing to rebel against except my stepfather, I tried to do that. At the age of twelve, after watching that man fall apart, I swore off alcohol, porn, and cheap cologne. Somehow, I got all the way through high school and midway through college before the alcohol took me, then I was off to the races. And who needed porn when there were strip clubs by the dozens? I did manage to avoid the cologne, though, but not for any reason other than it turns out I'm allergic. I can't even handle perfumed soap without suddenly becoming short of breath.

The first time I saw the eye, I was in a strip club. Farah was giving me a lap dance and doing a decent job of pretending to enjoy it. Obviously, "Farah" wasn't her real name. One night, during a moment of drunkenness, she confided to me that her real name was Joyce. When asked why she chose "Farah" as her stage name, she went into a diatribe on how Joyce is not, nor would it ever be considered a good stripper name. "No one would want a lap dance from Joyce, no matter how tight her ass is," she concluded in her makeshift Ted Talk.

Our relationship was as transactional as the one with my mother, only with Mom I purchased a peaceful disconnect that allowed me to go back to my rent-stabilized apartment guilt free. Whereas Farah, on the rare occasion that her weed dealer boyfriend couldn't pay for something she needed, would stop by the apartment and fuck me for a few hundred bucks. The price would vary depending on what I wanted to do. A lot of people would say I was being overcharged, but those people never fucked Farah.

"Move your keys," she instructed as she grinded against me. Naturally, I did as I was told. But the brief interruption in simulated sexual bliss caused me to open my eyes, which had been closed except for the random peeks at one body part or another. There it was, about the size of a football, floating just above the elevated strip club security camera about twenty feet away. The manicure scissors, also significantly bigger, were sticking out of it.

"Fuck!" I shouted. The music was too loud, and the other girls looked good enough, so no one but Farah noticed my exclamation.

"Not tonight, dude," Farah answered, apparently oblivious to my actual mood change. "I think my period is coming."

When I closed my eyes and I shook my head hard, it had disappeared. By now, the song had changed, which would be her cue. "You want another dance?" Farah asked. Shaking my head, I paid her and stepped away. "Maybe next week, okay?" she said, thinking I was upset at her refusal. I nodded and walked off without even saying goodbye, which, to be honest, isn't like me. But I was shook up and scared. Farah and a few other girls had told me that someone had been randomly spiking their drinks, and try as they might, security had not figured out who the culprit was. With that in mind, my immediate thought was that another fan of Farah's resented my tying her up for four songs and slipped something in one of my beers. But while I was sweating and my heart was racing, I wasn't sleepy or impaired in any way. In fact, I felt very alert, as if I had done coke. But I hadn't done anything like that. Just the two beers and a shot of Casa Migos Tequila.

"Not your night," I told myself. "Time to go home." And that's what I did after I settled my bar tab and retrieved my bag from the coat check girl.

I slid into the backseat of my Uber ride and closed my eyes, thinking I would be home in twenty minutes. Then, I noticed the driver took a turn I hadn't expected. Knowing good and well what the best way to my place is and not looking for the Uber guy to line his pockets by dragging me along the scenic route, I leaned forward and was about to say something. There it was again, on the dashboard. Even with the scissors still stuck in it, the pupil was able to move.

When I exclaimed something incomprehensible, the driver glanced in his rearview at me. "Sir, if you're going to throw up, please let me know so I can pull over somewhere."

"I'm fine, sir," I shouted instinctively. Sometime later, I'm sure he noticed that I kept my eyes shut for the rest of the drive.

Minutes later, the driver stopped the car and thanked me. Stepping out into the street, my breathing was still heavy, and I felt distressed. *I need to stop seeing this thing. Fuck you, Lucas, and your fucking eyebrows.*

As I stood at my front door jumbling my keys, I heard a scratching noise. "Please, God!" I said out loud. "I'm sorry, I'm like him. I'm sorry, I'm worse. Please, stop punishing me."

Finally inside, I slammed the door shut, latched the two locks, and then just stood there in my vestibule, waiting to see it again. Nothing to be seen. I took a few deep breaths and rubbed my forehead. Part of me was still scared. The other part wished I had stayed with Farah, so she could do the only other thing she does better than sex: keep my mind off how shitty my life had become.

The apartment floor creaked underneath me as I slowly walked through the house, making sure my stepfather's right eye wasn't going to pop out at me again. When I didn't see anything, I turned the TV on to the late local news. At some point, I fell asleep. I must have.

When I woke up, he was there on the TV, his angry face surrounded by the white noise. The eyepatch he had come to wear until the last day I saw him looked frayed.

"*No!*" I screamed as my hands clenched. I instinctively tried to back into the sofa cushions.

"I tried to be a father to you, you goddamn ingrate!" the apparition in the TV said.

I didn't say anything because I was too busy telling myself it was a nightmare. I was trying to wake up, even as a carnival version of the *Miami Vice* theme began to play just under his voice.

"I was just a kid! What do you want from me?" I shouted. "Go away!"

"I am not going anywhere." As he spoke, I felt something wet land on my face. When I looked up, I saw the eye floating almost three feet over my head. Blood had coagulated where the scissors had stabbed it except for a single, moist trail that ran to the edge and dripped down on me like a leaky faucet.

Leaving the angry visage of my one-eyed stepfather to stare at the couch, I sprang to my feet and ran into the hallway where the circuit breakers sat innocuously embedded in the middle of the wall on my left. Panicked thinking brought me to the sudden conclusion that if this monster was attacking through the TV, then killing the power should render the monster helpless, right? I was sure I had either seen this in a movie, or read it, or something.

"I am incomplete," I could hear him say through the hissing white noise on the wall-mounted flat screen. "I cannot go until I am complete."

Giving no thought to what that could have meant, I pulled open the little metal door and flipped the five circuit breaker switches, plummeting myself into darkness. My labored breath slowed as the full weight of my hasty decision to kill the power and leave myself in a pitch-black apartment being hunted by a ghost bore down on me. Blood pumped hard in my ears as I turned and took a few steps back into the living room.

Again, the floor creaked under my weight, seeming louder in the dark silence. I made it to the head of the hallway unmolested and looked around the living room. No stepfather. No bleeding eye.

My mind desperately searched for a logical explanation. The drug spike courtesy of a hater at the strip club was still a strong consideration yet seemed incongruous with my alertness. Dimly, I was self-aware enough to realize I sounded like Ebenezer Scrooge, the *Christmas Carol* miser who initially blamed the appearance of his long-dead business partner on something he'd eaten. He'd been proven wrong as I felt.

But ol' Scrooge had prompted his visitation by being a tightwad and an asshole, two things I had not been. Just ask any number of my ex-girlfriends. Yes, I can admit to being emotionally unavailable most of the time, but they got what they needed and wanted in terms of gifts, dinners, and trips. In fact, I had been damn entertaining to all of them. I was just never the shoulder to cry on. It wasn't a behavior I had learned.

As my romantic past leaped into the forefront of my thoughts, anger suddenly replaced my fear. The resentment of being abandoned because I'm not the most expressive man in the world made my fists clench up as I stood just outside my living room. I didn't deserve to be walked out on any more than I deserved to be haunted by a stepfather I hadn't spoken to in decades just because I did something stupid as a child. I did not deserve it.

"Fuck you, you half-blind, bushy eyebrowed, alcoholic bastard!" I shouted into the darkness. "Fuck you!"

My eyes adjusted just enough for me to make my way to the bedroom and lock the door. Now that I was in righteous indignation mode, it was easy to convince myself that I should be safe away from the television and in my bed.

Lying there with my heart and mind continuing to race, I told myself to keep my eyes closed, and it would all be over soon.

As I lay there, it hit me that I had never actually been told that my stepfather was dead. With that in mind, I figured this had to be my imagination. Something had activated my repressed memories, and this was how it manifested. Nothing more.

Then, I heard his voice. It was just as clear as if he had leaned in and whispered in my ear. "I want to be complete."

My eyes shot open. I wanted to jump out of the bed, but I was now frozen in place. While I couldn't see anything binding me, I was clearly restrained. Above me, something metallic floated. It glimmered, catching light from the open window before it fell fast toward my face, like the blade of a guillotine.

It was a pair of manicure scissors.

Breathtaking pain erupted throughout my skull, and I screamed as if I had been lowered into hell itself. Holding my bloodied face, with the manicure scissors and my liquefied eye slipping between my fingers, I sat up. Gravity seemed to take the manicure scissors, leaving me with an unspeakable mess and a new forever blind spot. With my left hand, I fished out my cell phone and dialed 9-1-1.

Before the call connected, I heard the voice again. "Now, I am complete."

Despite the circumstances and the throbbing agony, I could feel a weight lifted off of me. I was scarred for life, irreparably damaged, but a debt, one I have owed for decades, had finally been paid.

Hours later, lying in my hospital bed, sedated with the right side of my face bandaged up, I noticed my cellphone vibrating furiously on the night table by my bed. As I looked over with my one good eye, I realized it was a text from my mother:

LUCAS HAS DIED.

"Always straight, no chaser with you, huh, Mom?" I said out loud as I turned back to the TV. The night nurse had left me watching The Game Show Channel. An old episode of *Jeopardy* was on.

POWER OUT, WIND HOWLING

JONATHAN LEES

As I claw at the wind, the bruised sky spits in my face, and my boots stumble on the rotting earth surrounding the grounds of the dormant Mathis estate. The soil, as if remembering the contours of my sole, sucks at my boots with each step. The frowning face of the manor peers from behind impenetrable whipping branches, the architectural embodiment of the morose teenager I used to be, harshly reminding me why I refused to return after my eighteenth year.

Everything here looks depressed, as if it can recall what happened within its walls, as if it all gave up and died without a fight. The storm and the trees wail and wave at me not to continue. I ignore their cries and trudge toward the sore mouth of the house, regretting every step.

The floorboards that used to screech at just the slightest bit of pressure from our pajama-padded feet now shout upon my entrance. The foundation quakes as the storm yanks the door shut tight behind me, rattling the paintings in the hall. I wait to be ejected — no, expelled — and sent tumbling back down the hill. Everything reeks of dank fabric, the tang of wallpaper paste, and a meaty musk of black mold. My eyes can barely adjust to the gloom before I enter the rooms whose memories made up everything I ran away from.

My family often looked through the diamond-shaped panes of the lancet windows and down upon the town below they claimed as their own personal snow globe; hand-crafted, everything in its place, and ready to be shaken up whenever they felt like it.

Mathis Hospital. Mathis Middle School. Mathis Diner. Mathis Lumber. Mathis Cemetery.

We got you covered from birth to death.

Father's family started in paper, Mother's family thrived in textiles, two common industries for a New Englander in the forties. Dad's older brother, Joseph Janson Mathis, after the businesses failed to diversify and took a downturn based on losses to cheap imports, swiped some change from the coffers and took off on a world tour. An expedition of freedom, he called it, peppered with frequent postcards of my uncle proudly posing in various "hellholes," a flourish Mother added as she read the barely legible text on the back. JJ returned nine months later with a hitch in his speech, a glaze over his eyes, skin sticking to his bones, and not a cent left tossing around his pockets.

The family discovered him one evening, sitting in the living room, lost in the fire, nearly nude and soaking, his skivvies wrinkling around his privates, his skin so pale the fabric looked like ropey blisters about to burst. His neck, chest, hands, and legs had miniature lacerations, puckered and bloodless. I overheard Dad say they were no more than the size of paper cuts.

He wouldn't tell anyone what happened or what was in the ten crates pressed against the walls of the study. Mother said his head always swam with ideas, but his brain drowned at the bottom of that black ocean he traveled.

A lot of pacing and shouting alone in empty rooms, and within a couple weeks, JJ looked different, his complexion florid, his speech focused. The silt in his eyes disappeared, and the slouch in his walk straightened. He thanked everyone for their care at a crucial time, though I don't remember anyone really doing anything that could be deemed "care." He gave them no other explanation, and returned to his study, locking himself inside, rarely emerging except to check the front door for packages — of which there were many.

Five years passed; with his repeated jaunts to remote parts of the world no one in my family cared to even pronounce, never mind visit, JJ amassed a small fortune. Through investments and clientele to which no one was privy, his wealth grew to shocking proportions, bringing the family to the height of the New York City skyline by the time I reached adulthood.

Ten years later, every last member of my family had been erased, and I inherited all the empty rooms, all the unanswered questions, and the remnants of bad ideas.

❧

I lock the door of my childhood home behind me and draw the curtains even as the windows chatter, the glass shaking like steel cages in the hands of anxious inmates. The hinges whimper, begging me to open them and let the storm in to destroy the damned house once and for all.

The study looks the same as my uncle left it. Any visitor would find it spacious and refined if not a bit funereal. JJ's amassment of books, the only objects of profound interest in the room, are bound behind twisted piano wire, peering from gilded frames that canvas the massive walls. The nameless tomes beg for attention, their taut spines saturated in vibrant hues of red, brown, and black leathers, gold paint laid in the grooves with no numbers or letters to differentiate them. My hands sweat down the handles of the bolt cutters I brought with me.

"Pure madness," said a visiting tycoon whose liquor-filled gut brushed papers off the desk as he leaned in to squint at the collection.

I was seven at the time, trying not to breathe, hidden within the recess my uncle built behind the shelves. I gripped my teddy by the throat until the stuffing squeezed out of his sewn eyes.

"How do you even know what the hell are in these? Let me see one. Just one."

"Absolutely not," Dad responded, his pipe smoke obscuring most of the disdain on his face.

The tycoon harrumphed like the beady-eyed cartoon villains that transfixed me every Saturday morning.

"JJ would never know," he revealed as if no one in the family had thought the same.

My father brushed past the broad-chested buffoon and waved his bored wife on toward some of our precious cabinets, pens, and other possessions, to shift the focus. She eagerly admired the baubles, her painted claws clicking over each hint of a jewel and glint of precious metals.

The giant man with sipping-straw whiskers pressed close to the tense wiring, focused intently on the craft of the bound volumes. He leaned closer, his nose pushed past the cage, his flushed face looming closer to where I hid when I gasped, crushing teddy's neck for good. No one heard me since Mother said the tycoon's bellowing echoed all the way up to her dressing room on the third floor. By the time she got downstairs, the not-so-gentle-man had barreled out the door, bleeding profusely, with his wife dabbing his slit face with a red handkerchief.

The scene seemed comical to me, hand clamped over my mouth stifling the giggles, not knowing then that this is where the story of my family's end began, and laughing would become more of a luxury than what we were used to.

Today, I trail a finger along the wire, relishing its bite, then past it, and my finger jumps instinctively from the heat, a pulsing on the book spines throbbing like the veins on my wrists. Impossible.

They are everywhere and nowhere at once.
I turn off the lights so I can see their silhouettes approaching the windows.
These Night People.

The warnings were nested within lullabies from my uncle's raw lips, little whistles of air dancing around the refrains. I've seen his drawings of them, their eyes a shock of white in the darkness right before they are upon you. I've listened to his legends of magics and rituals conducted in regions where people's entire lives were spent looking over their shoulders. I've dreamt of their murderous ways, slinking around in the darkest hours, feeding people poisons. I've been told the stories of the Night People, and in front of me bound in cages, scrawled in the pages, are supposedly the remnants of their legends.

I look outside, and the old elms hide their approach. I know they are out there. These giant shadows, their profane mouths widening, a proclivity for violence lighting their eyes. At first, I am terrified, teeth jittering and my limbs alight with tremors. Me, Anderson Mathis III, the descendant of possible demons, an inheritor of their torment, shivering behind the moldering curtains, listening to them shout our surname once again.

A sound unlike any other, it was almost music that sang from the dense Manhattan streets below the Mathis Tower. A whirling, reverberating sonic assault with lyrics composed of muffled shouts. The heightening winds howled along with the chants of the growing crowd, defeating the reasons why his family chose the top floors, *as far above the filth as they could be*, Anderson's mother spit. *Away from these rats shoving and climbing over each other to get to the equivalent of nowhere*, his father proclaimed.

Anderson stirred his fourth gin and tonic while he slumped in a Darboux mirrored chair that faced the skyline. He thought of the Mathis house tucked deep in the quaint New England hamlet he was raised in. He could picture the vacant rooms all holding their breath for someone's return. The books, hundreds of them, behind razor wire, still and sweating, waiting to be touched. Within the play of light and shadow from the increasingly tumultuous weather outside of this luxury prison, his eyes darted around the space waiting for some of the darkness to take shape, the Night People floating out of blind corners until their phantom limbs wrapped around his own and pulled him in—

The lights went out.

Anderson Mathis III, ex-star quarterback, ex-media personality, ex-socialite, jumped from the chair and squealed. He fumbled with the flashlight, and the beam glanced over the painted war masks from Africa, the crouching taxidermized tigers, and furniture wrought from bones. His chest heaved with each wave of his hand, hoping his heart wouldn't give out when the solid light got interrupted by a figure standing on the other side of the cavernous suite. Since Anderson was a child, he had been taught that within absolute darkness is the waiting room for the lost. He knew one day the Night People would be done waiting, and they would step into the light.

The mighty winds knocked at every pane of glass so hard Anderson expected to see the giant misshapen hands of something unnamable slapping against the building. He pressed his face against the vibrating glass and saw the little people below overtaking the carless streets with their handmade signs, his family's name emblazoned on them, looking up at the most oppressive symbol of the Mathis legacy, an edifice most considered to be the city's middle finger.

Every artifact in his family's building contained a history he was not a part of. He had acquired it all against his will. His delicately carved face and body allowed him entrance to exclusive rooms, but his wit didn't keep the doors open very long. He was loveless, without a profession, and in control of too much money and possessions that meant nothing to him. His inheritance could not pay for anything that he did not already have. There was nothing more to gain by remaining here, hovering above the masses, who looked up to him only to see how high they could spit. The only emotion these riches provoked in Anderson was fear. Fear of what he was born into. Fear of what lay in the darkness waiting to emerge and the fear of what just moved in the corner of the room, what appeared by the window, what loomed just beside the light from his hand. They were here for him. The Night People.

He choked as a pair of open eyes floated from the other room. One blink, and they were gone again. Anderson placed the glass next to the bust of his uncle JJ Mathis and tracked the forms as they appeared and disappeared. Outlines of limbs faded in and out around him, a raised fist, a wide mouth, powerful legs, whips of hair, none of it attached to one body; an orgy of limbs flailed in front of his drained, disbelieving face. In the darkness, they all looked like black watercolor lines, breaking apart at the edges. He backed up against the window as the wind crashed against it and he felt his whole spine alight with tremors. The shouts of protest outside overpowered the gale. Anderson felt their hatred rise eighty-four floors. Hatred for his family, disgust for their privilege, and repulsion for what they imagined the Mathis clan had done to attain it.

The darkness around him vibrated, shadows on shadows on shadows flitted past his eyes; each jitter of movement closed his throat tighter. Anderson envisioned that this was what his sister saw before she hung herself, what his mother saw before she crushed all those pills in her gimlet, what his father saw when his private jet fell from the sky, what his uncle saw as he closed the caging on the last of the library he smuggled into their house. Anderson remembered the triumphant look in JJ's eyes when he emerged and, something beyond his own feeble understanding at the time, resembled something incomprehensibly evil. Something that still existed in that old New England home. The home he feared he must return to.

✤

The books look just as pristine as when my uncle brought them home. Everything else in the manor is decorated in dust, green with water damage, black with rot. Here, behind the shining razor wire, the spines are luminous, wet even.

As I raise the bolt cutters, I feel like an intruder in my own home.

The first wire snaps. I halt, expecting something to jump out to stop me.

The second wire takes a bit of work but finally pops.

I move my head so slowly when I hear the hiss. I look for the eyes.

There! In the corner, something shifts. Just outside of the cone of light, not a bright white grin but a dull gray row of square choppers, slathered in grime, and above it no eyes. I don't even see a mouth. Just teeth.

"Clack."

I flick the flashlight and, of course, no one. Nothing. The teeth hover in the dark, dodging the light.

Two more wires and I'll be able to reach at least a couple of the texts that brought as much horror as wealth into our lives.

Even the storm outside seems to hold back its breath, knowing what awaits me in those volumes, even if I only have the faintest clue.

"Snip."

This time I hear movement everywhere. Simultaneously, upstairs and behind me, I turn and point the flashlight in random directions hoping the unpredictability will catch one solid glimpse.

It does.

It takes me a second to realize what I am looking at. It doesn't dissipate. Standing behind an unlit lamp is a figure that hasn't fully taken shape yet.

"Goddamn."

Every molecule in my body shivers. How can something be recognizable yet retain no features? Just the outline and its stance remind me of her. So poised and so… rigid.

"Mother?"

Then it isn't her. It has my father's tight mouth. My sister's furrowed brow. Finally, my uncle's hypnotic stare filled with curiosity and pain.

It moves closer. I'd say stepped, but I don't hear a footfall.

My legs lock, my stomach tightens, and my breath comes out in little huffs. Despite the chaotic tornado of extremities I witnessed back in Manhattan, this phantasm composed of my family's features makes me even more nervous.

I pull the books from the shelves. The books that no one has touched except JJ Mathis since he laid them to rest, and here he was, waiting patiently for me to do it.

"Uncle Joe?"

My voice goes from playboy billionaire to playhouse kindergartner as I run the flashlight up and down the phantom. The figure has consistency, wet with a gelatinous drip. And for the first time, I see what my family saw, what haunted them until their deaths, the little lacerations from his face to his feet. Tiny, puckering, bloodless mouths opening and closing with the urgency of hungry children.

I open the first volume I can get my shaking fingers around and almost drop it when I recognize the book binding does not have the feel of leather. This deep umber hide feels tacky, hideously alive with moisture, like my hands have been licked. I bring it close to my face and that's when I notice the pores.

I open to the first page and see a pasted photographic plate of a young boy, his dark complexion yellowed with rot, along with what looks to be my uncle's tight, illegible writing underneath. The next is of a middle-aged woman, tawny skin ruined, with blood blotches in her eye sockets and mouth. The next page, an elderly man, a mahogany hide, purpling with bruises, his eyes open, mouth slack accompanied by tight illustrations of the places they were cut. These are the Night People. I know now because I recognize them. I've seen them standing over my bed and weeping in the corner of my room. Waiting in the closets and corners for me to understand why they were here at all.

There are over seven hundred slim books in this collection. It doesn't take me long to recognize a pattern. It takes me less time to rip my shirt off as immense pain lights up in various spots on my torso and neck. I look down in disbelief as little incisions appear in my skin and with each opening and closing a fresh hell.

I watch JJ's rippling face. It's Mother. Father. My uncle again. Then, something indiscernible, vacant.

My fingers trail along these new wounds, these silent little slit lips suckling at my tips and nails. I face my family for what I hope is the last time, the power out, wind howling, the wounds on my body singing, the Night People calling out to be set free, and I think, for once, about how I can end it all.

OLD SPIRITS AND FINE TOBACCO

JOHN P. COLLINS

Halfway through my second whiskey, I felt it. The fine, blonde hair on my arm stood on end as a creeping feeling brushed up the back of my neck. The taste of my drink soured in an instant.

"There's someone else here," I said, wondering if my voice sounded as shaky as it felt.

Charles paused as he brought a wooden match to his cigar. The flame, sitting inches away from the clipped end of the smoke, gave his already tanned face a golden rich glow. The wooden match's fire tried in vain to reach out and kiss the tobacco.

Max sat across from us, comfortably sunk into his leather chair. A rocks glass of scotch rested on the arm of his old recliner, and as he took a sip, his tumbler hid an amused smirk.

"Exactly how much whiskey have you had tonight?" Charles said, a small grin on his face. A laugh came from Max.

The cold breeze of the autumn night howled in the eaves of the house. The house held the heat of the fireplace well, keeping the room warm from the elements.

My cheeks felt flush under their kidding and playful scrutiny. The fact was that despite our friendship, there was always an underlying feeling of insecurity on my part. Both men were at least fifteen years my senior, well-traveled and successful — Max, an author of educational texts, while Charles had more than his share of success in the business world. I, myself, worked as a meager public servant, employed by the local county as a heavy machinery mechanic.

The day I met them, each of us enrolled in a group boxing class at the local gym, there was an instant comradery. Friendly conversations would result in a few pints at the local tavern, which in turn became our monthly get-togethers that carried on well past the life of our sparring sessions inside the ring.

Never once was I ever made to feel out of place or looked down upon. Both men were generous, kind, and free spirited.

The three of us would gather at least once a month for a night of good conversation along with fine tobacco and aged spirits. My wife, Leigh, understood how important these gatherings had become for me. She had even encouraged me to go. She knew my psyche needed these nights with good friends, my brothers.

In fact, I felt those evenings of music, spirits, and tobacco were as much an education as any classroom in which I ever set foot. During the spring and summer months, we would sit around the fire pit in Max's yard, under the stars. We fed the flames oak logs as we talked into the early hours of the morning. In the fall and winter, we were content to spend the time gathered around the red-bricked fireplace inside, chased indoors by the biting chill of the night. My monthly university class would never fail to reveal something about myself that I never knew or didn't honestly admit was there. Our friendship had provided me some of my most valued teachers.

At that moment, though, I wished that I could be anywhere but there. Making an ass of myself in front of two men who held my admiration.

"Maybe I didn't have enough," I said, trying to brush off the feeling. The conversation had stalled, and an awkward shiver washed over me. I couldn't help but feel Max's appraisal of me. Not in the form of judgment, but more like curiosity.

It was Max's house. A hundred-year-old farmhouse on the north shore of Long Island. The farm fields once tied to the house had been split up decades ago, divided into forty-five one-and-a-half-acre plots that Max had joked about—on more than one occasion—wishing he had a piece of the property back then. He had been living here for just under a year at this point, purchasing the place after living in an apartment for eighteen months following the collapse of his marriage.

The two-story building with its gothic arches and a sagging porch was, for the most part, in top condition. The building and land had been well maintained despite being empty for nearly two years. The housing bubble had been ruthless to property values on the north shore of the island.

Max had made large strides in whipping the house into shape. While Charles and I had both been inside on various occasions, tonight was his first night having us over, feeling comfortable with the condition of his home for one of our ritual gatherings.

The study where we sat was tasteful in its decor. Mahogany trim on tan walls, a large bookcase monopolized the wall opposite the brick fireplace, where cedar logs burned away. An antique roller desk, now converted to a nifty liquor cabinet, sat in the corner. Max did his writing in another room in the house; the study was, as he said, "perfect for entertaining."

And it was, as I could attest. The room had an air of welcoming comfort. David Bowie played through Bose speakers.

Footsteps from the upstairs cut through my whiskey haze. A chill raised the fine hairs on my arms. Raising my hand from the arm of the recliner, I cocked my index finger upward. "Told you."

Charles faced up toward the ceiling, a startled look on his face. The cigar in his hand shook with light tremors. "There *is* someone upstairs." His voice was dry and uncharacteristic in its weakness.

Max laughed as he lit his pipe. Captain Black's rich aroma filled the air. "No," he chuckled, "just the ghost."

Charles stared at him, mouth agape. "Come again?"

"The ghost," Max said. A smile on his face, he drained his glass. "It's an interesting story. One that deserves a refill."

Max, being the genial host, got up and went to the wet bar in the corner, coming back with a Kentucky Rye for me and a decanter of scotch for Charles and himself. He filled our glasses, as well as his, to ridiculous levels. Under normal circumstances, I would have protested. My head was already spinning. This talk of ghosts, along with my consumption of drink, left me lightheaded.

Max returned to his recliner. Relighting his pipe, he puffed away until it smoldered to his satisfaction. Always with a flair for the dramatic. We waited, a bit impatient, knowing that he would not start his story until he was ready.

"You know, the first time I stepped through the front door with the real estate man, I knew there was something here, something different. The feeling just settled in me."

"Like that pins and needles feeling across your arms?" The sensation had covered my arms like a blanket since the evening took this bizarre turn.

Max nodded. "Yeah, exactly like that. I can't explain it, but I also knew I was going to buy it, too. The sale went fairly smooth. The house had been on the market for so long I think the seller was happy to be done with it. The first night I spent here was, to say the least, exhausting. After unpacking the majority of boxes for the bedroom, as well as finishing two bottles of wine, I fell onto the bed. My head was spinning from the booze, and to be honest, I spent some time just crying."

Taking a sip from his drink, he then leaned forward, lighting the candle in the middle of the coffee table. Charles and I exchanged a glance as Max topped off his own glass.

"The whole idea that my marriage was over, dead and buried had become very real to me that night," Max continued. "I'm not sure if I totally blame Stephanie. I was a better man when we were dating, maybe? I thought I showed her enough attention. She never said anything to the contrary. One moment she was here, the next..." He shook his head, as if trying to knock loose memories that stole away from him.

"Anyway, it was more than I could bear, so I decided if I had to deal with it, drunk seemed like a good option. At least that night."

Charles reached over, patting Max on the shoulder. We had all looked to him for wisdom in moments of council. The oldest among us, he had been the veteran of two businesses, one failed marriage, along with all the pitfalls and peaks that a busy life will provide. He had the endurance of a centurion.

Recreating his life, he had found success in assisting unemployed professionals find new employment opportunities. A second marriage to a beautiful woman he had met on holiday in the Greek Isles followed, and he was blessed with two beautiful children to go along with three grown children from his first marriage. He had handled all the hurdles with grace and kindness. In every moment, he seemed to know the right thing to say in the most sensitive areas.

In this moment, he wisely chose to say nothing.

"I was splayed out on that bed. My arms and legs were lead, and the room spun. I was sure I was going to be sick, but then I saw a shape at the end of the bed. I couldn't make out any features, but I was sure it was watching me."

My throat went dry. The shadow in the corner of the room became sinister. My mind's eye saw thin arms reaching out from under the couch where I sat, waiting with bony fingers to grasp my ankles.

I didn't want to hear any more. I had a panicked need to change the conversation to another direction, talk about women, politics, anything but this talk of phantoms. It felt wrong to me.

"Somehow, though, I felt better. The next day I started doing some background research and found a woman named Amanda Weeks, granddaughter of the original owner."

Max noticed my glass, along with Charles', were both empty. Leaving his chair, he refilled our glasses, and also provided some small water bottles from the wet bar — always the good host.

"The original owner of the house was a man named Walters, Michael Walters." Max had his lecture voice on, the same voice he used during speaking engagements. "He was a farmer, a quite successful one at that too. He had land all over the island, but he and his family made their home here."

Nodding at us. "Drink up, gents."

My anxiety had not subsided in the least, but I drank anyway. The whiskey burned on the way down, making me feel a little better despite my trembling fingers.

Responding to my obvious discomfort, Max said, "You need to relax. Everything is fine." Leaning forward, he patted my shoulder. "I promise."

Taking another sip of scotch, Max leaned back, looking at the ceiling. "You know, there are nights I just sit here. Kind of like we are now. Some good booze, a little smoke, and some tunes. I hear a noise upstairs, maybe feel Michael go past the back of the chair, and I'm not lonely, even if it's only for a moment."

"Michael? You mean Michael Walters?" I asked. "The same man who built the house? Are you sure?"

A shade of annoyance passed over his face as he nodded. Seeing that expression, I imagined myself one of his students that dared interrupt one of his lectures.

"Yeah, I'm sure there's a story behind all of it. If you don't mind, please allow me to finish this part. It is not the easiest thing for me to discuss."

Charles nodded; his eyes focused on Max. I had often thought that Max was hurting. His marriage had imploded two and a half years earlier. Right before I had met them — they were friends long before I entered the fray — Max had gone through the emotional ringer. He had never spoken of the details of his marriage's collapse, and I had never pressed my friend for the story. He, in turn, had apparently never felt the need to share that story, and that was fine by us.

The pain was evident on his face at times. When the conversation steered toward our family lives, the hurt appeared, like a passing shadow over his green eyes. I often thought the collapse of a marriage was always the result of betrayal. Infidelity was not always the fracture that drove couples apart. Sometimes it was enough just to forget the vows that were made, the oath meant to be kept for the rest of one's life. That can be the most painful of betrayals.

Hurt had never clouded him, though: bitterness did not suit him. Max had begun to enjoy bachelorhood; his coming and goings were of his own design. Keeping the hours that he pleased benefited him as his career blossomed to new heights with a new focus on work. He had even been toying with the idea of dipping his toes into fiction writing.

"Michael had come here by way of Pennsylvania before the first World War. He had found great success there as a carpenter. Apparently, his craftsmanship had left him a solid reputation among farmers and city dwellers alike. This wasn't a man who merely raised barns, but created wooden works of art. The high arches, the delicate trim work, and the beauty of his polished interiors had made him highly sought after throughout his home state."

"He was also an adventurous man. Always looking for new ways to broaden himself, he had begun to study the farmers. The science that they applied to the planting and raising of their crops became a fascination for him. So, he searched for a place to start his new career and remembered his time on the island. He had landed here as a boy with his parents when they arrived from Denmark, so he made plans to return here."

Any trepidation I may have felt earlier had disappeared. Max was quite skilled in drawing his audience into his stories, and while his normal flair for entertaining storytelling was absent, the situation itself was engaging enough.

"Was he successful?" Charles asked, clear that he wanted to cut to the chase. The situation had apparently dismayed him as well.

"By and large, yes. It took him a little while, but he found success rather quickly. He, along with his wife, Tanith, and their children—two boys, Henry and Christopher, and two girls, Carol and Susan—had found genuine happiness here. They had enough money to hire only the best laborers to work the land along with a foreman, a man named

Gold, whom Michael had pried away from another successful farm by offering him a share in the profits as well as a salary. Michael was known as a fair and honest businessman who was generous to staff and community. You know the Methodist church? The building with the attached greenhouse?"

Charles and I nodded, both knowing the property.

"Donated and built by Walters. I believe there's still a plaque dedicated to him in the entrance."

A gasp of low noise came from upstairs. The house seemingly agreed with Max.

"One of the reasons he chose the north shore of Long Island to start this phase of his life was his love of fishing. Saltwater fishing, in particular. The Long Island Sound was a perfect gateway to the Atlantic as far as he was concerned. Living on the south shore, while closer to the actual ocean, was too unpredictable even with Fire Island acting as a barrier."

Living here, this was common knowledge. Having been involved in cleanups of many major storms, the haggard looks on the faces of the homeowners we assisted had convinced me I would never willingly live on the ocean for any reason.

"One of the first things he did when they settled here was to commission the building of a sailboat. Except in the winter, it was commonplace to see his sloop off the beaches of Rocky Point with several guests. The boat had to be manned by two people, but it could safely sail with ten. He would entertain his family, neighbors, and even his workers aboard the vessel.

"The Sunday before the Fourth of July, Michael, his oldest son, Henry, and Gold the foreman sailed out one evening, trying to bring in striped bass. In the summer dusk, none of them paid any mind to the storm clouds that came in from the northwest. The storm came upon them quickly. The water became very rough as the sky darkened, and they found themselves in a hell of a nor'easter."

Max took a deep swig of his drink. I noticed that Charles had no longer been drinking, just smoking his cigar. My glass had been emptied for a few minutes now and just as well. My appetite for liquor was gone.

"Somehow, Gold fell in. Nobody is sure how. If the water was as choppy as Michael's granddaughter had heard it was, he either lost his footing or simply slipped off right into the water." Pausing to take a deep swallow of his scotch, he went on. "Henry dived in without hesitation. From what Amanda told me, this wasn't a surprise to anyone hearing the story. He was well known in the area for his selflessness and bravery."

"Who told her this story? It's possible she hadn't even been born yet," I asked.

"Her mother, Susan, who was Michael's daughter; she was fourteen at the time. Amanda was born eight years later," Max said.

Charles reached over, grabbing my glass. "One more drink." It wasn't a question. There was a demand in his eyes. It said, *let him finish the damned story.*

Until that moment, I didn't recognize Charles' own aggravation. So wrapped up in my own discomfort, I had failed to notice his problem with the course of the evening's conversation. Spiritual by nature, Charles took the symbolic icons of the church with the most serious of mindsets. This discussion of the supernatural was visibly bothering him, but he was just too polite to end it.

Charles refilled our drinks, splashing booze into our glasses. Placing his drink on the table and handing mine back to me, he tracked a few feet to feed logs to the fire. Its flames were fading a bit. The dry wood caught on and began to crackle in the refreshed pyre.

"Thanks," I said, my voice low and ashamed. Charles winked at me; the corner of his mouth turned upward. *No problem.*

If Max had noticed the exchange, he said nothing about it. "Before Michael could even decide what to do, the boat capsized, sending him and Henry into the Sound. He screamed over and over for his son but couldn't be heard over the storm.

"When they didn't return that night, his wife contacted the local marshal, and a search party formed. They found the smashed hull of the boat on the rocks of the shore, but no sign of the three men. Searching the water and coastline for miles in both directions, the search went on for two days with nothing to show for it."

A trace of sadness hung in Max's voice. I wondered how long he had been holding onto this story, just waiting for the right moment to spring it on us. A ridiculous image of Max placing speakers around the house occurred to me. The sudden idea that we were being pranked was almost too good to be true. Nothing would make me happier than for Max to jump up and say "Gotcha," with a wide grin on his face.

"On the last day, they found Michael," Max said, his voice quiet as a parishioner during a sermon. "Still in the Sound, he was clinging to a channel marker. When they pulled him from the water, crabs had been at him. Everywhere below the neck had chunks pulled out. It was miraculous that he was still alive at all."

Max stared into his drink as if the continuation to his story rested at the bottom of his glass. If any weight was being removed from him telling us this tale, I saw no signs of it. The only thing my soon-to-be double vision saw was that he was still wrestling with some issues, allowing a grim story to have such an effect on him.

"He was brought home. Any medical attention was just going through the motions, to be honest. Michael was dying, and he knew it. Hell, everyone knew it. When the priest from his church came to hear his confession, Michael had said, 'I'm not leaving until Henry comes home.'"

The expression on Max's face was sober. Any joy he had at the beginning of the evening was gone. "His family sat with him in shifts, even his youngest daughter, Susan, never leaving his side as he lay in the master bedroom. A fever had set in, burning him up from within. All the while saying that he wasn't leaving until Henry came home."

"Three days after he was pulled from the water, an hour after dawn, Michael died. Tear-streaked and heartbroken, the loss was visible on his still face. Everyone from town, as well as the surrounding communities, attended his funeral. His generosity was so well known that attendees came from as far as Manhattan."

No grimace from the scotch's smokey bite as he finished his drink in one gulp. Max looked at the bottle sitting on the table before him. He reached for it and then, as if he changed his mind, brushed it away with a gentle wave.

"In spite of the heartache, his wife and children lived here for another four years. They all knew how much he loved it here and thought it would have been what he wanted."

He paused. The story had taken a visible toll on him as it had on me. I felt exhausted, just wanting the story to end. To be honest, I wanted to go home. The small of my back, along with my forehead, was drenched in sweat. The room felt too warm to me.

"Almost immediately, there were stories of ghosts. Soft cries coming from the woods, phantom lights, things of that nature. The story was that Michael would return to collect anyone who he thought could help locate Henry. The farmhands had told Christopher — he was running the day-to-day work of the property — that some of them could hear whispering on the property, usually from behind the closed doors of their living quarters. On mornings when one of those same working men and women failed to appear, Christopher, along with some of their co-workers, would investigate. They never found hide nor hair of those poor souls. The only constant thing in those rooms was a large puddle of salt water.

"The final straw came to the family after his oldest daughter, Carol, disappeared. They had found her before on other nights, wandering the coastline of the Sound, crying out for her father and brother. She was so saddened by her family's loss that she had become a blank slate instead of the lively girl she had once been."

Max sat up in his recliner. Reaching for a poker, he prodded the fire, sending embers up the flue like ascending angels towards the heavens.

"Her mother awoke to the sounds of whispers coming from behind Carol's door. Frightened, she woke Christopher after failing to open the door — its hinges seemed to have swelled as if waterlogged. After some hard shoulders to the door, he made his way in to find nothing. No Carol or anyone else, for that matter. Just an exceptionally large puddle on the floor.

"The remaining members of the family left, and the legend of the North Shore Water Witch was born."

The room shrank, became claustrophobic. The walls seemed to fold in toward me, looming over us, closing us off from the world.

"This Amanda told you all of this?" Charles asked. He sounded tired.

We both were. Never one for the fantastic, the story of the house disturbed me. The creeping feeling that filled me was uncomfortable in its unfamiliarity. Solid footing was my haven. The truth that the sun rose in the east and set in the west was a relief to me. It was a certainty, unlike this talk of ghosts and hauntings.

"Yes, well, her and Michael," Max said.

My glass fell from my hand, bouncing off my foot. Charles just stared at Max, his mouth agape.

Max said nothing for a long moment. Not smoking or drinking but looking at the glass in his hand. "I know what you're thinking. But it's true. That first night here, I heard the whole story. I knew I was drunk, but I also knew it was real."

Charles was stunned, apparently not knowing what to make of the situation. The bizarreness of Max's demeanor, the melancholy of his story had shown us a side to him we might have suspected but never saw.

"The two of you get to go home to your families after this. My chance for that is gone. In a strange way, it was like I was meant to buy this house."

The room became tomb silent. My heart thudded in my chest. Fear mounted for my friend. His life had taken a tragic turn I feared that he didn't have the strength to correct. Charles and I stared at each other. Shock had washed away any weariness from our faces.

"I think that's it for the night." Max got up. "Let me get your coats." Walking across the study, he entered the walk-in closet.

An escape from this crazy evening had opened. The tone in Max's voice told me that he wanted us to leave.

There would not be another gathering; cigars and scotch nights were now a thing of the past. I felt him pull away from us with every passing minute of his story, but I just did not want to accept it. He would never feel comfortable around us, having opened himself up the way he did. Max had placed his scars on full display to us—a final presentation of what lurked within his soul.

Max's acceptance of such a tragic story should come as no surprise. The sad and broken always seem to drift toward each other like cosmic sand in the gravity of a dark star. Michael and Max were destined for each other.

"Of course, I would like to help you," he said from within the closet. The smell of ozone singed my nostrils as the lights dimmed for a brief second. A rumbling of thunder came from the west. The atmosphere became static. My hackles rose in warning.

Charles rose from his chair, walking toward the closet in small, measured steps. Looking over his shoulder at me, he gave the impression of a man walking to the gallows. His face had pinched into a look of fright. He was afraid, and he wasn't the only one.

Grabbing the door, he swung it open wide. "Max, what's going—" His voice caught in his throat. Shaking his head, he backed away from the door's threshold, blinking rapidly as if trying to rid his eyes of something he wished he had never seen.

Looking at me, he said, "This is fucked."

✥

Three squad cars sat parked in front of Max's hundred-year-old, two-story farmhouse with the sagging porch roof. When the police first responded, it was only one cruiser with two uniformed officers. A few minutes later, another one had pulled up, and a third was only ten minutes behind.

I can't say I would have blamed them if they had just shown up out of curiosity. The whole thing was bizarre, and having been there to witness whatever the hell had happened was the only reason I believed it.

Charles and I both repeated the same story at least half a dozen times, only we did it outside under the sagging porch.

Max walked into the closet to grab our coats and never came out. When Charles got up to check on him, he was gone. The only thing inside was a large puddle on the floor. After looking through every inch of the house, three times, we knew we had to call someone.

The police searched the house from the upstairs crawlspace to the earth floor of the root cellar. Nothing. His car was still in the driveway. A wallet containing his driver's license, three credit cards, and two hundred-eighty-three dollars was on the dresser in the master bedroom.

After two hours of repeating the same story, going in circles like a runner lapping the track, we were told that we could leave. There were no signs of foul play, nothing to hold us any longer, so we were free to go though we would more than likely hear from the lead detective at some point.

Charles had noticed that he left his keys on the coffee table. Asking an officer to get them for him, he refused to go into the house. I couldn't blame him.

Over the next couple of weeks, we heard from the detectives. Nothing changed, except Max had now become a missing person. The police assured us that they would do everything in their power to find him.

"People go missing all the time," the detective told me.

"From their living room closet?" He had no response to that one.

The story became a minor media item. Charles and I were never mentioned by name. We have never said a word to anyone about what happened. One article quoted a "reliable source" within law enforcement. A famous television psychic, known for his hour-long show on basic cable, lobbied Max's out-of-state next of kin to allow him to come to the house and try to contact Max on the other plane. He claimed that

Max had found what he was always looking for. From what I have been told, Max's sister hung up on him.

Since that night, I have found myself quite literally on the edge. Shadows in the corner of the room now hold unknown danger. I can't enter a room without the light being on. I'm jumpy, wary of every sound.

My wife wasn't sure what to make of the story, only that something had happened that I could not shake.

For three weeks, my nights have been plagued by the same reoccurring dream. I'm sitting in a recliner, sipping whiskey while staring at an empty fireplace, when I hear a knocking at a door behind me. After the soft creak of the door as it swings open, I hear the soft pads of bare feet coming up behind me. As a hand lands on my shoulder, I wake up gasping.

Then Charles called me this evening to tell me that he was moving south. The opportunity was there to leave now, and he and his family thought it best. As he said goodbye, I asked how he was sleeping. He disconnected the call.

There is no ill will there. If I had the means to leave, I would. Things are strained between my wife and me now. I've taken to sleeping in the guest bedroom. My fear is that my sanity is slipping away, but I'm terrified that I'm completely sane. Mental illness would at least be a rational explanation for what had happened.

Even more so, the sound in my closet makes me nervous.

THE RED MARE
A Dr. Darque, the Spectralist Story

TEEL JAMES GLENN

There were seven of us arrayed around the table that midsummer's night waiting for the spiritualist's séance to begin. Lady Astral was a delicate thing with pale skin, red hair, and watery blue eyes that gave the impression of her health hovering on the edge of collapse.

I was not fooled.

I knew she was robust, for I had seen her earlier when her dress had caught momentarily, and she fell forward on the stairs. Her hand shot out, and she grabbed the banister with a firm grip.

Then she went back to her feigned weakness. Clearly a pretense to garner sympathy from onlookers for the medium.

So, there we sat, myself, the lady, her "aide" Simon, my confederate Jack Stone, Horatio Venture — a reporter for the *London Star* — and the Wentworths for whom the ceremony was being conducted. It was their daughter Katherine who had "passed on."

They were wealthy Americans come to live here whose child had died in a riding accident. Both were silver haired and well behaved for colonials save that she had a tendency for tears, and he smoked an inferior cigar.

I had been invited to the séance as a "noble skeptic" by the *London Star* to spark controversy.

"I welcome you," the little medium had said at the first meeting. "I have heard about your activities, Doctor Darque."

Her hand, so small in mine; her grip was firm.

"I have heard more about you, I am sure," I responded. "Your fame as a medium has eclipsed all other news, even reports of Mister Houdini's tours."

The red-haired medium blushed shyly. "I think not, Doctor," she said. "Your doubts make the headlines as well as Mister Houdini's campaign against true seekers."

"I do my humble best."

She was the celebrated "Seer of Kent" who had been pronounced "a true spirit guide" by the Wallman Committee.

I knew most of that committee, and they were a bunch of idiots, not trained, scientific observers like myself. I refused to let her carnival techniques bamboozle me. I had spent time with Harry Houdini, had, in fact, consulted with him on several cases of medium hoaxing.

"Have you come to look up my sleeves and rattle my chains, sir?" She ended her statement with a giggle in direct challenge to me.

I smiled genially. "Well, I shall observe and note, madam. I will leave the rattling to you."

With the sitting room curtains drawn and the electric lights shut off, a single candle on the center of the table cast dancing shadows. Incense belched forth a fragrant disguise for the musty scent of the room.

"We are gathered here," the mystic began, "in good faith to try and open a window to the other side."

Mrs. Wentworth sobbed, and Lady Astral graced her with a beatific look before continuing. "We hope that those who have crossed over will contact us. Sometimes the spirits are willing to talk through me, but many times they do not."

"Could the presence of a non-believer keep Kathy from coming through?" Mrs. Wentworth looked daggers at me.

All eyes in the room shifted to me. To her credit, the medium was confident, for she said, "Sometimes, Mrs. Wentworth, but the good Doctor is merely a healthy skeptic, not the least bit hostile." This left the onus on my shoulders.

"None hopes more than I for the genuineness of such contact," I said. "I will keep an open mind and open eyes."

The medium's sly smile told me she believed she had found a chink in my armor, that I would not stop her perpetrating her sham.

She did not know me if she believed that. I have a deep faith and, like Mister Houdini, would love to know without a doubt that there was a path to the beyond, but I was also repulsed by the charlatans who prey on the bereaved.

Meanwhile, the red-haired medium began.

First, her hands were lashed to the arms of her high-backed chair. Next, the tall, thin Simon placed Mrs. Wentworth to the right of the woman and the reporter to her left.

"This way, there can be no suspicion of the Lady Astral's methods," he said. His voice was as thin as he.

Next, he secured her ankles to the chair legs as proof against her using her feet to manipulate any hidden switches. He took pains to announce this to Horatio Venture, who took notes all the time.

I sat opposite the mystic, looking at her across the flickering flame of the candle. She had a serenely calm expression on her face, a half-smile on her rosy lips.

"The Lady Astral will require you all to remain quiet and calm," Simon said. "She must enter a trance state to open herself to the spirit guide."

"Who is her spirit guide?" Venture asked.

"My guide is Asad El-Adin," Lady Astral said. Her voice was already a little vague with a distracted quality to it. "He was an eleventh-century poet in Persia. He has reached through time to touch my essence." Her words began to fade away, and her head rolled back to rest against the chair.

"It begins!" Simon said with barely contained excitement. "I must ask you all to hold the hand of the person to either side of you and do not move from the table."

We all settled in, holding the hands of our neighbors. Jack was to my right and Mister Wentworth to my left. Simon was between the married couple and urged her and the reporter to place a hand on the forearm of the psychic to keep the 'chain' unbroken.

Lady Astral had begun to moan softly. Her head slowly moved back and forth as if in a fever dream. Her eyelids flickered, and a sound came from her that might have been a death rattle.

"Uhahhh," she moaned.

There was a rushing sound from all around us, and the candle flickered wildly. The medium gyrated violently.

The moaning increased from her, followed by gasps from the Wentworths.

Simon cautioned, "Do not move from your seats. It will disturb the aether!"

I had seen the same pattern at many of the so-called séances.

"*Salaam.*" A voice came from Lady Astral. It was a deep, masculine voice. Even her eyes seemed also to have changed.

"Who is that?" Mrs. Wentworth murmured.

"It is Asad El-Adin," Simon said. "We are here, great poet; what have you to tell us?"

"There is one among you who doubts," the gruff male voice said. Lady Astral's head turned to fix her "different" eyes on me. "He is blocking the vibrations."

"He must leave," Mrs. Wentworth said. "We have to hear from Kathy!"

"No," Simon insisted, "do not break the circle!"

"Mother!" The medium's voice had changed again, this time to a high-pitched, childish voice. A young girl's voice. "Mamma?"

Suddenly, the room went black as the candle flame was extinguished.

Almost at once, the table began to jump and move. A noise sounded from behind me, and a silver trumpet appeared to float over my head. A single long blaring note issued from it and then died.

"Mamma." The girlish voice came from above the table. "I miss you so much."

"I miss you, darling." The mother's voice was wracked with sobs. "I miss you so much."

"I miss you, Mamma," the plaintive voice repeated. "It is so dark and cold here."

"Baby!" Mister Wentworth gasped.

"You have to help me," the child's voice called.

"How, Baby?" Her father was close to hysteria.

"Lady Astral is the only way to me. I have to go! Ask Lady Astral."

"Kathy!" her mother cried.

The table began to vibrate again, moving violently up and down.

"Don't go!"

The table all but jumped straight up.

That was the moment I flicked the switch for the electric lights and exposed the fraud!

When the stark bright light exploded on the scene, the tableau was clear; the reporter and the bereaved father still held the forearms of the pseudo-psychic, but the head of the flexible vixen was bent forward under the table. It was the source of the "magical levitations" of the table.

Simon was so startled by the sudden luminance that he had no time to put his shoe back on; it was slipped off so that he could manipulate the hidden buttons on the floor that worked the trumpet.

The poor Lady Astral, I'm afraid, was so shocked she hit her head on the edge of the table and cursed in a very un-ladylike fashion.

"What is the meaning of this?" an outraged Mister Wentworth asked.

"Very simply put," I said with no softness in my voice, "this charlatan and her confederate were using elaborate carnival tricks to set you both up for financial fraud. They were never actually sympathetic to you or your wife, sir. Only to your money."

The mystic was struggling in her bonds now. "Get me out of these damned ropes," she cursed.

Simon had leapt to his feet and moved toward me with a menacing attitude but thought better of it, for though I was supple enough to pass Jack's hand to Mister Wentworth's hand and slip out of my chair in the dark, I was still several stone heavier than he.

Simon went to his mistress and began to untie her.

"You are an evil man," the petite medium hissed at me when she got to her feet. She had no fear, striding right up to me to look directly up from little more than my belt level. Her eyes were swirling pools of liquid fire. "You will never profit from this vile act."

"The pot calling the kettle black, my dear," I said. I am afraid my vanity allowed me to smile at her. She knew that with Horatio there, the true facts of her fraudulent career would be public knowledge by dawn.

She lashed out and slapped me hard across the face. "You will pay for this, Saxon Darque!" she said. "I put a curse on you!"

I laughed again, for the genuineness of her magic left me little to fear at that point.

"A remarkable story, Saxon," my friend, Jolly Stevens, said, "but how does that explain this package?"

We two stood in the study of my home with a large wooden box set on the table before us.

"I am not exactly sure how it explains it, Jolly," I said, "but the signature on the box is indeed from the medium herself."

"Could it be a bomb?" Jolly asked. His shock of white hair, round glasses, and bushy eyebrows gave him an owlish appearance.

"I don't think the lady is quite so obvious," I said. "But it might do to be cautious; let us take it out onto the patio." We picked up the long box and carried it to the side of the cottage.

"What exactly does the card say?" Jolly asked, when the two of us had set the ominous box on the patio table.

"To the man who mocks the spirits; may you enjoy the day of Aine and become a partner for the red mare."

It was signed, "Lady Astral."

"What in heaven's name does that mean?" Jolly asked.

"No good, I expect."

I spied a garden rake leaning against the side of the house and motioned for my friend to step back. I used the rake to unlatch the hasp on the front of the gift.

"Here goes," I said and flipped the lid up. We both winced in anticipation of some sort of trick, but nothing happened.

Jolly looked to me, and I shrugged.

"Well, I expected she would not be too obvious." Inside the wooden crate was a red pantomime horse head such as were worn in many pagan festivals.

"Aine is the Celtic goddess of the midsummer holiday — or Litha to the Irish," I said as I studied the contents. "The red mare is often her symbol. She is a goddess of sexuality, wealth, and sovereignty."

"What significance can it have?" Jolly asked.

"I revealed her tricks on Litha some four years ago, as I told you in my story. Tomorrow is that pagan holiday. I suppose it is her attempt at something poetic."

I tipped the box to reveal its contents to him.

"Seems a bit tame for a revenge gambit," Jolly said.

"It sure seems so, but we shall see if the siren of the spirits has a more devious plan for me." I set about examining the suit using a fountain pen to move it to and fro. I looked for any minute hidden traps within the box as well.

After a time, we carefully removed the horse suit and set it out on the table. It appeared to be just a cleverly sculpted horse head complete with straps to attach it over a sort of coverall.

"It certainly looks large enough for you, Saxon," Jolly said with a chuckle. "She seems to have anticipated your girth enlarging."

I laughed, patting my stomach. "She may be psychic after all."

"But what could it really mean?"

"I don't know, and perhaps that is the point."

"How so?" he asked.

"To fill our thoughts. A puzzle. This is one that might be intended to occupy my mind and, maybe, keep me from seeking some other revenge."

"A ruse?"

"Not a clever one, I think." I ran fingers along the cleverly crafted "skin" of the horse head. I felt a little sticky substance on it, which I sniffed but could not identify. *Some sort of packing material.*

"We will have to investigate where this woman is," Jolly said.

"Just so, then let us leave this silly thing. Don't you have to head to lunch?"

"Are you going to the bonfire tonight?" Jolly asked.

"I hadn't thought to, but now that I've been challenged by the Lady Astral, perhaps I will partake."

We parted, promising to meet later. From my garden gate, I saw the horse suit still set out on the table. It made me chuckle.

"I accept your challenge, good lady," I said to the horse head.

The glass eye of the equine glinted and almost might have been winking at me. I left the costume where it lay and went to the daybed in my study to have a toes-up. I was soon asleep.

And I dreamed.

In my dream, I saw Lady Astral, but she was standing at the edge of a great dark abyss in a flowing crimson gown. Her hair was a wild halo around her head, and her eyes glowed from within.

"Saxon Darque!" Her voice sounded like the wind. "You who defame the occult."

"I do no such thing," I said. "I respect religion; I do not respect criminals!"

"Enough!" the dream woman cried. "You ruined me! I was turned out because of you!"

"Well, you could have taken to the stage, my dear. You certainly have skill at drama."

"Drama!" she screamed, and a peal of thunder split the dream sky.

"I know this is a dream, madam," I said with exasperation. "I will not be flummoxed by your chicanery!"

"Beware Aine's power, sir," the Lady Astral declared. "You will pay for what you have done!"

Suddenly the figure of the medium became a red mare with watery blue eyes out in the center of the lawn. The red mare threw her head back and whinnied, then spun on her haunches and headed into the woods with me compelled to follow.

We raced through the woods and out onto the heath outside of town. It was a rolling swath of open land that was bordered by bogs. The red mare flew, her hooves barely touching the sod.

The Lady Astral-mare led me around a blind bend. I raced after her at full tilt.

I rounded the turn and went sailing off the cliff face she had led me to!

I cried in terror as I tumbled end over end down toward the jagged rocks fifty feet below.

I woke up screaming and sat bolt upright, my breath ragged and my hair wet with sweat.

I had no thought to where I was. Then I remembered the cliff.

It was – it was a dream?

I have real insight to how so many poor souls are duped by charlatans like Lady Astral now. Even a man of reason like myself is susceptible to her suggestions and hocus pocus.

I stood on unsteady legs and went to the sideboard to pour myself a stiff brandy, shaking my head to clear it, suddenly aware of the time.

I should get a hurry on else I shall miss the lighting of the bonfire!

When I reached the patio, however, I stopped short; the table with the horse suit was knocked over, and the lawn itself was a mass of divots as if a large animal had torn across it at full speed.

I felt panic rising but forced myself to calm.

I must have heard a horse run by and the table fall over in my dreaming state; perhaps the rider indeed knocked it over, and I translated the events into my dream. Yes, that must be it.

In the village center, there were revelers out, some of them in their midsummer celebratory costumes; elaborate bird masks, pantomime lion or dragon costumes, many elaborate in construction and coloring.

I put the nightmare out of my head by the time I gained the village green. On the swath of grass, a huge pile of wood had been assembled in a pyramid in anticipation of the coming conflagration.

The celebrants were milling about, many with mugs of ale in their hands. Jolly was chatting with Mildred Smothers, the town librarian.

"Ho, Saxon!" Jolly called. "I was afraid you had changed your mind."

"Evening, Mildred," I said. Jolly handed me a tankard.

"Good man!" I quaffed the first drink.

The younger members of the community were boisterous. There was music and dancing, many costumes, and much laughter. My investigator's eye was drawn to a familiar-looking girl across the village common, clothed in a green dress that was created to resemble the leaves of a bush.

It was an outrageous outfit, yet there was something in her carriage and the set of her head that made me think I had seen her before. Only when she turned around and faced me did I freeze with shock. The woman, who was masked, nonetheless looked exactly like the red-haired Lady Astral!

"You," I yelled. "Stop there!"

Jolly and Mildred swiveled their heads, but I ignored their questioning looks and raced toward the masked vixen.

The woman turned without comment and headed outside the circle of torches with unhurried steps. Once out of the torch light, the moonlight gave all a ghostly glow, and the petite woman was soon moving in and out of the shadows between the close-set buildings of the village.

This is absurd. I caught yet another glimpse of the longhaired girl on the street ahead of me. *It is just someone who looks like Lady Astral. She is just in my mind. Why would she come here?*

A high-pitched female laugh came from a pool of darkness off to my right.

"You really do have to cut down on the mutton, old fellow," the voice of Lady Astral came from the shadows.

"Show yourself, vixen. Tell me what you want."

"I want my reputation back."

"Reputation?" I spat. "You took advantage of innocent people—"

"I gave comfort to the bereaved," Lady Astral said, "so what if I did not exercise true psychic ability on those cases? Who was hurt?"

"Those who believed," I said with venom. "Those who hoped."

The medium stepped from the blackness to stand in a shaft of moonlight, her eyes appearing to glow. "Like you, Doctor? Could it be that you hate yourself for not being able to believe?"

She took my silence as agreement and gave a little laugh again that sent a chill up my back. "I will give you something you can believe in, whether you want to or not!"

"What was the meaning of sending me that silly costume," I said. "Did you poison me with something on the suit?"

"I did not poison you," she said. "It was you who poisoned the public against me. Now you will understand what you ridiculed."

Before I could inquire what she meant, a group of revelers came out of an alley nearby, laughing and joking. They swarmed quickly between us so that I was swept along with the crowd.

"Let's go!" someone yelled in the group. "They're going to light the bonfire!"

I felt stunned and looked back, but the green-garbed medium was gone. I moved along with the partiers feeling myself in a daze, the encounter with the Lady Astral feeling like another dream.

On the village green, the ceremony to light the bonfire had begun. The mummers dressed as animals and mythical beasts were dancing around the stack of wood while musicians played on horns, drums, and cymbals. The pagan splendor of the spectacle, lit by the full moon, seemed as unreal as the nightmare.

I pulled myself from the group when the green-garbed Lady Astral stepped out of the shadows and gestured to the ground before me.

Somehow the pantomime horse costume had been laid out on the grass.

"What's your rush, Doctor?" Her eyes were glimmering behind her mask. "You can't go to the party without your costume!"

I tried to speak, but the words stuck in my throat.

"Help him dress!" she cried to the crowd. She waved her arms to exhort the revelers to come toward me. "Help him dress!"

The group swarmed toward me and soon took up the chant, "Help him dress, help him dress!" and moved in around me.

I couldn't resist as they pulled at my clothing and tore it from my back. "No, stop!" I cried. "No!" I yelled, but my voice was a whisper. "Can't you see that witch is doing this!"

But they couldn't. They saw only a great jest as they forced me into the faux equine.

All the time, Lady Astral stood by and chanted. She clapped her hands and danced around while I was manhandled into the suit.

"You were the one who made me an object of ridicule," Lady Astral said. "Now it's your turn to know what it is to play the goat." She laughed again. "Or should I say, the horse!"

The crowd pulled the head of the rubberized suit over my head. It was like being entombed alive. The smell of the hood was vaguely chemical, and it made me momentarily flash on my suspicion of a hallucinogen or poison.

The crowd stepped away. I tried to stand with the false head on and stumbled. The rush of the revelers had moved to the unlit bonfire. The music suddenly stopped.

All the faces at the pile turned toward me.

Abruptly in the silence, Lady Astral called out, "Now the fool of the festival is ready to dance!"

"Dance!" the crowd called. "Dance!"

Against my will, my arms and legs began to move to a new rhythm as if unseen hands were controlling me, moving me toward the base of the wooden stack.

This is mad. She has drugged me. I have to get to Jolly. I have to get help!

The music throbbed inside my head, echoing into my soul to fill me up with desperation and despair.

I did an awkward dance around the lawn for the amusement of the crowd, who cheered and applauded. I felt as if I were a performing monkey in a carnival show.

I moved withershins as in an ancient summoning with a sudden horrid thought of the remembrance of pagan sacrifices of old, where a wicker man was burned to bring better crops.

I knew the tradition well as it paid to know the enemy, but I had known the ways of magick without believing in it. Now I felt the power of that magick, for I began to believe that this was my end.

But I just continued to gambol around the base of the woodpile while the villagers and guests cheered and sang.

My heart sank when I saw my friends laughing and cheering with the rest.

Then someone lit the pile.

The bonfire exploded into light with a great hiss and then a *whoosh* as the dry wood caught. The night was abruptly as bright as day, colored orange and black with a sharp line where the light from the flames met the darkness.

I heard the voice of the petite psychic again.

"Do you feel your mortality, Doctor?" she asked. "Do you know the fear of the dark? Is your body aware of the fragility of life and the power of the beyond?"

The woman's eyes caught light from the burning wood and reflected it back.

The heat from the fire made me dizzy. The sound of the music, the crowd, and the crackle of the flames roared in my ears. It was almost deafening but not so loud that I could not hear her whispered words.

"I know what it is to question and receive no answers. To question and wonder with no proof. But now you know. Now you have proof."

The bonfire blazed brighter, then the heat rose precipitously, and I stumbled toward it.

I had a last image of the green-garbed mystic smiling at me as the heat robbed me of all thoughts, and I pitched forward into blackness.

"It was almost the end of you, Saxon." The statuesque Mildred was standing beside my bed. It was the morning after the solstice celebrations.

"I thought so," I said. "Never expected to awaken from that fall."

"The suit dehydrated you, Saxon," Mildred said. "If we had not realized you were beneath that mask—" She shuddered.

"I wish I knew what else that vixen intended for me. This jest cannot be all."

"I suspect she has nothing more in store for you," Jolly said as he entered the room. "At least not if what I learned is true."

"What do you mean?" I asked.

"I traced the box which held the horse costume to the shipper," my owlish friend said, "who reported me a description of the woman you described, this Lady Astral woman."

"That pretty much cooks her goose then," Mildred said.

"Not really," Jolly said. "I checked with the police; it seems that the woman known as Lady Astral, real name Jenny Seaworth, took her own life in a fit of depression two days before that package was even mailed. She blamed you, Saxon, for the state of her life."

"The police are sure?" Mildred said.

"Definitely," Jolly said. "She put a bullet in her brain; it seems this was mailed to you by a dead woman!"

"I did see her; it was not a dream." I felt as if the room would spin. "It seems that the lady has done one last service to the world by making contact with me from the beyond. I suspect I shall never be able to debunk a medium with quite so much assurance again."

Somewhere outside my window, I heard the sound of the wind in the trees — or perhaps it was the sound of a vixen having the last laugh.

MOSHIGAWA'S HOMECOMING

GORDON LINZNER

Moshigawa Edo paused before the low rubble where the sloping outer wall of his clan's castle had stood. The long climb had tired him. Despite the chilling sea breeze, perspiration crawled under his leather breastplate and the loose folds of the hunting jacket his class usually wore in times of peace. The latter was his only attempt at disguise.

Edo was bareheaded; his elaborate helmet hung behind by its chinstraps. Bow and arrows he'd left with his Tohoku-bred mare in a thicket at the cliff's base. Although the animal had been raised among mountains, this path was too narrow and twisting for her hooves. The regular roads were, of course, barred to him by Hairo patrols. Besides, the crosswinds on a seacoast clifftop made bowshots uncertain. He had his dagger, thrust in his belt, and two fine swords: the long tachi and the shorter katana. A warrior of his skill needed little more; however, Edo anticipated no danger within the ruins.

Edo glanced back the way he'd come. Much of his path was hidden by boulders, stubborn brush, and thicker cover near the bottom. To the right, far below, was an open field once lushly green but now brown with upchurned mud, where he and other children of the clan sometimes held ferocious battles with self-made wooden swords and mercilessly teased any dogs foolish enough to intrude.

On special occasions, competitions were held there. That earth had been shaken by sumo bouts, horse races, and games such as the soccer-like kemari, as the clansfolk vied among themselves or with guests from nearby provinces. On one of these competition days, Edo decided there could be no lasting peace with the Hairo clan from the south.

Edo's likable but slow-witted cousin, Kiken, was particularly fond of tako, wherein kite-tails fitted with sharp blades were manipulated to cut the cords of opponents' kites. That year, a sudden downdraft had brought a kite down near young Kiken. Without a thought, Kiken grasped at it and lost his right forefinger to the second joint. Edo recalled his own cry of horror, saw again Kiken's parents rushing to his side as the child tried, through watering eyes, to tie his finger back in place with cloth torn from his kimono.

Above the cries of concern and distress came the braying laughter of Hairo Mouka, heir to Lord Hairo. Edo was tempted to challenge Mouka at that instant, despite the Hairo's advantage in age and weight, but Lord Moshigawa would punish any breaking of their truce with exile. Unfortunately, their paths did not cross afterward.

Now all but Edo were dead. No Moshigawa infant would chase dragonflies across that green again.

Edo turned grimly to his goal. The Hairo warriors had been thorough. Most of the castle's stones had been cast into the sea from the sheer western cliff. Only enough remained to outline the foundations. Pebbles, fragments of the only home Edo knew, crunched beneath his leather boots. Something glittered as the late morning sun found a gap in the clouds, and Edo stooped to recover an almost intact glazed tile from one of the keep's roofs. The shibi, or sea monster, decorating the tile was missing a tail and one foot. Edo tucked the fragment into his sleeve and stepped over a low pile of stone where the keep's wall had been.

He strode forward austerely, picturing the structure as it looked before he'd been called away, slowing only once as he passed the site of the arsenal from which, in his fifteenth year, his first real sword had come. That was the day he'd returned from the monastery after five difficult years of studying such manly pursuits as ancient history, calligraphy, and mastery of the horizontal flute.

He'd lost the flute to a storm at sea two years past and had not found time to replace it. At times he missed its solace. This was such a time.

At last, Edo came to the opposite side of the keep and the square that he remembered best. Because the castle was small, it possessed but one garden, theoretically reserved for the noble family to the exclusion of warriors and vassals who took on their lord's name. However, Lord Moshigawa was lenient in many things, and the province was remote; he did not have to impress other nobles unduly. Warriors, servants, even peasants visiting the castle on business — all could spend almost as much time in the garden as the noble family and their more honored guests. Mutual respect kept the sacred spot serene. Edo often wandered its footpaths, meditating or simply escaping the drudgery of his duties. He loved the garden more than anyone else in the castle, save the lord.

Now the tears he'd held back began to flow. A few of the hardier shrubs survived, their roots buried deep enough to permit regrowth: they were ragged and ugly out of context. Painstakingly arranged pebbles were irrevocably scattered, bridges burnt, islands smashed to dam rivulets. What had become of that ancient tortoise who'd led him, as a boy, to discover many of the subtler, more pleasing secrets that only the gardeners and, perhaps, Lord Moshigawa knew of? Worthy creature! He deserved a better fate than that of stew for the bellies of craven Hairo warriors.

A curse escaped Edo's lips, the first word he'd spoken in two days. *He* should have been here to defend his lord's castle, dying with the others if that was how it must end. Instead, there was that fool's mission for the Emperor, a three-year sea mission to study the feasibility of invading Korea. Edo accepted Japan's need for more land; the islands were so heavily populated now that it was difficult to reward bold warriors with appropriate domains. Yet Emperor after Emperor had looked hungrily across that dangerous stretch of water, without result. Attack Korea or let her be, but why drag the question on for generation after generation? Edo could not fathom the imperial mind. Moshigawa's province was too far from court for the lord to be sucked into meddlesome politics, though not far enough away to avoid certain obligations. Many of Moshigawa's best fighting men died in wars in which no gain could be made. Edo was conscripted for a spying mission ill-suited to his open nature.

For thirty months, Edo and his company sailed up and down the Korean coast in a small, poorly constructed ship, under orders not to remain in any port longer than was necessary to resupply, even during typhoon season. Countless sister ships were sunk by those storms, some within reach of land if the sailors could only have seen that land under the pitch-colored sky. Edo's own vessel limped into its home port at Hirado, barely reaching the dock. While he'd bailed endless buckets of water, his family, home, and lord were being destroyed.

At the garden's center was a wide pool which, Edo noted with surprise, retained its original shape except for a section of its northern shore. Water still filled the depression, but without the constant flow of man-made streams, it had stagnated. A thin green scum coated the

surface. Those extraordinarily beautiful fish that had dwelt here...
could any have escaped the slaughter? It was impossible, of course, but
Edo knelt, cleared a patch of scum with the side of his hand, and peered
below the surface.

At first, he saw only his own scarred face, its hardened eyes glaring
back at him. He moved his head aside... and a gasp escaped his lips.

His right hand clutched the hilt of his tachi, though he did not draw
the blade. The gesture was instinctive; no enemy threatened. Edo jerked
his head right, left, behind, up. Above was the cold gray sky; to the
west, the even grayer sea. Rubblework surrounded the last of the
Moshigawa clan.

A trick of memory, Edo thought. He looked again. Then he decided
that grief had driven him mad.

Reflected in the pool's waters were the upper stories of the keep of
Castle Moshigawa. Due to clever landscaping, the keep had been the
only part of the castle visible from the pond.

And the original no longer existed.

Edo dried his hand on wine-dark cotton trousers and drew the
glazed tile from his sleeve. The shibi's image grinned as if it knew a secret it would not tell. With the tile, Edo cleared a larger patch of pond.

Yes, that was the Moshigawa keep. The gently tapering lines of
the hipped roofs were unmistakable. Crude in comparison with the
magnificent castles built in recent years in open country, its simple
ornamentation warmed his nostalgic mood. Behind those shuttered
windows were the arsenal, storehouses, audience chambers, and private apartments of the lord's family. Edo had only heard second-hand
reports of the beauty to be found in the latter rooms, but he could
imagine it, had done so often. From the highest point of the keep, one
could on a clear day see past farms and forests to the highest point of
the keep at Hairo Castle.

A woman's face appeared beside his own reflection. Edo glanced
behind to assure himself that this was but another phantom of the past
rather than some silent assassin, then stared down at her. He did not
recognize her until she smiled, revealing fashionably blackened teeth.
Then it seemed incredible that he had not at once known his younger
sister, Yuki. When Edo left, Yuki was a month shy of her first eyebrow-
plucking. A few months made a great difference in women at that
age. The lord's fourth son, Edo recalled, had been attracted to Yuki even
then.

Such a waste! And he'd never have known what she looked like before her death, except for this curious window on the land of the dead.

Yuki smiled, but he could not smile back, thinking of what the Hairo must have done if she were too slow to take her own life… or even if she'd succeeded.

A sea breeze whipped across the plateau, turning the perspiration on Edo's back to ice. He did not shiver. He'd endured worse cold while training as a warrior. Even when the castle stood, these offshore winds often froze its inhabitants. Nonetheless, Edo found the atmosphere disquieting.

Why had he come here? To see for himself that the castle had been razed, of course, else he would not have believed it. To stand among the ghosts of those who'd mattered most to him. He'd not expected to see one of the ghosts, nor to discover that the castle itself possessed an otherworldly shadow. It was seductive to think he might sit here calmly, seeing things as they were, for the rest of his life….

Edo shook his head to clear it. The helmet's chinstraps chafed his neck. The long climb, after a perilous ride through what was now enemy territory, with little time for food and less for sleep, was taking its toll. He needed to rest… but not here. If he lingered overlong, he would not wish to leave. And the clan of Moshigawa must somehow be avenged. One man could not accomplish much against the combined might of Hairo, but he would do what he could.

One more glance into the pool, and Edo would leave his home for the last time. He hoped to send many Hairo ahead of him before he joined his fellow clansmen in the land of ghosts.

Yuki's face was gone, but another came forward. Edo started as he recognized the hated features of Hairo Mouka, he who'd mocked the unfortunate Kiken years before. Why was Mouka on the grounds of the Moshigawa Castle of the afterworld? According to all accounts of the siege, the heir had come through the battle unscathed. If the reports were false, so much the better, but would the arrogant Mouka be thrust upon those he'd wronged? Was there as little justice in the next world as this one?

Edo's absorption almost cost him his life. The scrape of a blade leaving its scabbard, however, was too familiar a sound for Edo to mistake for anything else.

Mouka's sword slashed air where, a second earlier, Edo's neck had been. Not entirely air; Edo felt a warm trickle below his left ear. He could not judge the depth of the cut, but it was not a death blow, and nothing less would save the craven who'd attacked from behind from a warrior's wrath.

Mouka laughed in the same high-pitched, braying manner that had burned itself in young Edo's mind that competition day. Seeing the accusation in his foe's eyes, Mouka said, "Any man who lets an enemy come so close deserves his fate."

"Who strikes from the rear is no man," Edo spat.

Mouka's laughter died. "My retainers saw you skulking through the hills. As future lord of Hairo, I felt it my duty to deal with the last Moshigawa. You knelt as if inviting death."

"I neither skulked nor advertised my presence. Hairo patrols trembled in the bushes as a true warrior rode past."

"I shall treat you as my clan did your castle."

"With words?" Edo mocked, rising.

No further words were exchanged. The roar of the sea seemed very far away, and even gulls shunned this place of slaughter. The two men faced each other, swords raised, legs braced, ready to fight and yet unmoving, each studying his opponent.

Edo's only armor was the leather breastplate, no surety against a well-made blade—and the Hairo heir would have no lesser weapon. Mouka wore the full war dress of a samurai, including a breastplate of lacquered steel and stiff greaves that rose above his knees. He'd been skillful to approach so near in that regalia without being heard. Mouka was also fresh. He'd ridden but a few hours to reach this place, along the gentler sloping main road to the fortress's former gates.

Edo felt a tremor in his right calf. He could not hold this position much longer, and he dared not show his weakness. Although he was not ready, he attacked.

Steel flashed, unaccompanied by the sound of metal on metal. In Japanese fighting, swords rarely touched; the weapons were not designed for defense. The best way to spoil a quality blade was to use it as a shield.

Mouka twisted his thick torso, allowing Edo's blade to sheer harmlessly past. He pressed his own attack at once. The Moshigawa barely recovered in time to withdraw and then could gain no respite; Mouka did not pause. The Hairo knew he had his rival. Edo's attack was clumsy. A few strokes would disarm him.

Edo sensed his doom but did not yield to despair. He cared little about dying. He'd even welcome the opportunity to join the others of his clan. To lose any hope of avenging them, however, was a bitter pill. He would be satisfied to take but one Hairo with him... especially if that one was Mouka....

He dodged a blow, knowing as he did so that he'd moved too late. Mouka's blade swung toward his bared skull, and Edo could do nothing to stop it.

Then a mossy rock gave way beneath Edo's feet.

Arms flailing, hand griping his tachi, Edo flipped backward into the stagnant pool. A spout of water enveloped him. He gasped for air, spat foul liquid, felt sharp agony as his elbow struck a stone on the pool's bottom.

Mouka waited at the pool's edge. Thrashing wildly, Edo might strike a deadly blow without trying. Or the Moshigawa could crack his skull and drown, saving the Hairo the trouble of running him through and having to clean his blade.

Edo splashed, putting more distance between himself and his foe before struggling to his feet. He cleared his eyes with a shake of the head. The pool was not deep; the water rose no higher than his thighs. He positioned his sword and watched for Mouka's next attack.

The Hairo heir did not relish wading in the stale, ill-smelling pool, but the near miss angered him. The game was no longer enjoyable; time to end it quickly. Edo would be even less of a match for him after that ignoble fall. Mouka smiled savagely and stepped forward.

"Prepare for death, Moshigawa," he advised.

Edo held up his weapon, despite the pain that shot through his sword arm. Mouka could easily parry whatever stroke he made now, following with a death thrust. Yet Edo had to lash out a final time. One did not give up a fight simply because it seemed hopeless, not when one's life depended on the outcome.

Mouka halted two sword lengths from Edo. The latter's eyes narrowed. Was this some new sport of the cruel heir? No. The confidence on Mouka's face gave way to horror. The man strove to come nearer but could not move his legs.

"What cowardly trick is this?" Mouka demanded.

Edo shook his head.

Mouka suddenly slashed the water with his long sword. The absurdity of the action so startled the fatigued Edo that he did not use the opening to attack.

Then Mouka was waist-deep in green water. Edo thought of quicksand, but how the gardeners could have created such a pit at the bottom of a pond built atop a cliff of solid rock was beyond him. It was purposeless, as well. Besides, he'd fallen in the same spot, moving further in to regain his balance. Why hadn't *he* been sucked down?

Mouka's sword hand dipped, and at once, the arm plunged down to the elbow, tachi and all. Edo slowly approached his rival. As he came alongside, Mouka cried out and vanished below the surface. Air bubbled up.

When Edo saw what had pulled Mouka down, he trembled without shame… though only for a moment.

Hands gripped the Hairo by ankles, calves, wrists. Burly arms wrapped around the warrior's chest, holding him to the floor of the pool. Another hand covered Mouka's mouth, even as the heir's death cry helped drown him… and this hand lacked a forefinger from the second joint.

Edo drew his dagger and slit Mouka's throat. The various hands seemed to relax their grips before the water reddened so that nothing could be seen below the surface. The last breathing Moshigawa turned and climbed onto dry land, his outer breeches stained with his nemesis's diluted blood.

Moshigawa Edo shuddered in the salt breeze as he fumbled for a scrap of cloth with which to dry his tachi. He perched on a chunk of masonry to contemplate the pool of death. More than insubstantial ghosts resided there. The hand that covered Mouka's mouth could almost have belonged to cousin Kiken, except that it was a left hand. Kiken lost his finger from the right.

Still, were not images reversed in a reflection?

Edo stripped to his loincloth and arranged his clothing flat on the stones to be dried by wind and sporadic sun. His spare clothing was with his mare, who had undoubtedly been found and taken by Hairo retainers. He had no reason now to leave the ruins. Mouka was head-strong, but he would not have come here alone without telling some-one. The patrols on the roads to Moshigawa would come looking for him.

Edo smiled for the first time in three years. Let them come, he thought. I shall not meet them alone.

The Moshigawa clan survived in their reflected images. They would not abandon Edo.

FETCH

Randee Dawn

Unearthly keening blooms deep in the Northern mist, billowing across the moors — a seeking, hungry sound born between dreams and nightmares. Hastening over the dales, it approaches a lonely cottage on the edge of a sprawling, isolated grand estate — and waits to be called.

Alfred starts from half-sleep, heart in a panic. He's stretched awkwardly on the flagstones of his cottage hearth where he fell some hours earlier. Long, low howls carom in his head and echo in his blood, the song of dogs on the hunt. Sounds that, as Head Gamekeeper for Lord M—'s Great House, he knows well. But there is no hunt now, no dogs loosed beneath the stars. The estate's foxhound pack is long gone, buried beneath layers of lime, rotting in the earth.

With soil-stained hands, he reaches for the whiskey bottle, dropping it once, and wonders at the state of himself. He's not yet thirty, yet he's shaking like a palsied geezer. Retrieving the bottle, he takes a long swallow, alcohol dribbling into his pale beard, and runs filthy fingers through his thick blond locks. Fire courses through his weary body. He spent all yesterday afternoon in the forest burying three blood-soaked shrouds, and afterward, it had been all he could do to stumble home and flop on the floor.

Sleeping in the bed was out of the question.

A yowl splits the night, a voice like that of his nightmare — but real and near. Not a foxhound. An animal with white eyes and a mangled ear. One that *cannot* be outside.

Aye, he's dead an' no mistake, Alfred assures himself. *Did it to hi'sen. Nae my fault.*

Alfred flings open his back door, revealing a walled-in garden bisected by a newly felled oak tree. The howl slices into him like an axe made of ice. His bones twist, his skin contracts. But there is no dog.

There will never be a dog here again.

Three springs earlier, Mary slipped into his garden cradling a bundle of kitchen rags, emerging from the fog like a silent wraith. Alfred gripped his shovel to combat the oncoming spirit—but no, 'twas only Mary of the Great House, a hopeful smile on her round face. A child-woman of thirteen, the same age Alfred had been when he'd first come to the estate, direct from the workhouse.

"Miss Mary!" he cried. "Tha gave me a start. Fer why are thee goin' out'doors w'nowt but a shawl?"

"Oh, Alfred," the girl tutted. "I do not require mothering. It's not so far a walk, and I've had my broth. Cook insisted." She wore a blue, high-waisted dress with a frilly collar, hair bound in a white bonnet.

His heart thrummed. "Yer *do* need motherin' and nae question. God rest her soul."

Mary hesitated. Lady M— had passed three months earlier of the wasting, coughing disease that banished people into their homes as it swept across the countryside. Gentry stayed safely put on their estates; Alfred, like other working folk, had fewer options. At least he avoided lodging with other servants—his position afforded him this cottage, which suited his naturally lonesome tendencies.

"A-men," murmured Mary.

"Aye." Alfred admired the clever rosy flush high in the girl's cheeks. "What'll I do fer ye this early morn?" Much as he enjoyed her company, he had chores: Lord M— had reduced staff, and he had to tend to the hounds as well as scout for potential poachers in the forest.

The girl unfurled her arms from her bosom. A brindled snout poked from the rag bundle, and two stark white eyes blinked. Alfred suppressed the urge to flinch at the ungodly thing. "What... what is it, Miss?"

After a moment's consideration, though, he knew: Lord M—'s house dog Asgard had whelped an undesired litter of seven some weeks past. Mary's father had been furious at Alfred; clearly, a foxhound had escaped and impregnated the Great House deerhound. Ruined her for future breeding prospects, too—a bitch crossbred was considered forever "tainted." On orders from Lord M— Alfred had drowned the newborns in a rain barrel, but after he'd finished the distasteful task and opened the sack to ensure all were deceased, there were but six corpses.

Now here was the seventh, wriggling from the cloth. One ear perked up smartly while the other dangled; it had a chewed aspect, as if its brothers had tried consuming it in the womb. *'Tis blind*, Alfred thought—but those white eyes stared at him steadily, as if it knew Alfred had been the instrument of its siblings' deaths.

Nae blind, Alfred decided. *Sees too much, maybe.*

"I *stole* him," said Mary with a child's cunning. "I paid footman Jerry a coin to only put six in the bag." Her chest rose and fell with excitement, eyes bright. The sweet pink in her cheeks glowed. "He lived in my room, and at night I spirited him to the kitchen to suck from Asgard's teat."

"Miss Mary!" Alfred gasped. "Ye should know n'owt o' such things." She had him all a-tangle. Of course, Alfred knew she wasn't here for *him*, even if they had been friendly in the past—she'd cooed and petted most of the property's animals—yet her words dried his mouth. A fleeting thought: *She wants a kiss, this one.*

Impossible, of course. Mary was still like a child and stood above him in station. For years, Alfred's physical dalliances had been with tavern maids in the village some fourmile away, but since the sickness, he'd not ventured off the estate. He longed for a touch beyond self-relief. But whatever fancies might play in his head, Mary could not be part of them. She would never be his, and there was no reason to think on it further.

Yet he did.

"Oh, you are a silly." Mary smiled. "Of course, I am familiar with such particulars. In all ways that matter, I am a woman. I will be fourteen soon, and with Mother gone, I am the lady of the House. So, you *must* listen to me." Her eyes twinkled, and the heat in his face raced to his nethers. "Meet Fetch." She handed him the bundle.

"Oh, Miss—no. I cannae. Dogs are *work* an'—"

The pup wriggled, and she did not retract her arms. "If Papa learns that he lives, he'll have him killed. He's such a tiny thing, Alfred—I do believe I've given him a piece of my soul. But I can't have him in the House. Let him be *your* dog. You care for animals—and he can be *our* secret. Promise?"

Alfred licked his lips. This wasn't really a request. All his life, his betters had told him what to do, where to go, how much he was worth.

His debt-ridden parents had landed the family in a stinking, overstuffed workhouse when he was a boy, and after three years there, both were dead. He'd taken the first glimmer of light that came his way—work at the Great House. Being employed in a time of sickness was a blessing, but he resented his own lack of choices in life. He would not *choose* the additional burden of a dog.

But he might choose to have a secret with the girl. She could owe him something, for once. And a crooked warmth blossomed in his gut. "I will care for tha's pup. But: tuh things. I'll tell Cook tae prepare food. I ken afford scraps for n'owt but m'self."

She nodded.

"An' tha will come t'garden tae play w'it. 'Twill be like tha's own pet, fostered here."

Mary clapped her small hands together. "Alfred, you *are* clever!"

"Come int t'early morn or late eve," he advised, thinking of how she'd slipped out of the House so smartly at daybreak. He relished the idea of her padding to his stone cottage, slipping through the rickety wooden gate. He would tie the dog to the oak tree in the garden, perhaps make a small shelter for it.

Alfred took the bundle. The dog's pink-gray tongue lolled from its furred snout. Gray-brown and sleek, it watched him. "Why… Fetch?"

"It's what dogs do, isn't it?" Mary glanced over one shoulder, already turned back to the House. In the morning light, she was almost pretty. "They do what their masters tell them."

Alfred huddles inside the cottage doorway. The calling is everywhere, a howl that comes from both moors and his own back garden. More than a calling, though—a *summoning*. But to what?

When he closes his eyes, the motley pack of dogs is there, rising from blanket bogs, bounding across marshy moors with determined fire in their gazes. Their bodies are coated in powdery, poisonous lime that glows in the moonlight. Noses low to the ground they seek, then stiffen, shifting direction, closing in on their goal. But that aspect is not what chills Alfred's blood; it is those high, swirling bays. Their music slips beneath his skin and chews upon his innards. He can no longer tell which cries are in his head and which are real.

He must *act*. He must *do*. But a frozen lassitude has crept into him. He might walk away from his home and escape this awful music. But where would he go? He has no family; he would be without reference for future employment, and there is the ongoing sickness.

Meanwhile, the distant pack sings eerily, harmonizing with the unseen beast in his garden, fashioning tunes even fae would recoil from. Yet he senses the calls are not for him, not exactly: They sing to one another.

Deep in the garden, back where the oak trunk lies, metal clanks then rings out. Alfred squints into the dark; he can hardly make out the borders of the yard. Mist has drifted over his stone walls, seeking and probing like the voices of the nightmare animals. He snatches up the now-empty whiskey bottle and flings it into the night.

"What d'yee *want*?" he shouts, but there is no answer, just the thud of the bottle on the soft earth.

A thin *scree* startles him, and he tumbles into the garden, raising a lantern. The gate latch has fallen open, and he slams it shut. There, he has acted. He should do more—

Something batters against the other side of the gate. The hinges creak with strain; the wood bends inward. A second strike, then a third, desiring ingress.

"Nae," he hisses. "Tha's nae welcome here."

Then something bumps against his calf, and Alfred screams like a child.

Mary upheld her side of the secret bargain joyfully, appearing every other evening or daybreak. Alfred took to leaving the wooden gate ajar so she might slip noiselessly into the garden, but the rattle of Fetch's chain stirred him each time. From his bedchamber window, he spotted the tethered dog leaping with delight at his savior, then cringed as the animal lapped at Mary's cheeks and lips. But she embraced the creature with such loving kindness that Alfred's repulsion turned to envy.

He began joining them. The girl sent the dog on a chase around the small plot with a ball, then devised a three-noted whistle to train it to command. "I read of it in a book," she informed Alfred smartly, puckering her lips together to make the down-up-down music, a tune Alfred began hearing in his dreams. She delighted in every aspect of her fostered pet, laughter ringing out strangely in the deep night or faint morning.

One day, Alfred wondered that she might be caught and punished for sneaking away from the House.

"Oh, Papa pays no mind to me," she said as the spent dog lay in the grass beside them. "We sup together, but he spends hours in the study, writing letters to our creditors. He has let several men from understairs go, you know. Days pass when the only people I speak with are servants—and you, Alfred."

"Ay, I am a servant too."

She glanced shyly to one side. "I don't see you that way." Her hand brushed against his. They were reclining on the patchy lawn of his back garden, the untended late summer blooms around the estate giving off a thick, overripe scent. By then, she had been coming for two springs, maturing as nature intended. Her dresses had filled out and grown snug, her face revealing comely planes and angles. The warmth of her touch against the back of his hand sent a dark heat through him like a root seeking nourishment.

Alfred sensed a crumbling between them, an invisible wall breaking down. A daring ambition rose within him then, and instead of shrinking his hand aside, he laced his fingers with hers, bracing for a slap. None came. She attempted to tug away, but it was clearly only out of propriety, for after a moment, she relaxed with a sigh and permitted him to hold her hand. A large moment, writ small: They had something new to share beyond the dog, beyond their different stations. Alfred's mind seethed with what it might mean.

Softly, softly now, he thought, holding on to her.

And he did not let go. Before year's end, his fingers roamed more freely on the girl, caressing parts usually covered by slippers or sleeves. The first time Alfred laid his lips upon her smooth, unmarked neck— then moved them to her eager mouth—longings rose in him unlike any he'd felt with tavern wenches. Ecstasy paired with eagerness, purpose with primal fear. He would not lose *this*. Not now.

That winter brought further change. Alfred now permitted Fetch to sleep by the fire during freezing Northern nights, which brought Mary into his lodgings. They relaxed on woolen blankets gathered by the fireplace, petting the dog first, then petting one another. One night, Alfred lifted Mary's dress. She jerked it back in place but did not resist when he raised the fabric a second time and plumbed her with his fingers, ensuring she was as eager for him as he was for her. Moments later, he had her pinned down.

"Say ye wish it," he growled.

She nodded. Or so it appeared in the firelight. In any case, she did not object.

Alfred plunged deep inside her, feeling imminent release —

Mary shrieked in pain.

Fetch leapt into action, sinking his teeth deep into Alfred's calf.

Alfred convulsed against her, then flailed at the animal, punching its head. It unclamped its jaws from his leg, tumbling into the hearth fire. Calling out, Mary wrenched from beneath Alfred and tossed a blanket over the dog.

The rest of the evening was lost. Alfred applied a yarrow and chickweed salve first on his own leg, then on the dog's burned hindquarters, binding both with cloth. Silent, Mary waited until the dog was quieted, then bolted back to the house. It was a surly end to what had seemed so promising.

Yet — not ended at all. Within a week, Alfred coaxed Mary into his bed for a proper romp, burying his lips against her mouth to squelch any further cries. But he heard nonesuch; her noises now were pleasure to his ears. She returned night after night, departures coming closer to sunrise each time. Afterward, while he drowsed, she spoke endlessly of her father's dark moods, his failing fortunes, of more servants being released.

"The House is so quiet now," she said.

This was not news to Alfred; the Great House's descent had been long in coming. Notes arrived in the weekly food baskets Cook sent over — notes that explained his lessened pay packet or detailed his expanded duties in the kennel. Caring for the hounds was a step down for Alfred, whose first job on the estate had been to feed them. Assisting the Head Gamekeeper had been an elevation; then, after the Gamekeeper died early of the sickness, Alfred had at last found himself in a position of respect and authority. His first act had been to evict the Gamekeeper's family from the cottage six days after the funeral so he could move in himself. Now he was back to feeding the hounds. And they were a drain, with feed arriving only every third day. He brought the beasts game from the forest when he could — otters, badgers, foxes — but their numbers slipped. Fourteen, eight, three. Each corpse went into a pit, and Alfred spread lime over them.

But Fetch ate well, because having Fetch happy meant Mary was satisfied. Not that the animal showed any appreciation; he'd never been friendly to his master, and since the night of the fire curled his tail between his legs whenever Alfred approached.

Early in the third spring, Mary became gravid with child. Inattentive though Lord M— might be to his sole offspring, he was not so blind as to overlook his daughter's expanding waistline. Mary fled from his explosive wrath and into Alfred's arms. "What shall I do?" she sobbed. "He has cast me out because he says he cannot *drown* me!"

"Oh, little plum. Tha has a home here."

Mary swept her gaze across the cottage as if seeing it for the first time and burst into fresh tears. But she clutched at him the way a woman lost at sea might catch a piece of driftwood. Alfred patted her shoulder while staring at the chained-up Fetch.

The dog's glowing white eyes gave warning: *Take care of Mistress. Or t'll be on your head.*

So, Mary came to live at the cottage. In years without sickness, such a scandal would have driven them both into the world, but these were extraordinary times across the land. Alfred wondered if anyone even cared about station and propriety anymore; all were focused on not falling ill. In any case, they were neither harassed nor acknowledged.

But the joy was gone. Mary sat listlessly in the garden while Fetch brought *her* the ball. She had no concept of cookery or housecleaning and was like another pet to care for. Alfred arrived home from a long day of many duties around the estate to find the cottage a shambles and Mary murmuring to her cur in a low tone, the dog's head on her lap. Eventually, the dog's head was pushed aside by Mary's burgeoning belly; despite the young woman's petite stature, the babe was enormous in her, and at night she took up much of the bed with twisting and turning. Alfred dozed in the chair by the fire, rising uncomfortably each morning, body and loins aching.

Finally, after weeks of abstinence, Alfred attempted to join her in the sheets. He reached around to cup her now-generous breasts—and she shoved him to the floor. Recovering, he smacked her across the face. The crumbled wall between them was now in ruins; she was the lady of *his* house now and no better than he.

"Tha'll do as bid," he growled. She reminded him of a fat turtle stuck on its back in the hot sun, flailing. Her fingers raked at his beard, but he was still the stronger of the two, and he held her down easily while he did as he pleased.

It turned out he liked doing it this way even more than when she was a slender whippet of a thing.

Urine courses down Alfred's leg as he whirls, the presence against his calf fleeting but in the precise spot where Fetch once bit him. His curses are croaked, half-formed guttural noises. Snatching up a lantern hanging in the doorway, he holds it high, light casting a faint halo that barely penetrates the misty dark.

The rattle from the back of the garden grates at him again. Clanking metal links slide across bare earth slowly, carefully. Alfred's gut clenches, and his eyes widen at what emerges: The mist has fashioned the shape of a dog, a barrel-chested cur stepping gingerly into the moonlight, head lowered, snout grinning, white eyes incandescent. Each misty paw touches the ground with a sharp jangle, though the creature wears no chain now. Within the spectral animal's body swirls a separate piece of mist, like a heart a-flutter, like a living thing.

A high, three-noted whistle pierces the night, then repeats. Mary's call to Fetch, a tune he once heard so often. The hair on Alfred's arms lifts.

I do believe I've given him a piece of my soul, Mary had said.

And it appears that Fetch has kept it.

Terror shooting through him, Alfred hurls the lantern at the beast, but it lands against the oak tree branches, paraffin spilling from its shattered glass housing. Fire crisps the leaves, and within seconds the rotted oak is ablaze, the night sky filled with the fires of hell.

And still, the whistling comes, down-up-down, down-up-down. The same three notes.

Then—it stops.

Out of the bright conflagration bounds the misty creature, white fangs a-gleam. Alfred scarcely has time to flinch away before the specter's paws are upon him, tumbling him to the ground. He lands awkwardly as it races over him, bolting to the gate. Alfred twists in the grass, wincing. The wispy beast is scraping at the wooden gate, which has bowed inward again.

Howls start afresh on both sides of the gate, the hungry bays of hunting dogs he has not seen intertwining with the specter's yowling summons. Alfred claps hands over his ears, and in the sudden muffled quiet, he has a vision: That this impossible beast he's raised since a pup neither loves nor hates his master. He only wants one thing — to run free across the moors, dive into the blanket bogs. To be with Mary again, perhaps. To return the piece of her she so willingly lent it years ago.

Understanding brings relief. Alfred has rarely, if ever, done anything that was not in part to service himself. Perhaps this is his chance for absolution. What if he can clear himself — undo all the wrong he has wrought — by simply *setting the beast free*? Tears course down his cheeks into his beard. Perhaps this is the one right thing he can do for all of them.

The moment he sets his hand on the latch, the great howling calms, ceding into whimpers and restless movement. Alfred imagines the unseen pack, come over hill and dale, through muck and marsh, baying with the voices of the unsouled to claim one of their own. To welcome Fetch on their mystical journey as they roam the moors forever as legends, as myths.

The gate presses inward, the old, rotten wood beginning to split. They desperately want their companion, who now sits with his head cocked at Alfred, white eyes simmering.

"Tha's a good boy," says Alfred in a generous tone as he releases the gate.

Two days earlier, Alfred burst from the cottage in a mad panic, tearing at his hair. He was escaping the muffled screams of Mary in extremis, sounds he'd endured for uncountable hours, their bed a shambled bloody wreck as she attempted to heave the babe from her body. They were on their own — even midwives were leery of stepping into strangers' homes amid the wasting disease — and once Mary's waters had broken, Alfred had feared to leave her, even to seek assistance at the Great House.

So, he'd steeled himself to be the midwife — had he not seen animals give birth before? — and retrieved heated water from the hearth, tearing clean rags into strips. But after so many hours, he was at his wit's end with the cries for medicine, for help, for relief. Some time ago, she ceased forming words, babbling like a madwoman. Alfred stuffed a rag into the girl's mouth to quiet her shrieks and fled into the back garden.

But he found no respite there; sensing the terrible struggle of his mistress, Fetch howled, thwarted from being with her by the chain keeping him linked to the tree. Alfred came upon the mongrel straining like to choke itself, digging an even deeper groove into the rotted oak's trunk. It hurled its body again and again toward the cottage, cacophony unceasing.

Alfred dashed through the gate toward the Great House, mist enveloping him. He'd intended to pay a call on the House for some time but had determined to wait until the babe was born, when he would have some claim on Lord M—'s attention. But now, he had no choice: The House was their last source of succor. He ran with all his remaining strength until, at last, the House rose before him, silent and solid as a gravestone in the gray morning light. Feet crunching on the outer driveway pebbles, Alfred stole close to the servants' entrance.

The back door stood ajar, paper rustling on the floor inside. "Hullo?" he called, voice echoing around the lower interior halls and kitchen. No servants emerged, so he ventured further, noting the cold ashy fireplace, emptied water buckets, and foodstuffs souring in baskets. A sweet, cloying scent wafted from upstairs, growing stronger as he ascended to the main floor. The sickly odor of decay led to Lord M—'s study, so pervasive that Alfred had to draw his neckerchief around his mouth and nose, gagging as he pressed open the door.

On the other side, he found the man of the house flung back in his chair, eyes emptier than Fetch's. A hunting rifle lay across his chest, Lord M—'s finger still on the trigger, muzzle indicating the gaping hole at the back of his head—a dried-out wound 'round which dozens of flies danced.

Alfred barely managed to lower his neckerchief before disgorging his supper on the Oriental rug. He heaved and released until there was nothing more to sick up, and by the time he moved away from his mess, some of the flies had flitted over to investigate.

The Lord is dead, thought Alfred, deciding Mary's father must have released all the servants just before releasing himself. Wheels turned as he realized: *Mary cannot inherit—but her son could. If she births a boy.* There were complex laws regarding bastards, but all could be smoothed over. Alfred knew things about the village pastor and his... predilections. He'd caught him in the forest more than once. The pastor could make a marriage certificate and date it six months prior. Alfred's smile was slow and curdled, his head whirling. From the workhouse to the Great House in his lifetime. He would trustee for his son until the boy came of age—

But only if the babe lived.

Newly fortified, Alfred dashed from the House — a place he already thought of as *my* House — calling for his darling Mary. The cottage emerged through the mists like Avalon, but as he neared, he slowed, expecting to hear cries and barking or perhaps a newborn's whimper. Yet his cottage was still as the House. The only noises he discerned were the *scree* of the unlatched back gate and the stealthy rustle of grasses.

Alfred ventured in through the garden, astonished to find the oak tree felled, sliced through by years of wear by the chain. His back door swung in its frame like a loose tooth. He followed the links that had once restrained the animal, a dog freed that might have escaped anywhere but had bolted into the cottage.

The tableau Alfred came upon inside took time to comprehend. It was like a great painting done in reds and whites and browns, obscenely garlanded in shining metal. Mary lay bent on the stained bedsheets, one arm wrapped around the iron bedframe. She had *begun* to birth their son, that much was clear; between her splayed legs, the head of a babe had emerged, and then… stopped. The babe lay half-in and half-out of its mother, face down in a pool of effluvia and blood, drowned as it took its first breath.

Alfred's stomach worked emptily.

Then he understood the rest of the story: Mary's free arm had fallen, resting atop the head of the unmoving Fetch. Its neck was a worn, bloody mess. It must have torn open its own throat in its urgency to be with its mistress, to assist in her last dying moments — and arrived just in time for her to leave it with one last caress. Now, the great large head lay flopped against the bed, tongue lolling from between stained teeth.

But its wide, white eyes that saw everything — they were bright and supernatural and settled on Alfred like lime dust as he fell to his knees.

They said: *Ye were warned.*

Alfred's hand has barely brushed the latch when the gate cracks in two, the wooden slats thudding against his body. Spectral Fetch leaps to one side as a flood of gray, misty dogs — hounds, terriers, mongrels, all baying in triumph — surge into the blazing garden. It is as if every tormented dog that had ever lived on the dales has answered the call.

The beasts stream over Alfred, knocking him to the ground again, hundreds of paws beating him into the earth until he stops trying to rise. At last, they describe a circle around his exhausted, prostrate form, and he peers up between swathes of matted, greasy blond hair. Fetch sits at the head of the pack, muzzle lifted, stark eyes glowing.

And then emerges one more from the flames, a coalescing of the mist that fashions a thin whippet of a girl in a blue dress, frilly collar, and white bonnet. She has no face—but Alfred knows exactly who she is.

Fetch barks once—and all goes quiet.

A high, strong whistle—three notes only, down-up-down—bleeds into the night. Mary, signaling to Fetch. He has always obeyed her, always followed her lead. She points at Alfred and whistles once more.

"Wait, now—" Alfred begins, but that is all he can say before the dogs tear him asunder.

IN THE MACHINE

Meghan Arcuri

Dear Lucy:
Can you help me? I'm a little lost, and I'm
not sure what to do.
Love and hugs,
Gram

> Who the hell is this?

Dear Lucy:
Is that any way to talk to your grand-
mother?
Love and hugs (and a bar of soap),
Gram

> My grandmother died two months ago. I
> don't know who you are. I don't know
> what you want. But if you don't stop, I
> will contact the police.

Dear Lucy:
Oh, my. You're right. I did die two
months ago. Time doesn't mean much to
me anymore. Especially because I seem to
have an endless supply of alcohol. They
started me on Long Island iced teas. Now
it's Jack Daniels.
Please don't contact the authorities, Lu-
Lu. I know this must be frightening, but I

need you to help me. You're my technology maven. I would tell my friends how
amazing you were—how handy it was to
have a granddaughter who worked with
computers. How is the new job, by the
way? You had just started two months
ago.
Love and hugs,
Gram

Who is this?

Dear Lucy:
It's me. Your grandmother: Jane A.
Murray. I lived at 22 Parry Road in Fort
Hudson. I had two daughters and a son
and five grandkids. I should have had
more, but your aunt decided becoming
an alpaca farmer was more important
than starting a family and giving your
grandfather and me more grandchildren.
These grandchildren are furry, she'd say.
As if I ever wanted to touch one of those
hideous creatures. They look like a cross
between a sheep and a camel, neither of
which is attractive in the first place. All
that spit and the like. Not to mention the
stench of feces.
Your aunt called them magical, saying
they hummed to her when she sheared
them. I think she was high.

I really shouldn't be saying these things.
It must be the Jack. They cut it with a little milk—just the way I like it—but it's
still pretty strong. Don't you snicker
about the milk thing, missy. You thought
it was pretty tasty when I let you sneak a
sip out of my glass on your eighteenth

birthday. Did you ever tell your mother
about that? I hope not.
Love and hugs,
Gram

Is it really you, Gram?

Dear Lucy:
Of course it's me. Who else would it be?
Love and hugs,
Gram

It could be spammers looking for money.
Or trying to take my ID.

Dear Lucy:
Spammers? What in the name of hope
and mercy are spammers? Are they trying to sell you that "meat" in a can? Pink
and gelatinous. That's how Spam always
looked to me. Isn't "gelatinous" a great
word? There aren't too many words in
the English language that make you want
to vomit simply by saying them. Gelatinous is definitely one of those.
Don't buy the Spam, Lu-Lu.
Love and hugs,
Gram

Spammers, Gram. Not Spam. Spammers
steal your email account and email all of
your contacts, hoping to get money.

Dear Lucy:
Oh. Like that Nigerian fellow I was
telling you about the last time you helped
me with my computer?
Love and hugs,
Gram

Yes. Him.

Dear Lucy:
He said he was in prison, but if I could get him out, he'd reward me with money. I know I'm not the most com- puter savvy person, but even I knew that was bananas.
Love and hugs,
Gram

You know you don't have to keep typing "Dear Lucy" or "Love and hugs, Gram," right? This is IM-ing. It's not formal.

Oh, thank goodness. I love you and all, but that was becoming a pain in my back- side. Even for me, the veteran grammar school teacher. What is IM-ing? No. Wait. Let me guess. Independent Musings. Internal Meanderings. Irate Marsupials. Insipid Monks.

An IM is an Instant Message. It's like chatting but with using the keyboard.

Didn't you try to get me to do that once?

Yes.

I hated it, didn't I?

Yes.

I said it was ruining the English lan- guage: all those wacky abbreviations, no pronouns, few verbs. If I wanted to grunt, I would've been a caveman. Not to

mention those emoji things. Don't even
get me started on them.

What is going on, Gram? How are we
doing this?

Hold on a minute…

Much better.

What happened?

They gave me another Jack and milk.

Who is "they"?

No one, exactly. If I want something, it
just appears.

Where are you?

I don't know. I was hoping you could
help me out with that.

Can you see anything?

I was losing my hearing, Lu-Lu, not my
sight—although those cataracts were
nasty. When you changed the size of the
flont, though, that really helped.

I think you mean font.

I'm sure I do.

I meant, what can you see?

Not much. I'm comfortable, but I can't
really see the chair I'm sitting on. I'm at a

desk, or some flat surface, but it's just out of my vision. Everything is a blurry cloudiness, until you want something... then it's right there.

Like the Jack Daniels?

Yes, or this laptop — although why I would want a laptop is beyond me.
All that doesn't tell us where I am, either. Maybe some wires got crossed or something. I did die at my computer, after all. Maybe I'm trapped in it — but you're at your computer, so that doesn't make sense.

Actually, I'm at your computer. Mom gave it to me when you died.

Well, there you go! I'm trapped in my computer.

I don't know... where are the drinks coming from?

I never question free alcohol. Except when it comes out of a box. Do yourself a favor, Lucy, and splurge on the bottle. The boxed stuff is for cheapskates and psychopaths.

Psychopaths?

Uncle Phil. Need I say more?

Nope.

It's almost like I'm in a holding area, waiting for the next step — a new start —

and they're giving me things to keep me
comfortable.

Who's "they"? People? Angels?

Angels? You didn't really buy that trash
they sold you in Sunday school, did you?

You taught the class!

I know, but it was bullshit.

Gram!

Pardon my French, but it was.

You were a convincing teacher.

Back then, I believed it. I lost my faith
after your grandfather died. No one
should have to suffer like that for so long.

I know...
Tell me more about where you are. Is it
kind of like Purgatory?

Jesus. Enough with the Catholic refer-
ences, Lu.

I'm trying to get my head around this. It's
kind of weird, don't you think? You
being able to send me instant messages?

Kind of weird? It's batshit bonkers,
Lucy-lu-lu. What's especially weird is
that I even have a laptop at all. They've
made me comfy, plying me full of liquor,
but here I am at this laptop. At this device
I never wanted in the first place, but I

knew I needed in order to keep up with everyone… and I knew you would help me.

                                        I was happy to.

I know. Except for the time when I thought my computer broke because I had too much mail in my inbox. Or when I clicked on that weird attachment in that weird email from your mother. Or when I accidentally changed my password and forgot what it was. Twice.

                                        Twice?

Okay, three times.

                    I know you never liked the laptop, but maybe some part of you wanted it right now because you thought I could help you. And the laptop was the way to make it happen.

Yes! Beautiful and brilliant. Just like her grandmother. Ooo!

                                        What happened?

They gave me an amaretto sour. Jimmy Thompson taught me an awful lot after a few amaretto sours.

                              Who's Jimmy Thompson?

I met Jimmy Thompson before I met your grandfather. At my first teaching job. His classroom was right down the hall from mine. All the other ladies swooned in his presence. Not me. Don't get me wrong. He was handsome — in a Rebel Without a Cause type way. I was too focused on my job to care. He asked me out, anyway. Probably because I ignored him. You know how men are. To my surprise, he was a very nice young man. We got on well, and one night, after he'd made me a few amaretto sours, he asked me if I wanted to… well, you know.

Oh, god.

So I said yes.

Gram…

You might think his popularity with the girls is a little bad or gross. You know, the dirty dick thing and all.

Gram!

We were safe, though — as you should always be, young lady! The benefit, though, of being with a ladies' man is he knows all the tricks — and I mean all of them. He introduced me to something.

Oh god, what?

My clitoris.

Jesus!

I'm never sure: is it CLIT-or-is, or cli-TOR-is? I've heard both. Do you know?

NO!

Oh, come on, dear. Lighten up! This is the
good stuff.

It's weird seeing you use those words.

Because of your grandfather, I didn't
drink a lot. When I did drink, though, I
was known to let loose a little.

A little?

Yes, dear. A little.

"Dirty dick" is hardly a little.

Touché.
Ooo!

Lemme guess... they gave you a Rob
Roy.

Good try, but no. They gave me a Manhattan. Now we're talking! Manhattans
remind me of Matthew McDowell...

Gram. Focus! Did you see anyone give it
to you?

No. It magically appeared on the table.

Do you hear anything?

Nothing but the clicking of the keys on
the keyboard.

How many drinks have you had so far?

Four? Five? Six? I don't know.

Seriously?

Seriously. Strongest Manhattan I've ever
had. Now. Let's talk about getting me out
of this machine.

I think I know what you need to do.

Tell me.

I don't think I want to.

Why not?

Because I like this. I like talking to you
again.

We're not really talking, dear.

You know what I mean. The thing is, if
what I tell you to do works, you'll disappear. And I'll have to deal with losing
you. Again.

I know, sweetie. But I'm only getting
drunker. And I'm gonna start spelling
things wrong. And I'm embarrassed I'm
starting sentences with "and" and "but."
Not to mention typing "gonna." Maybe I
am a caveman.

You're trying to be funny to make this
easier.

I'm trying to be funny because I'm
wasted. And I'm starting to have naughty
thoughts about Jimmy Thompson again.
Don't get me wrong, your grandfather
was an amazing lover…

Gram!

Ha! I knew that'd get a rise out of you. I knew how to get a rise out of your grand-father, too, if you know what I mean.

Please. Stop.

Okay, okay. Good manners trump dirty grandma speak. Your grandfather was the funny one, by the way. I always knew the alcohol had a lot to do with it—and my whole life, I only knew him as a drinker. When he became clean and sober, though, he was still funny. I was kind of relieved. I think he was, too.

I always thought you were funny.

That's because you're an easy touch. And you were my favorite.

You were mine, too.

I know, Lu-Lu. And that's why I need you to help me out now. I don't know why, but I know I can't stay like this forever. It's not permanent.
…
Lu?
I can hear you thinking.

I love you, Gram. I miss you every day. I don't know how I can live without you.

I love you, too. I'll always be there, never far from your mind: every time you sit down to write at my computer; every time you help an older person with a

computer question; every time you say
the word clitoris.

                                    GRAM!!

Sorry.

                                    It's okay.

So whaddya got, Lu? How am I going to
get out of here? Get my new start?

                    That's the thing. You need to reboot.

How's that now?

                    You know. Restart the computer. Do you
                    remember how?

Control-Alt-Delete?

                                    Yes.

Wow. You've gotta be impressed. Especially given the number of drinks I've
had.

                                I'm totally impressed.

Well, Lucy-Lu. This is it. Thank you for
helping me with my (hopefully) one, last
computer problem.

                            It wasn't a problem for me.

Nor for me. I love you, sweetie.

                                    I love you, too.

Good-bye.

Bye.

...

Gram?

...

Gram?

THE BELLS

MARC L. ABBOTT

From the second-floor bedroom window, Victoria saw the woman in black looking up at her from the garden. Her pale skin clashed with the lace dress and veil that draped down her back. She held her hands folded in front of her and stood still.

"Lexington? Who is that woman?"

Lexington Stanley joined his wife at her side to look at her. The moment he did, the woman turned slowly and began to walk back across the garden toward a grouping of trees.

"I have no idea."

"Your neighbor, perhaps?"

"Our closest neighbor is miles down the road," Lexington said.

"Shouldn't we go down there and find out who she is? She may need help."

"If she needed help, she would have knocked on the door. Forget her. I want to clear up the last of these things and get home."

Lexington left her side and returned to the interior of the bedroom where a steamer trunk sat open. He neatly folded his father's clothes and placed them inside.

Victoria turned from the window and began to walk around the room, marveling at the large oak bed with its tall columns holding up a canopy. Her eyes turned from there to the massive armoire and other beautiful hand-crafted furniture.

"Seems such a shame to sell all of this. It's in perfect condition."

"My father insisted that I tend to this place after his death. He practically ordered me to return here to put to rest an outstanding debt he ran up a long time ago."

"What debt?"

"Damned if I know. Outside of some bills he owed, I didn't find anything among his things at the hospital that pointed to a substantial debt. But then again, he was a private man and really didn't let me in on a lot of his affairs. Knowing my luck, I'll probably stumble across it someday by accident."

"But do you really have to sell this place? We could just move in here, Lexington. It's a beautiful home. It just needs some sprucing up. And when we have children, they will have that large garden and all these grounds to play in."

Lexington closed the trunk then turned to his wife. He gave her a crooked smile as he joined her in the middle of the room and embraced her.

"You really like this old house?"

"You say old, I say it has character."

He sighed. "To be honest, I have never been fond of this place. Too many painful memories roam these halls, my love. My father fell into madness when he got older. Albert, our last caretaker, said he would walk the halls at night talking to himself. He'd have arguments by himself in his den. At one point, he wouldn't even let me come in the house when I came to visit. That was close to the end. For me, this place is a reminder of the vanity of a man who squandered his wealth rather than use it for something good. Besides, we would need at least three servants to help keep this house in order, and I'm just not..."

Victoria cupped his face in her hands. "I understand. You're not your father. I'm not saying you should be. It's just that we have often talked about having a bigger place, and I figured this would be better than having to go search for one."

"We will find a home that will suit us. We get a good price from selling this place, we'll use the money to buy a bigger house."

"Why not open the place up to tenants?"

"I thought about it, but I fear that would be more of a hassle. Best to sell it. Speaking of, I need to go down to his office and find the deed." He took her hand. "Come, I'll retrieve the trunk before we leave."

Victoria walked a step behind Lexington as he led her out of the room and down a long, dimly lit hallway. There were three larger rooms along the corridor as they made their way to the stairs. At the far end of the hall was the fourth.

"How big are the other rooms?"

"They're guest's rooms, really. That one at the far end was a servants' section. There are two rooms through that door."

They passed a portrait of Lexington's father, Conrad Stanley, looking distinguished in his younger form.

"You favor him, you know. He was very handsome," Victoria said.

"He was also a cad."

Victoria slapped him on the arm. "That's your father!"

"And what, he couldn't be a cad?" Lexington chuckled. "He was very much a ladies' man. It broke my mother's heart. They used to fight about it all the time. How he would go to parties and flirt while she was right there in the room." He let go of her hand when they reached the top of the stairs. He took hold of the railing as he descended. "It's what drove her to leave us."

He paused on the stairs to look at the portrait of a beautiful woman with raven hair, holding a bouquet of red flowers as she stood at attention with Conrad behind her. "I used to stare at this picture a lot when I was a boy, wondering where she could have gone."

"She was stunning."

"She was. You would have to wonder why my father would want any other woman besides her." He looked at Victoria. "Don't worry, his behavior does not run in the family."

Victoria smirked as she continued to stare at Lexington's mother. There was something about the way she stood that seemed familiar to her, but she couldn't place what it was. She locked eyes on the woman. "You don't really favor her, though. You look more like him. Did Conrad ever speak about where he thought she would have gone?"

"No. He said she just left. I was in town that day with Mrs. Fairweather. She was our cook. I came home. He was here crying and told me she had walked out on us."

"She never tried to reach out to you?" Victoria turned to him. "She was your mother, after all."

"Honestly, if she really cared, she would have done so. But I guess cutting ties with my father meant the same for me."

Victoria placed her hand on his shoulder for comfort. "I'm sorry if I've brought up painful memories."

"It's quite alright. Let's look for that deed and get out of here."

❈

Conrad's den was a mess of old books, newspapers, and documents thrown all over. They had to step over piles of hardcover journals just to get to the cluttered desk at the far end of the room.

Victoria watched as Lexington moved to a large window covered by drapes, pushed them to the side, and let in the light from outside. Dust particles filled the air like snowflakes.

"Why is this place such a mess?" Victoria asked.

"I have no idea. He used to keep it immaculate. This looks like someone went rummaging through here looking for something."

"You think someone broke in here?"

"It's possible. Someone may have noticed no one was coming and going from here and picked the lock to get in rather than break a window. No use worrying about that now." Lexington moved toward the desk. "Okay, I know he kept all his records for the property in the desk drawer." He turned to the journals. "I think those journals are the financials from the business." He took a key from his waistcoat and unlocked the desk drawer. "Let's see what we got."

Victoria slowly moved through the clutter, tugging on the side of her dress to lift the hem so it wouldn't drag. As she passed the window, she looked out and saw the woman in black again. She was only a few feet from the window, watching them.

"She's back."

"Who's back?"

"That woman in black. She's standing outside in the yard." Victoria turned to him. "She's watching us."

Lexington placed a pile of papers on the desk. As he looked up, something in the drawer caught his attention. He reached in and took out a mahogany box large enough to hold documents.

"What's this?" he said.

"Lexington, come here."

"Hold on a minute." He raised the lid and reached inside. He retrieved a stack of envelopes, all addressed to Conrad from someone named Katherine Sullivan. "Victoria, look at these."

"What about the woman?"

"Don't worry about her. Whoever she is, she's not bothering anyone." He held up the letters. "These are from my mother. Sullivan was her maiden name. I never knew he had letters from her. They must have been letters she sent him during the war. She was a nurse, you know. Yes, they're from an address in England."

Victoria moved toward him but paused when she saw the woman in black slowly walking away from the house. She tried to yell to her but realized the window was too thick for her to hear. She continued to Lexington, who handed her the letters. She undid the string, removed the first letter, and placed the stack on the edge of the desk before opening the envelope. She carefully removed the letter and read it silently. A smile grew on her face.

"She's telling him how much she misses him and how someday they should visit the seaside village she's stationed near."

"There are more letters in this box." Lexington read the face of the envelope. "This isn't from my mother. This is from someone named Laura Pewter." He raised the envelope to his nose. "This had perfume on it."

"One of your father's many loves?"

"I guess." He opened it and looked at the top of the letter. "This is dated July 1918."

Victoria looked at the top of her letter. "Your father married your mother after the war?"

"They married in December of 1918." Lexington looked down at the letter and read it quietly. "I can't believe this. This woman... she writes how she can't wait until their wedding day and how she has a dress all picked out."

"Your father was engaged to another woman before your mother?"

"That's not possible. How could he have been if he married her two months after the war ended? This woman, Laura, would have had to have known he was already engaged."

"Unless..." Victoria picked up the stack and went to the last letter in the pile. She opened it and looked at the date. "This one is dated June 1917."

"What does that mean?"

"I thought for a minute that maybe this was her last correspondence. Maybe he thought your mother had been killed in the war, and that's why he took up with another woman. But this was almost a year before her final letter. Which means—"

"My father was running around with another woman behind my mother's back. No surprise there." Lexington pulled the last letter from his pile and looked at the date, then read it. "Oh no."

"What?"

"This one is dated April 1919. It's Laura's last correspondence with him. This one sounds more like a threat. 'I will never leave you or this home we have built together. Katherine might be your wife by marriage, but I am your one and only true love. Every time she looks into the face of —'"

They were interrupted by a loud knock at the main door.

"I wonder who that is." Lexington started for the foyer. Victoria followed.

Lexington reached the front door and opened it to find no one there. He stepped out onto the porch and looked back and forth on the driveway but only saw their Packard Twelve that was parked a few feet from the door.

"Who is it?" Victoria asked as she walked up beside him.

"No one. I don't see anybody out here." He turned to her. "Someone did knock, right?"

"I heard it."

"That's odd." He looked at the letter in his hand. "I can't believe this. My father had a bastard child with someone. Somewhere out there, I have a brother."

"What do you think she meant by this home we built together?"

"Maybe she meant it figuratively. Like her heart is their home or something."

"I wonder who she was, Laura, I mean."

"We'll pack the letters up and take them with us. We can sit down and read through them together and find out what really went on."

Somewhere on the upper floor of the house, a bell rang. It sounded like a call bell. It was faint, at first. The second time it rang, it was louder.

"Did you hear that?" Lexington said.

"I did. Where's that coming from?"

The bell rang again, echoing through the hall above them. "Up there. It's coming from the guest room."

"I don't like this."

"Remember I told you there were once servants' quarters? Well, each of those rooms had a call box with a bell in them. I bet that's what it is."

"Why would it be ringing by itself?"

"The house is wired in the walls. Could be rodents chewing on the cable or something. It's been known to happen."

"All this is making me a bit peaked. I'm going to step out into the yard for a minute."

"You want water?"

"No, I'm fine. I need some air. Go ahead and finish up. And bring the letters. This is fascinating stuff."

"Okay. I'm going to check on that call box first, then find the deed. You stay outside."

Victoria leaned in and kissed him. She walked toward the car as Lexington closed the door. She took a deep breath, filling her lungs with the early autumn air, then exhaled slowly and strolled past the car and into the yard along the side of the house. She stopped to reread the letter she was still holding. When she was done, she looked back at the house then up at the bedroom window from where she had first seen the woman in black. She turned to look in the direction she had seen her walk.

Standing inches from her face, staring at her with eyes as black as sackcloth, was the woman. She seized Victoria by the wrist and said, "Come hear the dead speak."

Lexington reached the top of the stairs and proceeded toward the first guestroom. The ring of the bell changed its location. He followed the sound to the servant's quarters at the end of the hall. The bell rang louder.

He made a beeline for the door, stopping just before it. The bell rang again, but it was followed by another sound, the muffled cries of a woman.

"Help me. Please, help me!"

As he reached out to open the door, the knob turned on its own, and it slowly opened. The bell and the screaming stopped. Lexington paused. He looked down at his hand, which now trembled. The door opened a little more. He could see a small hallway and another door to the left, which led to one of the servants' rooms. On the other side of that door, the bell continued to ring.

Lexington turned to leave and froze.

At the far end of the hall, under a dim light, stood a woman in black. She stood perfectly still, staring at him.

He took a step forward. She raised her arm slowly then pointed at him. He took another step forward.

She dropped her arm and ran at him, screaming like a banshee.

Lexington abruptly turned, ran through the doorway, and slammed it shut. He took two steps back. The woman materialized through the wall, still screaming. Her right arm shot out, and her hand seized his shoulder.

He threw himself into the servant's door to pull away from her. It flung open, causing him to fall to the floor. He rolled over and came face to face with a pair of pale feet. Trails of blood ran like rivers over the top of them. He looked up, seeing the blood-soaked hem of a white nightgown at first. His gaze continued to travel upwards, the blood now more pronounced near the midsection, then he saw the ghostly white eyes of a woman staring down at him. Her stringy hair was wet and clung to the side of her face.

"How dare you enter this room?" Her voice was raspy. She looked away from Lexington and straight ahead, not talking to him. "Get out of my room!"

Lexington rolled out of the way and struck the wall. He sat up with his back against it, too terrified to move as he watched the two women stare at one another.

"You're hemorrhaging, Laura," the woman in black said from the doorway. "You shouldn't be up so soon after childbirth."

The ghost of Laura stepped back. "You're jealous of my strength. You vain, barren woman."

"You will not live under my roof with that bastard, do you hear me!"

"I gave your husband, my lover, the one thing you couldn't. And if you think he's going to remain married to you, Katherine, now that I have given him a son, oh, think again. He loves me. He always has. His love for you died when the war ended."

Katherine entered the room and slapped Laura with so much force that she fell back onto the bed behind her. Then she moved to stand over her, grabbed a pillow, and held it tight.

"It's a shame you didn't ultimately survive the childbirth. But don't worry, I'll take good care of our son!"

"Help me!" Laura screamed and rolled toward a call box button that had been installed for her. She managed to press it before it was too late.

Katherine brought the pillow down over Laura's face to suffocate her.

"Sleeping with the hired help! I won't allow two bastards in my home!"

Lexington watched as Laura flailed under Katherine's weight. Katherine's shrill screams filled the room. He put his hands over his ears and rose. He found the courage to move toward the door. The screaming stopped. He turned around, and Katherine was facing him, the pillow at her side, Laura's lifeless body behind her.

"Where are you going?" Her voice had a low resonance to it. "You're not leaving this property with that." She pointed to the letter he still held. "You will not publicly embarrass us with that outside these walls. Her blood is on Conrad's hands, not mine."

"What?"

"You should not have come back here. Everything here belongs to the dead. And with the dead it shall remain." Katherine dropped the pillow as she rose off the floor, levitating before him. "The sins of Conrad must remain contained here, and you" — she raised her ghostly hand and pointed at him — "are the product of that sin." The bell began to ring within the room. Its eerie staccato rhythm was matched by her slow movement toward him.

Lexington began to comprehend what Katherine was saying. His fight-or-flight response kicked in, causing his heart rate to increase, his body to shiver, and his eyes to well up with tears. He shook his head rapidly while his hand seized up around the letter as he screamed, "No!" He glanced at Laura's body then began weeping. "Mother." He inched backward as his gaze shifted back to Katherine. He wildly swung his fist back and forth at her. "God damn you!" He nearly tripped as he turned on his heel and fled the room.

Victoria burst through the front door just as Lexington turned the corner and started down the stairs. He stopped when he saw her.

"Lexington! Oh my God, where's the letter you found?"

"I have it right here."

She held up the letter she was holding. "You need to put them back and come with me. Hurry before—"

Disembodied footsteps running down the hall caught their attention. Lexington turned. Katherine rounded the corner, her arms out in front of her, and pushed him.

Victoria screamed as she watched Lexington lose his footing. He tumbled wildly down the stairs. He attempted to stop himself, landing hard on his elbow on one step then on his shoulder on the second to last. He rolled to the center of the foyer.

Victoria rushed to him. Sliding her arm around his back then under him, she coaxed him to his feet. Lexington, wincing in pain, began hobbling quickly toward the door, practically carrying her in the process.

They crossed the porch and put enough distance between them and the house, then stopped. Victoria looked down at Lexington's hand, wrestled the letter from him, and ran back to the house.

"Victoria, no."

When she reached the door, Katherine appeared, blocking her path. They stared at one another before she put the two letters together and handed them to Katherine.

"The rest of them are in the den on the desk. I'll do what you asked. I'll explain it all to him. You have my word," Victoria said. "Now get out of here and leave us the hell alone."

The two women stared at one another. There was disgust in Victoria's eyes. In an unladylike move, she spit at the feet of the ghost. Katherine moved back into the house. She looked down at the letters in her hand, began to weep, then dematerialized. The door slammed shut, and her wailing echoed through the walls. The faint sound of bells could be heard along with her cries.

Victoria turned, her eyes red and swollen from tears. She wiped them away then walked quickly toward Lexington, hunched over by the car.

"I have to show you something," she said.

"What the hell was that just now?"

"I made a deal and a promise I have to keep."

"With the ghost?" He cowered slightly from her. "What deal?"

Victoria didn't answer him. She stepped in and put her arm around his waist, then took his arm and put it around her neck. Then she guided him to the woods, where they walked along a short path until they came to a clearing where a large beech tree stood. One of its thickest branches hung over a small stone monument roughly two feet high. An angel, covered in cracks and ivy that had grown over it from years of neglect, sat weeping atop a pedestal. They stopped several feet in front of it.

"What is this?"

"This is your mother's grave," she said.

Lexington began to tear. "The one Katherine killed."

Victoria turned to him in shock. "You know?"

"I saw it happen in the upper room moments ago." He lowered his head. "I'm having a hard time grasping all this."

Victoria looked back up the path and her face turned pale. "Please don't, I didn't know he knows. I was about to tell him."

Lexington followed Victoria's gaze. Walking slowly toward them was Katherine. In her hand was a rope that had been fashioned into a noose. The closer she got, the more tranquil she looked.

They watched as Katherine glided past, ignoring them as she moved to a large tree opposite the monument. She turned and faced them. She threw the noose over the thick branch of the tree, slightly adjacent to the angel, then affixed the rope around the trunk. She then glided over to the monument and began to climb it.

Victoria and Lexington watched in silence as Katherine put the noose around her neck. This prompted Victoria to speak loudly in a panic.

"Katherine couldn't stand the thought of Laura living with her bastard child in the house. She killed Laura and claimed that she died hemorrhaging." Katherine stood above them, securing the noose, and then she waited. "She wanted her thrown in a pauper's grave, but your father built this monument for her and buried her under it. Back then, all of these trees around us were not here. Katherine had to look at this every day, a reminder of her crime. She raised you as her own until you were five. Then you began to resemble your mother. Your father was seen out on the town with other women. It became too much for her to bear."

"Oh God, no! No, no, no." Lexington moved toward the monument. "Don't!"

"She told him she was leaving him. Then she came out here and—"

Katherine leaped from the angel. The slack in the rope around the tree tightened as the noose seized around her neck. They heard a faint crack as her neck snapped. Her body twitched for a couple of seconds, then went lifeless, swaying back and forth above them.

Victoria's tears flowed as Lexington screamed with a mix of terror and grief.

"He lied to me."

"Katherine came to me outside the house." Victoria glanced up at the swaying body. "She told me to follow her here and explained everything. Then she made me promise to tell you before she hung herself. She's made me watch her do that twice now." She placed her hands over his. "Lexington, your father knew about Katherine's suicide. He was the one who found her out here."

Lexington looked at her. "I saw them. I saw Katherine kill Laura in the servants' quarters."

"That explains why she disappeared moments after she hung herself. She went back to the house."

"I don't understand. I have never seen either of these women as ghosts before while I lived here. Why now?" Lexington peered at the monument. "The debt."

"What?"

"I told you that my father mentioned a debt that was due. The debt was the truth about me. My whole life, he did everything to keep me from finding out who I really was and what happened to my mother. Well, mothers, really." He took her hand as he rose to his feet. "He wanted me to discover the truth. That I'm a bastard. None of this truly belongs to me. When word of this gets out, my reputation will be ruined."

"It won't get out. The only people who know the truth are either dead or kneeling here right now. We'll keep the house. Keep its secrets safe. Your father is dead, and there is no one else who knows the truth."

The ghost of Katherine had vanished. Lexington took Victoria's hand and led her out of the clearing and back to the car. He paused only for a moment to glance at the house.

"I should burn the place down," he said. He turned to Victoria, who was staring across the yard. He followed her gaze and saw Katherine and Laura watching them.

"Would that send the ghosts of your past away?" Victoria said.

Lexington got into the car and started the engine. When Victoria joined him, they sat in silence for a moment. She reached over, gently touched his hand. He pulled away from her. Their eyes locked, with Lexington giving her a cold stare.

"You're never to speak of what happened here today," he said. "As far as I'm concerned, I have no past in this place."

"That doesn't change—"

"That's enough!" he said through clenched teeth.

Lexington put the car in drive and sped away from the house. Victoria looked back. And saw Katherine crossing the ground.

"The ghosts would beg to differ," she mumbled.

SCHRÖDINGER'S GHOST

ALP BECK

Death.
That's how many ghost stories begin.
This one is no exception.
There will be a death.
There will be a ghost.
And there will be a story.
I can promise nothing more.

The green countryside sped by occasionally peppered by brown clusters: *so many cows*, he thought. The automobile's white leather seats contrasted brightly against the body of his chili-pepper red, '65 Chevy Corvette convertible. His dream car. The one he'd yearned for since his awkward, pimply self spotted it, shiny and new, on his snobby neighbor's driveway. It had taken thirty years of misery and subservience to make it his, but this did not diminish his joy, and, as the wind whipped through his few remaining hair follicles, Bob Burchwald grinned, tightened his grip on the steering wheel, and hit the gas.

Irene fussed nervously with Bob's overbed table. She filled the blue plastic pitcher with water then busied herself rearranging the rest of the items.

How much time had he lost? His brain felt fuzzy. His thoughts read like a badly erased blackboard. *How much time had passed? Days? Weeks? Months?* He was not sure. Bob's sense of time had become an elastic party trick.

His mother continued organizing the tabletop, her chatter constant and aimless. She swapped the small box of tissues with the cup as she spoke, then back again, all the while avoiding eye contact. He knew her patterns. Something was off. She was not telling him something.

"I'm so happy you're here with us, Bobby. For a minute there, we weren't sure—" Her voice trailed off. Then, uncomfortable in the silence, she resumed. "It really *is* a miracle you're here." She reached over, touched his arm lightly, then snatched her hand back as if burned, folding it back into the sweater that draped her bony shoulders. He watched her as something picked at him: he did not remember her ever making that trip before, especially alone.

"Did you *actually* drive here, mother? From Delaware?" he asked. "By yourself?"

"Oh, honey, it's not that far. It's closer than you think once you're used to it." Then, noticing his doubt, she added, "You'd be surprised how well I get around these days."

His mother visited daily, but her presence did not help fill the hole in his memory. If anything, the more he saw of her, the more he felt the insistent scratch in the back of his mind that something was amiss.

Bob awoke distinctly aware that something had changed. His soul vibrated in anticipation. He knew immediately—without being told: *he was getting out.*

He glanced at the chair beside his bed, where his mother always waited for him to wake. As expected, she was there.

"Mother...?"

"Yes, dear?"

"What happened?"

"Hmm?" She would not meet his eyes, but he could tell she knew what he was asking.

"Mother? Please look at me. What happened? How did I end up here? Why can't I remember?"

Irene finally looked up and drew in a deep breath.

Oh, God, this is going to be bad, he thought, and for an instant, he pushed the information—already forming in his brain—away because he knew what she was about to say before she said it.

"She didn't make it." Irene's voice was flat as she said this.

She—? Bob thought, but he knew.

SHE. The hollow space where memories of a daughter should have been, filled with regret.

As the knowledge slammed into him, he gasped, and reality descended, obliterating everything in its wake: his past, present, and future.

His daughter.

His beautiful daughter.

She had been beside him in the car.

One reckless moment of impulsive disregard and the one remarkable thing in an otherwise unremarkable life had left him.

One minute she had been beside him and then —

He closed his eyes, attempting to block out the image. *The blood.* Her body splayed on the road. A broken rag doll with legs akimbo, her beautiful hair hid her face from him as the blood seeped and spread around her head in a crimson halo.

He didn't remember the details of the *before*, only the moments *after*. The loss and guilt paralyzed him, leaving him gasping and unable to breathe as his lungs turned to stone.

His gentle girl, *Amelia*.

He had killed her.

Lowering his head, he tightened his jaw and drew in small, haggard breaths, tamping down his emotions. Once back in control, he raised his head and whispered:

I am sorry.

Sometimes I think he sees me.

His presence moves soundlessly throughout the house. It is easier for me to spot him later in the day, particularly late afternoons and evenings. I don't know why.

I catch a whiff of his scented hand soap, and my stomach roils with revulsion and anxiety.

My father's presence here is unbearable — a cosmic joke. A year has passed, and the imprint of his private education still haunts me. To have to share these rooms with him still is maddening.

I was almost free.

I grit my teeth, take a deep breath, and force myself to relax.

These rooms hold many memories; dark, muted moments to which only he and I were privy.

And *she is* with him. Of course, she is. *She would never leave her baby boy behind.* She is harder to see, but it makes an odd kind of sense since she's been gone longer than him. I glimpse her behind him: a faded spectral silhouette that chills me still.

My dear grandmother: *the enabler.*

Her words echo in my consciousness:

"Your father is in the study. Why don't you go and keep him company? He's had a long day and needs to relax. I'm sure he'd love to spend some time with you. Go, Amelia, be a good girl and sit quietly until he's ready for you."

Irene knew of his tutoring, I was sure. I also suspected she'd taught him, as he had me.

Does this infernal space hold wonderful memories for him?

I scream into the void.

"Did I not give you enough? Did you not take enough from me?"

The responding silence is loud.

His mother: the woman for whom he was everything and I nothing. As a kid, I'd occasionally catch her disapproving stare. Our eyes would meet, and I'd challenge her to say something, anything. She'd harden her stare and turn away as if I were nothing more than a temporary inconvenience. I sensed competition for my father's attention, but in time, she found a way to demote me. Her encouragement of my father's actions put me in my place. Well, she could have him, *all* of him.

Even after my arrival, her routine never wavered. Her cloying presence buzzed with excitement whenever my father's keys jingled in the lock. Her mothball-scented figure fussed over his arrival like a stale bride, making contact lightly with her nervous, fluttering hands, armed with possession and satisfaction.

And *Bobby* loved all of it.

A year ago, I was free; a freshman at Pembroke University, I'd left the past in the past. Then I got the call.

"She's been gone four months," he said. Sadness outlined his words. He sounded lost; small, in a way I hadn't heard him before.

"We're placing the gravestone on her grave this week. Had to wait for the ground to thaw."

I didn't answer.

"She loved you, you know."

I couldn't help it. I laughed.

He begged.

"Please. Just come for the ceremony. It would mean a lot to me."

I grumbled something and resisted.

"Please…" his voice cracked.

—and I relented.

Once home, he took me to the garage and showed me his prize. His eyes glittered with pride, and as he caressed her curves possessively, I shivered.

"Look at her. How could you possibly resist taking a ride with me in this engineering marvel?" Father asked. The shiny ragtop seemed out of place in the rundown garage.

One lousy, fatal car ride, and once again, I was trapped in this bloody house with the two of them.

There is no escaping a bored universe wielding fate for its own amusement.

He bent over a worktable in his study. The task light illuminated the small body panels of the 1966 Chevy Nova Pro Street model. He'd found the unopened kit waiting for him, sitting on a dusty shelf when he'd arrived home from the hospital.

"You'll need care," his mother said, and he didn't protest. He agreed to stay with her although he couldn't remember why. It didn't matter, anyway.

Losing Amelia had drained him.

Without his memories, he felt unfocused; disconnected from his old life. The only lingering imprint on his psyche was that of his daughter. The sadness and loss he harbored there was a massive anvil wedged deep in his heart. He missed their time together, their closeness. He had never felt that intimacy with any other living being. Her warmth and innocence lingered and haunted him.

Lately, hope had been rekindled and, because of it, the skewed perception of time's passing no longer had a hold on him. He felt freer than he had in years.

Amelia was here. He was sure of it. He sensed her, especially in this room.

His mother seemed unaware of her presence.

As he carefully picked up the car's rear bumper with the tweezer, he caught movement from the corner of his eye. He angled his head slightly, and his heart jumped into a staccato flutter. In the darkest corner of the room, she stood, vague and familiar all at once. He could not see her clearly; only her outline but, like a Seurat painting, he recognized her. He would have known her anywhere.

He thought he heard her breathe.

She stood there, a mere shadow, right by the wooden chest where Amelia would patiently sit as he worked on his models. She would stay quiet, familiar with their routine.

Quiet.

Until he was done.

Quiet.

Until he was ready for her.

Quiet.

Until their special time.

Just as his mother had taught him.

What a good girl she had been.

A flash of warmth ignited his loins as the memory flashed through him.

He nodded his head in acknowledgment.

The figure froze then rushed out of the room.

Amelia.

The whisper remained unuttered.

I *want* to frighten — no — *to terrify* him. On those occasions, I open cabinets, doors, and drawers and slam them shut. I toss silverware into a stockpot and shake it until the clatter is unbearable.

He looks up, startled at these antics. Maybe he hears me or at least senses me. But then, it might just be a reflex because he shakes it off and goes back to what he is doing. The anger and frustration snake up my spine like a wild, unbridled current.

Sometimes, I get lucky, and he drops whatever he's holding.

But in his study, I freeze.

The paralysis is familiar. The compulsion to stay quiet is overwhelming. Occasionally, when I can move closer to him, I peer over his shoulder as he assembles his precious models, and I lean in and whisper:

I am here... next to you. Your precious Amelia.

You fucking bastard.

He pauses his model-building, and I think he senses me.

Can you feel me?

Do you want to?

I reach out and touch his shoulder. My fingers travel through his body like vapor: insubstantial and transparent.

He shudders and looks around, then focuses on the spot where I spent hours waiting for what was to come.

The memories chase me out of the room before I can see the longing in my father's face.

Most of the time, though, I stay away.

A year.

One long, miserable year –

– trapped in this house.

The memories live here with me.

The dark corners of recollection are as solid as the antique furniture.

The day he called me into the bathroom, then he shut the door after me.

The three of us... still.

I could leave this house. But I will not give him the satisfaction. He doesn't deserve it. It's all I have left. I'll be damned if he gets to keep it.

He would have won then.

I have a right to be here. I earned this house. It is mine.

I paid for it with my innocence.

Then, the doorbell rings.

She had been in the car with him.

He had glanced over. Amelia's face reflected joy as the car sped through the curves. Her chestnut hair blew behind her as her cheeks flushed with excitement.

How much he missed her.

She was beautiful.

He sighed softly.

His daughter.

So sweet.

So soft.

So willing.
So close.

He reached over and placed his hand between her thighs, squeezing lightly.

Amelia whipped her head around, startled. Her eyes revealed the pain of the betrayal. Then, she reached over, grabbed the steering wheel, and yanked it violently toward her. And in those last few moments, he saw...

... her rage.
Ah, yes. He remembered now.

His mistake.

He'd promised to never touch her again.

Downstairs, the doorbell rang.

The mailman waited under the portico, listening for signs that someone was home.

After a moment, the door opened, and a woman stood there, leaning on a cane.

"Yes?" she said.

"Registered Mail? It needs a signature."

"Ah. Sure thing."

He reached in his breast pocket, pulled out a pen, and handed it to her.

"Here... and here," he said, pointing on the form.

She leaned forward, signed, and took the delivery from him.

"Thank you."

Then she backed into the doorway and gently closed the door.

I close the door and make my way to the dining room. The damned leg is throbbing again. Next week I'm scheduled for the final surgery. Maybe then, I can lose the cane. I take the letter opener from the credenza and rip open the envelope.

In my hands are the final papers from the lawyers. My fingers tremble with relief. My father's estate is finally out of probate.

I let out a deep sigh; the nightmare is finally over.

TAPS

PATRICK FREIVALD

Molly froze, her backpack half-in and half-out of her locker. It came again, a series of taps and scrapes behind the wall, a repeating rhythm that reminded her of the classic jazz drummers on her dad's old CDs, Billy Higgins and Jack DeJohnette, Art Blakey and Buddy Rich. The old guard who'd inspired her to pick up the sticks while her friends gravitated to the clarinet or the flute, the tomboys maybe braving the trumpet or sax.

She'd played the drums her whole life, straight through to her junior year, and she knew a great beat when she heard one. It sounded again, almost urgent, then cut off in a shriek of metal on metal.

"Hey!" Kirsten's voice cut through the rhythm like a scythe. The five-four brunette bounced on her heels and clutched her geometry book against a pale green sweater that matched her fingernails. "You're late for class."

"Speak for yourself." Molly pocketed her cell phone and produced a blue slip of paper. "I have a pass." She nudged her locker shut with her hip and hustled into step with Kirsten, the rhythm a memory hammering at the back of her mind.

"What did your mom say? About Saturday?" Kirsten's voice held too much hope, and Molly hated to crush it.

"She said, 'No.' And not the *maybe* kind of 'No.'"

"Did you tell her there wouldn't be any boys?"

Molly nodded. "Yeah, and she agreed. And no girls. Or animals. Or pizza delivery. 'Just because it's February Break doesn't mean you don't have work to do.'"

Kirsten stopped dead in front of Mrs. Bigg's room. "Oh, c'mon, how will she even find out from Atlanta?"

Shoving past, Molly ducked inside so that Kirsten couldn't see her eyes rolling. Even from her conference in Georgia, Molly's mom would learn of any transgressions against The Rules. She had neighbors checking in at all hours, a task force of busybodies with one relentless goal: ruin all fun.

Mrs. Bigg glanced their way long enough to notice the blue pass and then let them sit without interrupting her speech, something about congruent triangles and the stability of bridges. Molly sat next to Chris DeSouza and looked over his shoulder to copy the notes she'd missed.

In the back of the room, the heater pinged and hissed, the metal cycling through hot and cold phases. As it expanded and contracted, the incessant shudder transitioned into the tapping rhythm from her locker, then back into random noise.

"Did you hear that?" she whispered.

Chris shook his head without taking his eyes from the smart board.

She tapped the rhythm on her desk. The heater answered, then they did it in unison.

"Miss Fitzgerald?" Mrs. Bigg's voice cut through her concentration, and the beat disappeared with it. "Can we keep the percussion in the band room?"

Molly cast her eyes down to her page. "Sorry, Mrs. Bigg."

Sounds followed Molly down the hallway to the drinking fountain: a rattle as the winter wind shrieked past the window, a jingle of keys in Principal Lawson's pocket, a subtle tapping down the lockers, each with the same distinct pattern. The hair stood on her arms, and an electric shiver coursed up her spine.

Kneeling to collect her *Anthology of American Literature*, she ran her fingertips across the thick white cover, then put her nail against the back of the locker and tapped, hard, repeating the pattern as she'd heard it.

Silence, not even her own breath, held in anticipation of a reply.

A hand grabbed her wrist, stark white and ice-cold. Molly shrieked and fell back. Her head rang, and pain blasted the back of her skull, a black void filled with frozen stars, their cruel light reaching down to rob her of warmth and love and humanity.

Black tendrils wrapped her, squeezing and lifting her up into the darkness. She screamed again and tried to punch, kick, bite.

"Whoa!" Chris stumbled back, hands raised in a defensive posture, as the world slammed back into place, too bright and too real.

"What... I...?"

His face scrunched with worry, he knelt to pick up her fallen bag. "You hit your head."

She rubbed her wrist, numb from the cold, and looked into her locker. Aside from her books and folders, it held nothing but her coat, with no room for a person or a void or stars. The *Anthology* sat undisturbed in the bottom.

"You okay?"

She dragged her eyes away from the book to look into his baby blues. "Yeah, I think so. Just a spider, freaked me out."

He scowled toward her wrist. "I've never seen spider bites like that. Maybe you should go to the nurse. Get some cream or something."

She looked down at the string of hot, mottled-pink welts rising from her skin. They looked feverish but felt like frostbite. "Yeah. Thanks."

He kept pace with her to the end of the hall, then turned left to go to history. She went to the bathroom, locked herself in a stall, and took deep, steady breaths to calm her racing heart.

Fifth period, Molly dumped her lunch in the garbage can—chicken nuggets and mashed potatoes with lumpy white gravy and a side of boiled broccoli—and headed for the band room, ears pricked for tapping sounds that didn't come. Mr. Stevens turned away from the shelf on the back wall, the one that hid the ugly metal access door between the practice rooms, and gave her a cursory wave on his way back to his desk.

She sat. The smooth sticks belonged in her hands, and her right foot found its home on the pedal to the love-worn bass drum.

A heavy beat rolled from the bass as her foot pumped. Twirling the sticks once, she set into the snare with a *piano* drum roll, building it up to a *forte* before launching into an improvised solo. The rhythm flowed out of her, a fire in her arms and legs to defy the cold grip of... whatever the heck that was. Sweat beaded on her forehead, so she switched tempo and brought it down to a dull roar.

The sticks writhed in her hands, and as she struggled to control them, they hammered out a rhythm of their own, *the* rhythm, and cold dread shot through her bones. Her wrist throbbed in time. She forced an improvisation, but of their own volition her arms and hands flowed back to the driving beat. She looked up in alarm to see Mr. Stevens standing at the podium, arms crossed, a bemused look on his face.

She stopped with a crash on the high-hat, letting the discordant clang jar through her teeth like fingernails down a chalkboard.

"Where'd you get that groove?" A baby-faced twenty-something, his light brown goatee helped keep people from mistaking him for a student, but Molly always thought his gray eyes hid a weariness he never quite revealed.

Squirming under the scrutiny, she set the sticks down and met his eyes. "Not sure. Why?"

He chuckled. "It's Morse Code. I did two years as Signals Intelligence in Qatar."

Everything in her screamed not to ask, but she had to. She licked her lips. "What does it mean?"

He tapped it out on the podium. "F. I. N. D." He paused, then started again. "M. E. Period." He played it again and again, speeding up with every repetition, and the room shuddered in time. Eyes closed, he didn't seem to notice the shaking walls, the oppressive darkness as gray clouds swallowed the midday sun, the deep throbbing pulse of blood in her skull.

"STOP!" She pressed the heels of her hands to her ears to block out the sound.

His hands hovered above the podium, the smile frozen on his face. Sunlight streamed through the windows, blinding against the snow blanketing the hillside. "How about this?"

He started again, a different pattern, longer. She waited for him to finish before speaking.

"What did that say?"

"It said, 'Codes are for hiding things.'" Slumping to rest his chin on the back of his hands, he glanced at the clock—twenty-two minutes to the bell—and scowled. "Where'd you say you heard that?"

She shrugged. "I don't know. Just sort of came to me."

"Hell—um, heck of a coincidence, getting every letter. Even the punctuation."

"Yeah, that's really weird. Maybe it came from one of my dad's movies or something and has been bouncing around in my head."

"War movies?"

Nodding, she picked up the sticks and stood. "Yup. Vietnam and World War Two, mostly. He loves the old classics, and documentaries."

Mr. Stevens grimaced. "Never saw the real thing, did he?"

She shook her head. "No. Grandpa served in Korea, though. Mom's dad, too."

"I thought as much." Eyes raised to the clock, he clucked his tongue. "Time flies, and I've got work to do. Feel free to play until the bell."

"Thanks, Mr. Stevens."

He walked back to his desk and picked up a stack of sheet music off his chair, then sat.

FIND ME. The words flashed through her mind as she picked up the mallets and turned toward the xylophone. FIND ME. She shivered, closed her eyes, and launched into a cover of Copa Cabana, upbeat and airy and not at all dark and cold.

Behind her, the wind rattled the window, and she understood what it said.

FIND ME.

Molly opened a math book on her dresser, turned up the volume on her iPod, and ignored both in favor of her laptop. Fingers soft on the keys, she typed in "Morse Code Translator" and hit "Enter."

She tried a phrase, listened to it, tapped it out on the bedframe, over and over to commit it to memory. Then another phrase, and another.

An hour later, she fell back, head on the pillow, and stared up at the white ceiling, tracing routes through the uneven glossy patches. Beads of sweat cooled on her forehead, and she breathed hard as the songs faded into memory.

No. Not songs. *Messages.*

The next morning, Kirsten met her as she got off the bus. "How you feeling?"

Molly shrugged. "What do you mean?"

"Chris said you hit your head pretty good yesterday, and I didn't see you at all after. Figured you went home."

They meandered toward homeroom on scuffed, faded tiles. Lockers jiggled, shoes shuffled across the floor. Heating vents flooded the hall with tepid air. Molly pricked her ears at every sound, but in the cacophony of human voices, she couldn't pick out any patterns.

Fingernails dug into her shoulder.

"Ow!" She flinched back and gave Kirsten a wounded look. "What the heck?"

Kirsten let go and let out a theatrical sigh. "What planet are you on? Have you heard a single thing I've said?"

Shaking her head, Molly tried a sheepish grin. "Sorry? Just a little distracted, I guess."

Kirsten rolled her eyes. "Yeah, well, don't be rude."

They walked in together, said the Pledge of Allegiance after the bell, and suffered through thirty minutes of group work with Chad and Tom, the least mature boys in the history of ever. Their constant, childish snickering tore through Molly's head until she just couldn't take another moment. Her hand shot up.

"Yes?" Mr. Brown raised his eyebrows but didn't look up from his newspaper.

"Can—may I go to the bathroom?"

He looked up at the four of them, a dubious frown dragging on his expression. "Are you done?"

"It's an emergency."

She ignored Tom's chuckle and hurried to the door the moment Mr. Brown nodded.

Alone in the hall, she walked toward the bathroom but stopped at the first locker. Reaching out with one fingernail, she tapped a pattern. WHERE ARE YOU?

Nothing happened. She laughed. *What'd you expect, Mol? You're just going crazy.*

She took two steps, and at the end of the hall, a door opened with a scattershot creak—more dots than dashes. A little seventh grader, wide-eyed in glasses way too big for his face, stepped out and walked her way. The door squealed closed with the same rhythm as the kid disappeared around the corner.

Looking both ways, she pulled out her phone and put the pattern into the translator.

Goosebumps crawled up her arms as the temperature dropped ten degrees. Something scraped against the inside of the locker, mouse-feet rustling almost too quiet to hear.

BENEATH

Molly reached back, hesitated, then repeated the word with her fingertip, adding a question mark. BENEATH?

Another pattern. She plugged it into her phone as humid air condensed on the screen.

SO COLD

Teeth chattering, she tapped, combining the new word with one she'd memorized. BENEATH WHERE? Her breath billowed in white clouds as she waited for a reply.

SO COLD

The temperature dropped again, and ice crystals crept across the windows.

The kid with the huge glasses rounded the corner, staring at her with wide eyes. She let out a breath she hadn't realized she'd been holding. "What, kid?"

His eyes frosted over, a cataract of ice crystals. She stumbled back, and he grabbed her wrist, his touch icy daggers ravaging her skin straight through her sweater. The chittering noise that came from his mouth belonged to another world, a world of shattered glass and pain and rocks cracking under the force of new-formed ice.

She jerked away and ran. Locker doors thundered an unrelenting staccato FIND ME as she ran past. Windows and door locks rattled FIND ME. The air in the vents whispered underneath and around the maelstrom of noise, repeating the boy's words in time with her throbbing wrist. Clutching it against her chest, the hall blurred through a sheen of tears.

She busted into the bathroom, shut herself in a stall, and huddled there. Squeezing her hands over her ears in a desperate attempt to make it stop did nothing. Even the dripping of the fountains pressed their command. FIND ME

She closed her eyes and replayed the boy's message in her mind. Hands shaking, she brought up the translator and fed the pattern into the phone.

I HEAR YOU PLAY

Noise flooded the room, human noise, girls chatting and arguing, classes changing in the hall. She let out a relieved sigh and opened the stall, joining the typical press of girls trying to freshen up in their allotted four minutes. She washed her hands, wincing as her sweater rubbed raw on her wrist, and ducked out into the hallway without speaking to anyone.

❈

Heart thundering, Molly hurried past the janitor's cart, muffling the keys' jingle with her hand, praying that nobody heard in the din of students grabbing last-minute things from their lockers and heading for the buses. She slipped the keys into her coat pocket, the metal cold against her shaking fingers, too cold, like the janitor had just been outside.

Principal Lawson returned her tight-lipped smile with pearly teeth and a hearty, "Have a good weekend!"

The kid's message rang in her ears. Where could you hear her play, behind foam-covered walls and thick, noise-isolating doors? What hidden place held those answers? Only one.

She shuffled toward the exit, then cut right, through the internal fire doors, and around the corner to the band room. After a soft knock, she pushed her way through. "Hello? Mr. Stevens?"

With no answer, she pulled her practice sheets from her cubby, a tiny space for music and spare sticks dwarfed by those for the saxophones, trombones, and tubas. She stuffed the loose papers into the bottom of her bag, under her textbooks and folders. That done, she walked over to Mr. Stevens's desk, grabbed a sheet of paper from the printer, and opened the top drawer for a pen.

A silver oval caught her eye, the dull metal held by a beaded chain. She picked it up and read the dog tags. MARTIN, JAMIE E. The letters scraped their way through the shelf in the back of the room as she read them; she didn't have to look them up, didn't have to translate them.

Hands trembling, she took a picture, put them back, and wrote a quick note.

MR. STEVENS,

I LOST MY PRACTICE MUSIC. CAN I GET ANOTHER COPY ON MONDAY, PLEASE?

THANKS,

MOL

She closed her eyes, took a deep breath, and turned toward the far wall. Between the two practice room doors, a black metal shelf held a legion of dusty trophies dating back sixty years. From tarnished brass to cheap plastic, they chronicled the victories of every competition and ignored the countless others where they found only defeat. She slid the shelf to the side, legs screeching against the floor to reveal the portal behind. Marked AUTHORIZED PERSONNEL ONLY in bold red letters, the peeling paint gave her an indication of how often anyone used it.

She pulled the ring of keys from her coat, the jingles spelling out HERE HERE HERE as she searched for the one that matched the number on the lock. Her fingers blistered as frost rimed the metal, and she shivered in her coat at the bitter cold. Jamming the key into the lock, she hissed against the pain and turned it. A jerk, a sigh of freezing cold air, and darkness yawned in front of her.

A steel ladder descended into a square hole in the concrete floor, the bright yellow paint faded from years of neglect. Black mold smudged the walls with angry splotches. Breath frosting, she pulled out her phone and used the flashlight app to blast the bright white LED down the hole.

Molly gasped.

A skeletal hand rested against the bottom rung. Beside it lay a caved-in skull on patchy gravel. She rubbed her wrist and frowned at the rusty handcuffs linking the arm to the unyielding metal. The body wore the tattered remnants of a uniform, dull gray-and-white camouflage just visible in the mold and rot. Her eyes grew wide as the finger twitched, the signal ringing out on the metal.

RUN

She stumbled back and slammed the door, groping for the keys. The ring fell from her fingers and clattered to the floor. She knelt to pick them up but instead grabbed the shelf and jerked it back into place. A trophy tottered as the band room door opened. She caught it and set it down next to the blazing heater. Suddenly too hot, she swooned, light-headed. Pushing the keys under the shelf with her foot, she stood.

Mr. Stevens raised his eyebrows at her, the exact look he gave anyone late to class or goofing off instead of playing. "Looking for something, Miss Fitzgerald?"

She swallowed and tried not to gasp in a breath, instead pulling it slowly through her smile. "Hi, Mr. Stevens. I can't find my practice music. Was just leaving you a note."

He pulled the cart loaded with music stands the rest of the way into the room, let the double doors close, then pushed it against them. Wiping his hands on his shirt, he walked forward. "From the floor?"

A nervous giggle escaped her lips. "No. My shoelace came untied. The note's on your desk."

He glanced at it, picked up the pen, clicked it a couple of times. "From my drawer?"

She shrugged. "I didn't have one."

"You saw the dog tags, then."

"Dog tags?" Playing dumb never came easy to her, and he didn't look convinced.

He took another step, picked up the trophy, and then leaned in too close. Staring down at her, he licked his lips. "You're not special. She talks to me, too, you know."

She met his eyes, blank brown orbs, flat under the fluorescent light. "What?"

He brushed his knuckles across her cheek, then settled the hand on her shoulder and tapped, his fingernail sharp against her neck. He spoke the words as they seared across her nerves. "I. Loved. You." His grip tightened on her shoulder, twisting her coat until it pulled tight under her arm. "She looked like you, a little. I mean, not anymore."

Molly screamed. He swung the trophy, and the world exploded in hot white light. Pulling herself from the floor and unsure how she got there, her eyes came to focus on the line of red drool hanging from her lips. Searing pain shocked through her chest as his shoe impacted her ribs, again and again. He dragged her to her tiptoes, her scalp on fire, his right hand tangled in her hair, the left still holding the bloody trophy.

Feet dangling, legs useless, she tried to reach him, tried to claw or hit, tried to scream through the iron tang of blood in her mouth.

"No one can hear you, Molly, not through these walls."

She knew it. The soundproofing and thick wooden doors did more than prevent dead spots. Words came, thick and hard to understand around her swollen tongue. "Please, Mr. Stevens. I don't know—"

His face twitched, a spasm gone as fast as it came. "Don't play dumb. You're smarter than that, and it's… it's insulting. Jamie insulted me, near the end, after all we had and all we went through. She said she loved me, lived for me, but didn't show it, not after a while. Little niggling, nagging, grating insults, day in and day out. That's not love." He shoved her backward without letting go, and she tried to protest around her fat lip. A tooth shifted and a jolt of pain shot up her jaw.

"Please, Mr. Stevens. Please, don't."

"Too late for that. She talked to you, you listened. You think you're the first? You're not. You're not special. You're not first. Just the first to find her. Maybe she wants company."

He pulled a handful of pills from his coat, pried open her mouth, and stuffed them in, jamming his fingers past her bite, forcing them to the back of her tongue. Tilting her chin up, he plugged her nose and rubbed her throat. She tried not to swallow but swallowed. He held her against the wall, cruel hands crushing into her neck until the world swam and her tongue grew thick in her mouth. A cloud bore her to the ground.

Dark eyes stared down at her. "Goodbye, Molly."

Cold. Too cold to shiver, too cold to breathe. She reached out in the darkness for something, anything to hold on to. Her fingertips brushed something smooth. She stretched, reaching, and pulled the orb toward her. It scraped across the floor in the pitch black, and a tear escaped as her fingers traced over the top to the brow, eye sockets, empty nasal cavity, and ruined teeth.

February break. Friday afternoon through the following Monday morning. Ten days, give or take. Ten days before anyone would look for her in school, and no one to miss her at home. Ten days in the frigid dark, with black mold and Jamie Martin's skeleton for company.

She couldn't feel her toes, and her ankles burned through her socks.

The skeleton next to her shifted, a faint rustle almost too quiet to hear. Its finger rang against the ladder, staccato taps she couldn't put together without the translator. Molly reached for her phone, thrust her fingers deep into empty pockets, and let out a sob.

Frigid air slithered through her lungs, stagnant and precious proof of life.

Jagged shards of white-hot agony shredded her chest as she tried to lift herself from the ground. She collapsed next to the skull, panting. She'd broken her leg in Pee-Wee soccer a long time ago. This felt like that, only all over.

Cheek against the ice-cold floor, she reached out one-handed, feeling in the dark for anything that might help her. Brittle clothing crumbled at her touch, revealing naked bone beneath, jagged and splintered where Jamie's ribs had fractured. An old belt, stiff in the cold, the metal buckle frozen to the floor, but no bags, no tools, no walkie-talkie or phone or radio.

She moved higher, tracing the outstretched arm over the handcuffs to the twitching hand, tapping away a fervent message too fast and too long for her to understand. It calmed as her hand covered it, and it tapped a single word.

WARM

She tried to speak, but no sound escaped her ravaged throat. Instead, she slid her index finger past and tapped a memorized phrase on the ladder. WHO ARE YOU

Images flooded her mind, a young woman in an Air Force uniform, short red hair, and a beautiful smile. A helicopter ride over the desert. Mr. Stevens in uniform, on his knees, holding an open box with a gold ring inside. Fighting. Broken bones, a shattered jaw. Wounds hidden from family and friends back home.

Warmth and sorrow slithered into her, a life wasted and dumped in the eternal cold, seeking release. Seeking justice. Comfort. Warmth. With the memories came patterns she hadn't had enough time to learn, the dots and dashes like second nature to a Signals Intelligence officer.

She tapped on Jamie's shattered skull. HOW DO WE GET OUT?

The skeletal hand tapped on the rung.

FIND ME

Molly joined her, and they tapped together.

FIND ME

Again and again in the dark, desperate, until hope faded and the cold took her and plunged her into hard, unrelenting nothing.

Molly woke in the darkness, alone and too warm, unnaturally warm. Her skin burned, like chapped lips from too much skiing, but everywhere and nowhere, a disembodied pain that encompassed her entire world. Pushing through the agony, she felt but couldn't see her breath frosting against the back of Jamie's skull, the dead girl silent for the time being.

"I'm f-freezing. Can you—can you h-help me?" A piteous voice just rasped from her throat, sore like poisoned needles in the back of her mouth.

The skeleton made no reply. Jamie repeated the phrase.

Its finger twitched under her palm, lifted to the rung, and tapped.
HELP ME

"Yes. C-can you? Help me?"

HELP ME

"No, you don't understand. I n-need you to help me. I need to get out." The last phrase faded to nothing as her voice failed, throat too damaged to continue.

Jamie tapped.

GET OUT HELP ME HELP ME HELP ME GET OUT

Molly groaned and tried to stand. Her body protested, every motion a new study in just how much damage Mr. Stevens had done. She couldn't move her legs enough to sit, even pushing against the wall. She couldn't lift her arms enough to push up, and even trying sent spasms through her body.

Tears froze in her eyes. Words formed on her lips, too quiet for even the dead to hear. "You brought me here to die with you."

WITH YOU

WARM

WITH YOU

She closed her eyes and slept.

"Hello?" A man, somewhere above, muffled and too quiet.

Frost crusted her eyelids, held them shut. She couldn't move, not even to lick her lips, as the voice called again.

"Molly Fitzgerald, you in here?"

Voices bantered back and forth, strong male voices, Principal Lawson, and others she didn't recognize.

"She has to be. Cameras show she came in here, never came out."

" — her necklace in his car. We took him down to — "

" — nothing here."

"Maybe she — "

She tried to scream, to make any noise, but nothing came out. She tried to reach for the rung, but her hand didn't move. Her lips moved against the ice-cold skull, a desperate plea with her last shred of energy, movement without sound. "Help me."

A faint rustle and the skeleton shifted. Then bone rang on metal with sharp peals.

HELP ME

HELP ME
HELP ME
A voice above responded. "Do you hear that?"
"Morse code?"

Jamie tapped on, repeating the phrase again and again while Molly lay still, broken and unable to move.

"Is that a door?"

"Help me move this thing."

She tried to open her eyes, hold them open long enough to see the light, but the tapping faded, and she knew no more.

The screaming wouldn't end. High, then low, then high, it shook her body and threw her side to side. She only knew pain, pain, and unending screams. It hurt to move. It hurt to lie still. It hurt to breathe.

But she breathed, sweet country air tinged with bleach and the acrid bite of medicine.

I'm alive.

"She's waking up." A male voice, soft but urgent.

"Good. They'll want her statement at the hospital, if she's up for it."

Divine light blinded her, white and pure, and the shrieking faded to an ambulance's unsteady wail.

"Molly, can you hear me?"

"Yes." No sound came out of her raw throat. She tried again, and again, and squeezed her eyes shut against unbidden tears, hot on her skin. He shushed her.

"You're going to be okay. You've got some frostbite and hypothermia, a lot of broken bones, but we're keeping you warm and giving you fluids. They say you know Morse code. Can you tell us what happened?"

She reached out, and he took her hand. Molly didn't know Morse code, no more than a few phrases. But Jamie did. Tracing her fingernail to his palm, they tapped.

AFTER TREVOR VANISHED

ROBERT P. OTTONE

Deirdre and Drew needed to escape the city.

They had spent the summer working. Drew, teaching summer school in Queens at a facility for special needs children, and Deirdre, who skipped teaching this summer to help her younger sister Audrey execute her wedding, were both in desperate need of some rest and relaxation.

"Remember when the DJ pressed a button on his MacBook Pro and transitioned from 'Blue' to 'What Does the Fox Say?' Masterful work, no?" Drew asked, steering down the backroads to the lake.

"Which wedding was that?" she asked, genuinely unsure.

He shrugged. "All of them?"

They shared a laugh.

Some time at her family's lake house would do them some good, even if Deirdre hadn't been there since the accident.

"Don't be so nervous, kid. This'll be fun," Drew said, eyes on the road. "Did I just miss the turnoff? You remember 'fun,' don't you?"

She rolled her eyes. Drew's weak attempt to get her to lighten up only made her tense further, but she forced a smile anyway. Stress from work. Stress on the two of them. "Fun" was a luxury she didn't have much stock in lately, even with the diversions of summer weddings, parties, and more.

"The lake house always was a good time," she offered. "I remember, in high school, just feeling so…" she trailed off.

"Free?" Drew offered.

"As if the natural world didn't matter. That unfettered release."

Drew nodded. "The good ole' days."

"Exactly," she said, thinking back to the sounds of a lakeside summer. Splashing, shouting, music blaring from a nearby CD player, waiting all afternoon for the radio station to play her favorite songs. Then she thought of Trevor. His smile. His warmth.

The lake claimed a life every year. Deirdre never expected it to happen to her, personally, nor did she even believe in the superstitions of the old folks who repeated the story over the years, but when Trevor vanished, she knew some legends just might be true.

Deirdre thought it was because of an unmapped cave system fed from the ocean, but local legend chalked it up to a Native American Princess who desired company after white men killed her long-lost love during colonial times.

She didn't know which to believe. She only knew that her teenage boyfriend, Trevor, was never seen again after a post-homecoming party at the lake filled with the usual teenage debauchery and mistakes of youth.

The night he vanished, they had made love for the first time and told one another how much they loved each other.

That last weekend with Trevor had been as close to perfect as Deirdre ever experienced. Stolen kisses, admissions of love, planning for college admissions, the future laid out before them perfectly, a wide-open expanse of possibility.

After Trevor vanished, that expanse closed in quickly and became a slow march to adulthood, which Deirdre felt came on altogether too quickly.

College turned into grad school. Friends began to settle down. Grad school turned into a teaching position. Four years after landing the position and locking down tenure, Deirdre found herself in therapy, discussing the loss of Trevor frequently. Her analyst felt there was a direct connection between Deirdre's loss of self and the night Trevor vanished.

The last time Deirdre saw the house on the lake had been the last night she truly allowed her guard down and had legitimate "fun."

Drew had been driving about two hours and pulled the seat belt away for more space to stretch his aching back. The trip was taking slightly longer due to summer traffic heading eastbound on Long Island. Since crossing the bridge, they hadn't said much to each other during the ride. Drew had been the one to push for the trip to the lake house. They had needed some time together, for sure, but she was hoping for literally *any* other location. Nevertheless, here they were.

"How many times do you think we heard 'Yellow Diamonds' this summer?" Drew asked, breaking the silence.

"First of all, it's not called 'Yellow Diamonds,' it's called 'We Found Love,' and we easily heard it four times," she said, adjusting her Ray-Bans and smiling. "I'm good if I never hear it again."

"But Dee, *we* found love in a hopeless place. I'm hurt you'd say such a thing," he said, teasing her.

"Mr. Fowler, as your department chair, I'm shocked to hear you refer to P.S. 153 as a 'hopeless place,' and will be recommending you for immediate disciplinary action."

"God, I hope so," he said, winking at her.

She couldn't help but laugh. The busy summer barely gave them time to spend together, and even though their hours were roughly the same, at the end of the day, they found themselves settling into the couch, watching season after season of *Ancient Aliens* and eating leftover Thai food in gym shorts and sweatpants. Not the sexiest of summers.

They pulled onto Bloch Lake Dr., nothing more than a gravel road carved through the densely wooded region around the lake itself, and Deirdre found herself staring into the thick woods around them. The trees stretched high above and created a natural canopy over the road, which had certainly seen better days. Fallen branches and some smaller, dead trees littered the road. For a moment, Deirdre thought she saw a figure in the woods, nude, skin sagging and wet. Shaking the thought loose, she blinked, and when she looked again, it appeared to be a plastic bag or a hammock left behind by some campers.

"I love the sound of the tires going over gravel," Drew said. "Gravel roads are so awesome, babe. I'm having fun already."

She laughed at him again. Dumb comments like that were one of the many reasons she fell for a co-worker in the first place. This was the first time Drew was seeing the house, and Deirdre began to feel hints of excitement to show it to him. When they pulled up, Drew's eyes went wide.

"Babe, oh my god, look at this place!"

The two-story house was a simple chalet-style home with large windows, allowing whoever was inside a view of the lake no matter where they seemed to be. Deirdre's parents had remodeled a few times, adding updates and upgrades here and there, and a stone fireplace complete with a painting of Deirdre and her sister as kids, staring, somber-faced, eyes wide.

Drew jumped out of the car and ran to the trunk, gathering their bags, and carried them to the door. She followed after him, pulling the keys from her jean shorts.

The place didn't radiate the discomfort Deirdre expected. Deep down, she didn't know exactly what she'd find once she opened the door, but a million horror movies prepared her for any variety of ghouls, goblins, or whatever lurking behind every countertop or hiding in every closet.

The truth was, the house was as painfully plain as it had ever been. Memories of chasing her sister around the marble countertops flooded her mind. Eating s'mores in the backyard. Kissing Trevor along the shore. Deirdre found herself smiling.

"I knew you'd love it," she said, unlocking the door. He bounced up and down like an excited child, waiting to check out the interior and sneaking a peek through the windows.

When she opened the door, he ran inside and started looking around. He gestured out the sliding back door at the lake in amazement.

"Babe, look at this view!"

"I know, this is my family's house, remember?"

Drew rolled his eyes and continued his excited examination of the house, darting from room to room.

There were only two other houses scattered along the water, and they were far from Deirdre's family's place.

One rested on the opposite side of the lake, seemingly forgotten by whoever owned it, since the windows were boarded up or smashed.

"I'm gonna' have sex with you here, and there, and on those steps," he said, throwing their bags onto a nearby couch and pointing at the various places in the cabin. He picked her up and kissed her all over her neck and face. "And possibly, if you play your cards right, on that landing, and *definitely* on the kitchen counter."

"We might have to take down the creepy painting of me and my sister above the fireplace if we're gonna' do it on the couch, cowboy," Deirdre said, laughing at his amorous advances, and thankful that her family wouldn't be popping in any minute.

"Nah, let 'em watch, they've got to learn!"

She laughed and collapsed backward onto the couch, Drew's hands shaking with adrenaline as he removed her clothes.

�֍

Splashing from the lake awakened Deirdre.

It wasn't overly loud, but the distinct sharpness of the sound was familiar enough to jolt her awake. She rose, and in the fading light of the evening, walked, wrapped only in a blanket, to the large sliding door leading onto the back patio of the home. She left Drew behind, blissfully asleep, barely wrapped in a sheet.

Outside, birds chirped, singing an evening tune that tinkled in the air like a wind chime, and Deirdre shivered, a light chill in the air. She stepped closer to the railing of the deck and looked beyond, where about fifty feet of land eventually dissolved into the lake, turning from grass to rocky gravel to muddy sand. There were some Adirondack chairs her father built resting next to one another on the grass, and Deirdre would usually lay in them, watching the lake each night.

Before Trevor vanished.

The commotion in the water stopped, and Deirdre stepped off the patio onto the grass. She made her way to one of the chairs and sat down, draping herself in the blanket. The wooden chairs felt cold against her nude body, so she tucked the blanket around herself like a toga and watched for the movement in the water again.

For a moment, she thought she saw her breath in the cool evening air.

Ker-plunk.

Deirdre imagined it might have been a large bass in the lake, emerging and dunking, but the fading light cast impossible reflections across the surface.

For a moment, she thought she saw a slender hand emerge from the water. *Impossible*, she thought, closing her eyes and shaking her head. She breathed deep and prayed that when she opened her eyes, there would be nothing in the water.

"Dee?"

She jumped at Drew's intrusion. She turned, her heart racing, and looked up at him. He was nude, standing in all his glory.

"Boy, you better put something on," Deirdre said, pulling him down onto the chair and wrapping some blanket around him.

"Why? There's no one around," he said, kissing her. "What're you doing out here?"

"I used to watch the lake at night when I was a kid," Deirdre said. "Thought I heard some splashing."

"It's comfy out here." He continued kissing her neck and chest. "We should absolutely do it right here."

"You're such a creep," she said, laughing. "What if someone sees?"

"Again, let 'em watch," he said, slipping lower on the blanket, kissing his way down between her legs.

She felt nervous, thinking someone could be watching, maybe from the woods, but was overcome by the feeling coursing through her body while Drew enjoyed her. There wasn't anyone around, at least not that she could see. She felt like a teenager again. The thrill of having her boyfriend go down on her in an open space where someone could see was exhilarating.

The thought of a thousand eyes in the woods around her made her self-conscious, and her mind and body wrestled with the notion of pleasure and discomfort she felt being out in nature.

She fought the discomfort back and let Drew continue, letting lust take over.

As Drew's head bobbed lower, over the top of his tousled hair, she saw something poking out of the water.

A head with glittering pink eyes fixed on her.

She screamed, and Drew rose from under the blanket. "Holy shit, babe, what?"

"Nothing," she said, looking for the head. It was gone. "I'm sorry, let's go inside, okay?"

"Sure, yeah, okay..." he said, helping her up from the chair, and wrapping her in the blanket.

The following day, Deirdre and Drew shopped at a local market, getting supplies for the evening when the rest of her family would be arriving.

"In Queens, I don't get the opportunity to be a grillmaster, so, of course, I must take the opportunity to impress you with my ability to burn meat," he said, holding up a pack of steaks.

"My sister is a vegan this week, but I'm all about seeing your meat skills," she said.

"Damn right you are," he said, smacking her rear as she turned to gather some seasoning for the steaks.

She rolled her eyes and walked down an aisle, examining the rows of seasoning. She pulled a tin of Old Bay off the rack and started looking it over.

Then she heard the sound of wet feet slapping on tiled floor.

Splosh-slap. Over and over.

Slowly, Deirdre turned her head down the aisle toward the front of the store and saw nothing. The wet slapping continued, this time, from behind, and she found herself caught off guard by the sound, jumping.

She walked, backward, toward the front of the store, looking around for the source of the *splosh-slap* sound. Cold air swirled around her. She looked up, thinking she'd find an air conditioning vent above her, but there was no vent to be found.

Splosh-slap.

When she saw the wet footprints on the tile before her, appearing step by step toward her, she screamed, and the periphery of the world around her, the fluorescent lights overhead, the rows of brightly colored items, all blurred into darkness.

Drew knelt over her, head encircled with fluorescent light. He smiled warmly and kissed her forehead.

"You slipped, Dee. How does your head feel?"

"What? Slipped?"

He nodded. "Floor was wet. Stock boy must've missed a spot."

She saw the manager nearby, holding a first aid kit.

"Slipped?"

"We're so sorry, ma'am, we've called an ambulance already," the manager said.

Slowly, she sat up and looked around. A small crowd of people were gathered nearby, watching, eyes wide. Some whispered amongst themselves.

"No, no, it's okay," Deirdre said, rising slowly. "I'm okay."

"Take it easy, babe. You hit your head pretty hard," Drew said, rising, holding her by the arm.

"Please, here's my card. If you need anything, don't hesitate, everything in your cart is on me, alright?"

Deirdre, with blurry eyes, stared at the manager, a look of true worry on his face.

"Oh, okay, thanks," Drew said, tucking the card in his pocket. "Let's get you home, kiddo."

That night, Deirdre lay on the couch, her sister Audrey and her new husband, Spence, nearby.

"You slipped on some wet floor? We should sue the shit out of them. We could be market owners, Dee," Audrey said.

"They're not a mega-corporation. I don't want to ruin a mom-and-pop operation," she said, chuckling. "I'm fine. I just got dizzy and slipped."

"I'm glad you're okay, Sis," Spence said, smiling. If a golden retriever could be a human, it would be Spence. Dopey, happy, blond.

"Thank you," she said, bristling at Spence's use of "sis."

The smell of grilled meat hung in the air, wafting through the open sliding glass door. Drew stood, wearing a "Kiss the Chef" apron he snuck into the cart before leaving the market. Deirdre had talked him out of the chef's hat he wanted but conceded to the apron.

He finished grilling, added a dash of pepper, and placed the meat onto a large tray.

"Audrey, I've prepared a delightful medley of carrots, sliced onion, and cucumbers finished with a balsamic vinegar reduction for you," he said, placing the steaks down on the table and producing a bowl from the refrigerator.

"Isn't that just a salad?" Audrey asked.

"Dammit, Dee, she guessed it."

Deirdre laughed and rose from the couch.

After dinner, Deirdre and Audrey sat on the Adirondack chairs, watching the lake. During the day, twentysomethings had occupied the house across the lake and now raged, jumping off the dock into the water and doing keg stands.

"It's good to see the Party House is still a fixture. Remember when we were like that?" Audrey asked, sipping her rosé. "Those kids always had the best coke."

"I was *never* like that," Deirdre said, smiling. "That was all you, kid."

"I guess so," the younger girl said. "It happened so long ago. You seem tense being here."

She nodded. "I think I saw him, Audrey."

Audrey stared at her sister. "Who? Terry? Did he still have that bubble butt, or do ghosts not have bodies or whatever? Was he just a mist? What's the afterlife like?"

"His name was Trevor," Deirdre corrected. "Maybe I'm going nuts, but I'm pretty sure."

"Where?"

"In the water," she said. "Then at the store. Sorta'. I mean, I saw *something* at the store."

"What did you see?"

"Wet footprints."

Audrey stared. "Did you tell Drew?"

Deirdre shook her head. "Tell him what? I'm seeing the ghost of my dead high school sweetheart at the lake where he disappeared? That's totally normal, right?"

Audrey nodded. "Yeah, that's a boner killer for sure."

They shared a laugh.

"I don't go for that supernatural shit, Dee, you know that," Audrey said, finishing her glass. "There's no such thing as ghosts or goblins or Draculas or whatever."

"Dracul*a*. Singular. He was one person."

"Ugh, get fucked, don't be a teacher right now," Audrey said, rolling her eyes.

She smiled. "Do you think I'm crazy?"

"I've been saying you're crazy *for years*, so, obviously."

"He had pink eyes," she said, after a quiet moment between the two of them.

"Who? Whatever you saw in the water?"

Deirdre nodded. "I just feel so guilty."

"Trevor drowning or whatever isn't your fault. He probably hit his head on the deck and was pulled under. How is that your fault? We were kids. Shit happens."

"I didn't even notice he was gone until the next morning," Deirdre said quietly. "What kind of person am I to not realize the person you're supposedly in love with is missing?"

"Dee, it was high school. You're allowed a lapse in judgment. You have kids all the time who make stupid fucking mistakes, right?"

"You don't ever miss how things used to be? You don't *ever* want to go back, give up all the bullshit of what we have now and just go *back*?"

Audrey shook her head. "Onward and upward. Or, like, forward and frontward. Whatever, I dunno'. I don't think about the past. The present is too important."

"Is it, though? What's so important now? Our jobs? Our spouses and partners? Our bills? Rent?"

"It is what it is," Audrey said, finishing her glass. "Fuck, I'm out."

The two sat in silence a moment.

"What color eyes did he have for reals?" Audrey cocked her head. The telltale sign that she was invested in Deirdre's mystery.

"Trevor's eyes were gray."

"So, there you go, you're trippin' balls."

Deirdre shrugged. "I'm glad you're staying here tonight."

"If any spooks or specters try to fuck with you, I'll light some sage and kick their asses out."

The sisters hugged and poured some more rosé, eyes on the lake.

Deirdre walked slowly along the shore of the lake, watching as two kids at the party house snuggled on the pier, kissing and enjoying each other.

As she walked, she could hear Drew, Audrey, and Spence chatting, laughing, and hollering while watching YouTube videos in the living room, one of Drew's favorite pastimes and not one of her own. Deirdre tucked herself into her sweater, a cool breeze whipping up around her. She shivered in the darkness and looked out over the water.

Flecks of starlight glistened, and she smiled to herself. Her head felt better, and she felt more relaxed after chatting with her sister. A sense of comfort washed over her.

She allowed the memories of Trevor and their time at the lake to flood her mind. Moments spent staring into each other's eyes, reading poetry aloud, snuggling, getting closer. It felt true in the way teenage romance always does, that somehow their love could last forever.

Deirdre relished that feeling and wondered if her students felt it with their partners, or if that puppy love-type of romance had been washed away by sexting, Snapchat, and the attention-grabbing social media apps every student seemed obsessed with.

The love she and Trevor had was pure. Unfiltered and exploratory. Scary but comforting. That comfort sensation entered her being, and she sighed in the darkness by the lake, smiling and breathing deeply, remembering her lost love, the night relaxing her spirits.

Until she saw the wet, bloated figure standing on the water. Its pink eyes shimmered, standing out against the darkness of the woods, lake, and sky.

The figure stood, feet resting atop the moving water, flesh sagging, blotched and wet. The face was a jigsaw of flesh, bone, and murk from the lake's depths.

Whatever it was seemed to be smiling, hand extended to Deirdre.

"*Deeeee...*"

"No..." she said to herself, shivering. She closed her eyes and rationalized that whatever this thing was, wasn't there.

When she opened her eyes, the figure was gone.

Deirdre awoke with a start and looked around the room. Drew lay asleep next to her. She shivered in the darkness and rose, heading for the thermostat on the wall, her breath visible in the air as she breathed.

It glowed digital-green and read "35."

"Jesus," she said quietly and raised it to "70." Stepping back toward the bed, her foot landed in wetness.

In the darkness of the room, the only light from the full moon outside, Deirdre looked at the floor. She knelt down and touched the puddle, about eleven inches long, not particularly wide.

Grabbing her phone, she turned the flashlight on and recognized the puddle beside the one she was standing in as a footprint.

She followed the prints along the floor and found that two prints, side by side, stood next to the bed, on her side, facing where she had been sleeping moments ago.

Trembling, Deirdre swallowed hard and traced the steps backward to the doorway of the bedroom. As she followed the prints out into the upstairs hallway, then down the wooden steps into the house, she moved slowly, seeing her breath linger in the air as she moved, regretting not putting on a hoodie or sweatpants.

Downstairs, she noted the footsteps came from the sliding door and into the house.

Standing at the edge of the water was a pale, wet, slender figure facing the lake. Its body was blotched with green patches and terribly emaciated, ribs sticking out, the flesh of the buttocks saggy.

As Deirdre stepped closer, all moisture vacated her mouth. She found herself choking on her breath, her body seizing and reacting to the impossible creature before her. She waited for the flight or fight response to tear through her body, but it never came. Instead, she found herself stepping ever closer as though being drawn in.

"Where have you been?" the figure asked. Its voice tremored, as though something obscured its throat, the words barely able to scrape into the air. The voice was familiar, distant, as though dragged through decades of waves and muddy shores.

"Who are you?"

"You know who I am," it said.

She stepped closer. The water lapped at her feet, and she stood beside the figure. She leaned over to get a look at its face.

A nose barely there, deteriorated by years of neglect beneath the waves. A small hole where his cheek once was. A skeletal face.

Trevor, in what remained of the flesh.

"Oh god..." she whispered.

He cast his eyes to her, radiating the pinkish hue. "I've been here. All these years. Waiting for *you*."

Deirdre's body shook violently. She felt as though her feet were frozen in blocks of ice, and the feeling ran up her legs to the small of her back.

"All these years. Waiting. The princess kept me. Kept me close. Her plaything. But then, the following summer, she claimed someone new. And I've been waiting for you ever since."

"Trev... I'm sor—" she started. He placed a slender, half-missing pointer finger to her lips.

"You're here now. We're together now."

Tears began to swell in her eyes, and she stared at the being before her. The swell of nearly twenty years, her mind racing as to what became of her first love washed over her. It was a tidal wave of emotion, warmth, and desire, and her body was racked with agony.

"Why does it hurt so much?" she asked, her voice barely above a whisper.

Slowly, he leaned in and kissed her. Musk and decay entered her mouth, and she gagged a moment before the icy feeling found its way to the base of her neck. Trevor ran his cold hands up her spine, his grip firm but radiating frost.

In the recesses of her mind, Deirdre felt the urge to run. But she couldn't. Somewhere inside her, she knew that this was exactly where she needed to be. In Trevor's arms. The compulsion to remain by his side, lovers again, tied to one another, a flame rekindled. The desire and carefree youth she desired was here before her and possibly, always would be.

His body was slick with water. Or sludge from the depths of the lake. Deirdre couldn't tell which, but it clung to her. Insects and other crawling nightmares skittered around Trevor's ankles, crawling over her own.

"Now we can be together," he whispered, the funk of nearly two decades of rot on his breath. Slowly, he began to remove her night-clothes.

"I'm sorry for not noticing..." she muttered. "I'm sorry for leaving you here. Take me away, just... I want to go with you."

He nodded and kissed her forehead. A radiating wave of cold tore through her skull, passing down her spine, locking her more in place. She only nodded, unable to move, unable to do anything but shiver.

"I l-l-love y-y—you..." she tremored, struggling to get the words out as the coldness overtook her being.

The following morning, Drew, Audrey, and Spence looked for Deirdre. In their cars, they drove around the lake and when they came up empty, called the police. With officers in tow, they searched the woods and nearby area. Again, they came up with nothing. No cell phone towers could triangulate her position. No security camera footage from nearby businesses uncovered anything. Highway monitoring systems, the same.

The only remnant of the woman that could be found was a small pile of clothing beside the lake.

It was eventually determined that Deirdre had, at some point, possibly due to too much alcohol, slipped out for a night swim and drowned.

Nobody else disappeared at the lake the rest of that year. Nobody at all.

After Deirdre vanished.

THE SPECTACLES

LOU RERA

Nathan pushed his hands through his hair as he bent face down over the interview table. In a frozen moment, he saw dozens of coffee stains, rings from cups overlapping each other, layer upon layer, creating a history of lost hours. He thought, *There's one way out of this hell – but they'll never believe me.*

He bumped one of the cups. Wet cigarette butts bobbed up and down in the iridescent filth of a nasty habit. *Who's going to tell these guys they can't smoke in here?* The stench, the heat, the rancid cigarette breath from talking mouths spewing accusatory words. He sat, stoic, in the metal chair, his mind elsewhere. No windows, no air. He'd been confined for hours in this interrogation room with two detectives hell-bent on getting him to confess to a crime committed before he was born.

"You claim someone provided you with this information," number one said as he shot a sideways glance at his partner. "You said you had directions, is that correct?" He looked down at his notes. "The truth, Mr. Clark." The detective appeared annoyed. He squeezed the bridge of his nose and closed his eyes briefly, then lifted his hand to rub his forehead. A nauseating musky odor rose from the men.

"I found the body like I've told you. Julie gave me the directions," Nathan said bluntly. He paused as he noticed a spider making its way along the black vinyl baseboard. "I want another coffee," he demanded. Detective one glanced at his partner. He shoved his chair backward, then bolted from the room. The men would leave the interview session at alternating but random intervals. Nathan glanced up at the circular dirt ring on the wall where a clock once had been. He tapped the swizzle stick inside his empty cup. Detective two said, "While you wait for your cup of burnt coffee, tell me about Rifkin."

"I've never been in contact with Joel Rifkin," Nathan said. "Julie can tell you that herself, that is if you see her." The moment those words left his mouth, he could see the look on detective two's face. The detective smirked, then slammed his fist on the table. Cups bounced. "Bullshit!" Nathan knew his explanation sounded crazy. *I wouldn't believe me either.*

"Rifkin was caught with WhatsApp on a burner. We can't trace shit on the fuckin' thing. I think you dumped your burner after you and Rifkin dreamt up this little scheme," detective two said.

He leaned close to Nathan's face, then screamed, "You and your hero Fucknuts planned this. There's no record of how you contacted that crazy murdering fuck. How'd ja do it?"

Detective one, returning with a fresh cup of coffee, said, "The owner at Ting's told us you were like a little prissy fanboy when it came to Rifkin. You drove all the way there just to sniff the ass of history."

"I told the other cops the same thing and, no one believes a shittin' thing I've said." Nathan continued. "If you'd seen her, you'd never be able to sleep again. Never. It's those goddamn glasses. And you can't see her if you just put them on. There's a trick to it. Or magic, if that's what you wanna call it. She controls all of what you see."

Detective one jumped up and grabbed Nathan by the throat, lifting him off his chair. Nathan struggled to breathe. A hard knock came from behind the two-way mirror. The other detective's arm shot out from where he sat and grabbed detective one's wrist. Without a word, the first detective let go. Nathan choked and coughed as he rubbed the top of his chest and throat, his face red. Sweat poured down the sides of his head.

Detective two said, "Let's all calm down here." He drew in a deep breath and continued. "So, you're telling us Julie-the-dead-girl and a pair of glasses led you to the place where Joel Rifkin buried Julie's body, is that right, Mr. Clark?"

"If it weren't for Julie, I'd have never found her."

"Enough! Investigators never found Julie's body. Rifkin confessed to detectives twenty-seven years ago that he'd cut off Julie's head! If you're asking us to believe you, how the fuck could she 'tell' you without a head?"

This cop is catching on. If he thought about what he'd just said, it's as crazy as what I'm asking them all to believe.

Nathan Clark's troubles had begun in the fall. He and his girlfriend had decided to drive up to Lake Placid, then on to Vermont to bask for a couple of days in the vibrancy of the season's change. But all along, Nathan had something else on his mind. He wanted to head further north on his way back through New York State. His real destination had been the small village of Dannemora. Since 2015, most people had heard about the Clinton Correctional Facility located there. The prison had made headlines because of a made-for-TV escape. The two cons had avoided capture for weeks as swarms of law enforcement closed in. The end had been the stuff of television drama: the gruff con, shot dead as he peered through the scope of a stolen hunting rifle. Two days later, the other con took a bullet in his right thigh as he scrambled toward the Canadian border.

The prison escape story had riveted the nation, but Nathan had been fascinated with another bit of trivia regarding the village of Dannemora; of the four-thousand residents, three thousand were in prison. He couldn't shake the weirdness of that idea. A festering population of murderers and thieves, held at bay by a ramshackle, dirt-poor community.

That day, as his girlfriend checked her makeup and fussed with her hair in the visor mirror, Nathan said to her, "What would happen if the walls of the prison just, 'poof,' disappeared?"

When they arrived in Dannemora, the skies were gray, overcast with a dampness that burrowed deep into their bones. The chill he felt exuded from his girlfriend, too. She refused to leave the car, her attention focused on selfies. She'd been a pill of a companion for the last few days, and Nathan knew this little foray into *lovey-dove togetherness* would conclude their month-long tryst. The end-of-relationship markers had been there from the beginning. He read, she didn't. He liked burgers; she was a vegan. Nathan had perpetual bedhead and lived in the same clothes. She was drop-dead gorgeous and wore Christian Louboutin. He accepted the notion she probably had been attracted to his class clown bit, and then the newness of the sex, but he also sensed it was doomed to fail because they were so different.

Nathan left her and walked alone in the dismal village of Dannemora, and from the vibe he was getting, he vowed he would never return again. It wasn't just the gloom and the sense of poverty, but a desperation that traveled through the air like an unescapable pathogen. Like most small towns in America, Dannemora had a Main Street. The weak pulse of the so-called business district beat like an old heart ready to stop. Most storefronts were closed, some boarded, and one had blackened timbers. Then, like a beacon, Ting's Curios popped up on the corner of Milieu and Main. The building appeared run down, paint chips curled away from the rotting clapboards, but the contents of the window display piqued his interest. Years of grime fogged the thick plate glass, but he could still see the hodge-podge of bric-a-brac behind it. A red sun-bleached sign read "Bud's Taxidermy. Inquire inside." Two grizzled fox heads stared at him: one, frozen in time, biting its tongue, and the other, with a portion of an ear shot off.

A male mannequin's head wearing a MAGA hat and sunglasses hung by two pieces of wire. He saw a crude salt map of what appeared to be a model of the prison. In what looked like water-damaged original packaging, Gumby and Pokey grinned and waved. There were a few flashlights, and a shotgun cracked open with spent slugs lying around helter-skelter. Taped to the glass near the door, a yellowed index card posted a scrawled, handwritten message: "We have curios inside, just like the sign says."

When Nathan stepped through the door that day, the world as he knew it changed. He didn't feel any different. He didn't feel tingly. There were no blaring trumpets. There were no harbingers, nothing at all to tell him of his future. Yet he had been chosen to discover the truth. A truth no one would believe.

His soon-to-be ex-girlfriend shrieked when he opened the passenger's side door.

"Nate, what the hell's wrong with you? You scared the shit out of me!"

"Sorry, I need to get in the glove box."

"What for?"

"Does it matter?" He paused, perturbed. "I need the key for the compartment behind the back seat."

This silly tit-for-tat argument went on until she moved. Nathan tossed the key up and caught it in his left hand like a kid popping a baseball. He walked around to the back of the car.

When he'd bought the ole' station wagon, the used car salesman never told him about the row of hidden seats in the back, which could be flipped up from under the floor. Like a trunk in other cars, there was a storage compartment under those seats he used to stash things.

Today in Dannemora, it was cleaning day. He removed some trash, then walked it over to the dumpster behind Ting's. He placed the three items he'd purchased at the curio shop in the compartment, locked it, and this time put the key in the front pocket of his jeans.

After their argument, she apologized for being obstinate over something so trivial. She admitted his description of Ting's Curio Shop frightened her. When he asked why, she said, "Women's intuition." He should have dug a little deeper about her clichéd answer; there was some real meat on the bones of her fear. But at the time, he shrugged and decided that once they returned, his fledgling relationship with her would be over.

"What'd you buy? Anything cool?" she asked.

"Now you're interested?"

"Aw, come on, don't hold it against me because I was a little creeped out."

"I bought an 'official' Clinton Correctional Facility baseball-style cap. I think it's a knockoff, but it's still pretty awesome. Five bucks. I think the grease stain was put there to make it look more authentic. The guy in Ting's said it was from an actual guard over there."

"You gonna wear it around?"

"I doubt it. Maybe just hang it on my wall next to my poster of *The Shining*. I also bought what is supposed to be a real human finger bone. If it isn't real, it's a damn good replica."

"You're a sick man." Then she giggled, trying to lighten her earlier mood. "I hope it's not real; I mean, where would they get such a thing? Was it cut off from a prisoner in a gang fight?"

"That's nothing—the last thing is sick. If this is genuine, it's a collector's item. One so cool, I could probably get a grand for it on eBay from some death-cult sicko. I only paid one-fifty for it, so it's more about the story behind it that makes it fuckin' awesome."

"It's not a human skull, is it?"

"Nope, guess again."

"I can't, Nathan. Just tell me."

"Do you know who Joel Rifkin is?"

"Did he play for the Yankees? No—he was on Seinfeld, I think."

"Well, you're partly right. He was on Seinfeld—kind of."

"I can't remember. Who is he?"

"He's a serial killer who killed somewhere around seventeen women. Cut 'em up in pieces. Did weird shit to their bodies. He was stupid and got caught."

"What did you buy?"

"His glasses. You know, eyeglasses. Or at least one pair. I've seen a picture of him wearin' the kind just like the ones I bought. Besides, the guy in Ting's showed me a photo of Rifkin wearing 'em. They look exactly the same."

"How do you know the glasses aren't some old pair from the guy who owns the place?"

"He said a guard stole 'em from his cell and gave 'em to Ting's to sell. The guard gets half."

"And you think they're Joel Rifkin's?"

"Yep."

Nathan called it quits with his girlfriend before he got back to town. They'd fought about it, but in the end, she'd agreed not to disagree.

His road trip cost him steady sex, but it provided him an option to grab onto some extra cash. He'd tinkered with eBay before, but mostly from the purchasing end. The only thing he'd sold was a Spiderman comic book his father had given him from his collection. Nathan's father would be disappointed if he knew his son had sold the comic book, livid if he knew he'd sold it for half of what it was worth.

When he got home a day later than he expected, he placed the three items on his desk: the grease-stained guard's prison hat, the "real" human finger bone, and the eyeglasses. He had known all along the glasses were probably the most valuable, especially to those who wallowed in a mindset of darkness, people who liked to live vicariously through the terrible deeds of others. He planned to place the glasses on black cloth, then shoot a few angles with his iPhone. He'd download a picture of Rifkin wearing the same type of glasses. He was sure he could get a bidding war going.

Then he had a cool idea. He would post all the pics but add one more of himself wearing the glasses. Maybe even wear the prison hat, and hold the human finger bone up near his mouth as he made a sinister face—like he had just eaten the skin and flesh off the bone. He wasn't sure, but he'd remembered something about a policy against selling human body parts on eBay.

He waited until nightfall for the best atmosphere for the photos. He owned a fog machine from a Halloween party he'd thrown a few years ago and used it to haze up the living room to make it all the creepier.

The glasses were dirty, and the lenses needed to be cleaned, but Nathan knew better than to clean them. A pair of glasses owned by Joel Rifkin would be filthy, possibly with a few of his prints. *Too bad there isn't a speck of blood from one of his victims on the glasses – wow!* That would make them out-of-this-world valuable.

Slowly, he slipped on the eyeglasses. He adjusted the fit, using his index finger to push the frames up onto the bridge of his nose. He blinked a couple of times, then opened his eyes wide. His vision swam in blurred images from the prescription lenses; everything was out of focus. Some of his skewed vision must've been caused by the smudges of finger grease on the lenses. He was wondering about those fingerprints when he heard a woman moan from behind him.

He whipped around to see who was there, and when he spun back, he saw a blurry vision of a headless woman sitting on the ottoman in front of his leather chair. There was no blood, no gore, except for the fact she had no head. He could see the red cavity with whitish areas toward the back where the bone would be. She appeared nicely dressed, short skirt, legs crossed as she bounced her forward leg up and down. The back of her shoe hung off of her heel, and the front kept dangling off of her toes. From her demeanor, she seemed to be waiting. He expected her to be chomping on gum, but her head was gone. When she spoke, the sound of her voice came from behind him.

"I'm Julie Willington."

Nathan jumped up and turned around again. There was no one. He jumped back a few steps, then tripped and fell over the edge of his printer table. He hopped to his feet and yanked off the glasses. To his relief, she was gone. But she wasn't—he could still hear her voice.

"Nathan, please put the glasses back on."

"What the fuck kinda joke is this? Who are you? Did my ex-girlfriend put you up to this?"

"You know that's impossible. Now put the glasses on, Nathan."

He slowly brought the glasses back up to the bridge of his nose. As he did, it was like magic. Above the tops of the glasses, no one was sitting on the ottoman. But as he lifted the lenses higher, in front of his eyes, he saw the out-of-focus woman, headless, sitting there as calm as before, her legs crossed as if waiting for Nathan to come to his senses and have a conversation with her. Every time she spoke, her voice came from behind him.

Maybe it's because she has no head?

"You're right, Nathan. My head is disembodied, so to speak."

"Can you read my mind?"

"No, you actually said that out loud."

Nathan knew he did not.

"I am Joel Rifkin's second victim," she continued. "The police never located my remains, and Rifkin either forgot, or he wouldn't say. If you want to get rid of me, there are two things you'll need to do. I'll tell you where my remains are located, and I want you to tell the police."

"I read about all the crazy shit he'd done. You've been dead almost thirty years. What's left?"

"Enough, and you're smart enough to know that."

"What's the second thing?"

"I'll ask you later. It's a question you must answer."

"How do I walk into a police station with that kind of information and not become a suspect myself?"

The ghost of Julie Willington wailed like a banshee in pain, an ear-shattering sound, shrill and frightening, bouncing off the walls, echoing like the sound of fading screams in a canyon. Nathan froze, either unwilling or unable to move. His heart pounded, and he struggled to breathe. He had certainly said something he shouldn't.

"Are you kidding? You weren't born until four years after my murder," she said.

"Why me? Why so long? Why didn't you visit the guy at Ting's?"

"No one ever did the things you did."

"What things? All I did was put the glasses on."

"No, Nathan, you did one other, special kind of thing."

"Why'd you go with him anyway? Didn't you sense Rifkin was a maniac?"

"When Rifkin started to beat me, we struggled as he tried to get a firm hold on the piece of wood, the same one he used for his first murder. He tried to strangle me. When his glasses dropped into my hair, he grabbed them, gripped the table leg, then clubbed me into oblivion."

The headless Julie adjusted her skirt and switched her crossed legs in moves so normal, Nathan rubbed his eyes again, hoping she'd be gone.

"Of course, when the guard stole Rifkin's glasses, Rifkin went ballistic. In an unreported incident to the press, he rammed his own head against the cell bars, split his skull open, and had to be treated in the prison infirmary as he drifted in and out of consciousness. The infirmary doctor thought he was just out of his head like half the cons in the place. The prison psychiatrist blamed his wild outburst and self-mutilation to another of Rifkin's psychotic episodes."

Nathan tried to ask the headless apparition why she had chosen him, but she had disappeared. As the day wore on, he thought he was losing it. He believed he'd had a hell of a nightmare, that his imagination had run amok with his ideas about selling ghoulish shit on eBay. He couldn't remember when he'd drifted off, but he must have.

"Man, people write stories about weird shit like this," he said out loud to no one.

He received a No Caller ID text. The message contained only longitude and latitude coordinates. Nathan remembered his nightmare and found it too coincidental not to pay attention to the message. He pulled out his MacBook, opened Google Maps, then typed in the numbers. The location was in the northern part of Long Island, east of Oyster Bay, in a place called Lloyd Harbor, inside the Caumsett State Historic Park Preserve on the Long Island Sound. It was an out-of-the-way place near an area where hundreds of thousands of people lived.

Nightmare or dream, whatever. He loaded his station wagon with a new pickaxe, a shovel, a bolt cutter, some plastic bags, and to do it right, he purchased red utility flags to mark off the territory. If he was going to do this, he wanted the police to see he was being professional about the whole thing.

He had been to the park many times in high school. Luckily for Nathan, the parks commission had installed Wi-Fi everywhere. It made it easier for hikers to locate help when they needed it. Nathan could punch in those numbers and find the exact spot. He'd know very soon if the ghost's information was for real.

When he got there, he propped his flashlight in the crook of a tree. He dug at the location of the coordinates. Within an hour, he found what he thought was an upper leg bone, a section of what looked like a vertebra, and a hip bone. Even though he had failed basic biology in college, he was positive; the remains were human. Nathan figured he'd be a hero in the history of Rifkin's murders. Unfortunately, he misconstrued how law enforcement would interpret his find. He photographed the scene and made a notation as to the location. Then he contacted the Hempstead, New York Police Department since they'd originally handled the Rifkin cases.

"Nathan Clark, you're under arrest for aiding and abetting in the murder, disposal, and the coverup of the Willington murder. You have the right to remain silent, anything—"

His arrest followed shortly after he called the Hempstead Police Department to report his find. He was placed in interview room one, awaiting his public defender.

"You realize I wasn't even born when she was murdered," Nathan said.

"Tell it to your attorney."

"I should be getting a medal or something. You guys were used to finding Rifkin's murder victims on Fire Island and the rest, mostly south of 495. It never occurred to you forensic geniuses that Rifkin might try something different."

"And exactly how were you in on Rifkin's secrets?"

Nathan casually held out his hand as if he were inspecting a new manicure. He appeared calm, almost bored.

"Were you getting on the job training from that asshole while he rots in jail? By the way, genius—where is your girlfriend? No one has seen her since you returned from your trip up to Dannemora."

"Like I told your partner, we broke up. I don't keep tabs on old girlfriends. If I did, you guys would call it stalking, right?"

Two days later, Nathan found himself sitting in a conference room, much nicer than the hot, claustrophobic interview room. On the solid mahogany conference table, bottled water was placed in front of each chair. A man entered the room who reminded Nathan of the character Jack McCoy, from *Law & Order*. He was accompanied by two women, one with a recording device. The man who introduced himself as the

District Attorney then peppered Nathan with questions about the whereabouts of his girlfriend and about his fascination with serial killer Joel Rifkin.

"It's going to be difficult to make the case that you murdered your girlfriend because of the corpus delicti rule. No body, no evidence, equals no crime," the DA stated. "We could put you before a jury, and we might even get a conviction because of past precedents. But we'd lose on appeal. Again, no girlfriend's body."

"Well, I can go then?" Nathan asked.

"Not quite. We're charging you with conspiracy and aiding and abetting in criminal activity associated with serial killer Joel Rifkin."

"Get your fuckin' ass in that cell, buddy boy," Guard Bradley shouted.

"Gotcha, boss," Nathan said.

"You watch too many fuckin' movies, asshole. You achin' for a few whacks?"

"No, sir, just giving you the respect you deserve."

"It's Guard Bradley, shithead. I know all about your little bullshit with Rifkin. And there ain't no way on God's green earth you and that psycho fuck are ever walkin' the same concrete. You got that?"

"Loud and clear, Guard Bradley."

The next morning, Warden Horton visited Nathan in his cell. He didn't come alone. Bradley and another guard, who held what appeared to be a taser, came too. The warden didn't gamble with inmates. Paperwork only told him so much; he wanted to see for himself which cons might turn out to be batshit crazy.

"I don't know why they did it, but you pulled a sentence here, only one block over from Rifkin. I wouldn't call that cosmic justice," Warden Horton said.

Bradley chimed in, "That little fuck weasel probably went down on the sentencing judge to be near that murdering asshole." Horton's expression shut Bradley's mouth.

"They'll find your girlfriend's body. You know that, don't you? Then they'll add twenty-five more," Warden Horton said.

"I've been tellin' them, she moved," Nathan said.

"Don't be coy with me, son." The warden nodded at Bradley, then walked out of the cell. He stood there jiggling the change in his pocket as he looked at the gray concrete. Bradley rammed his night sick into Nathan's gut, hard. Nathan let out an "ooofff" sound, his breathing short and shallow. He leaned over to steady himself on the edge of the sink when Bradley whacked his knuckles. Nathan's time began in the way it did for most cons: with a lesson in brutal obedience.

One night, half-asleep, Nathan woke. He felt as if someone had tapped him on the shoulder, and he thought he'd heard someone say, "ssshh." At first, he thought he had dreamed it. He propped himself up on his elbow and put on his reading glasses. His bedside clock displayed 3:00 a.m. He was startled, then shoved himself against the wall at the head of his bed.

There she was again. The headless woman sat in the only chair in his cell, against the bars. She was exactly how he remembered her.

"Julie?"

"Nathan, do you have something to tell me?"

There was not enough room behind his head and the wall for anyone to be there, but nonetheless, her voice came from behind him.

"I found your body where you texted me it would be. I guess they didn't find your head. You must know how that worked out because you're here."

"Can you tell me about your girlfriend, Nathan?"

"Geez, you're stuck on that, too?"

A low guttural scream, mixed with a high-pitched wail, bounced off the concrete walls of his cell, reverberating in the central corridor.

"Okay, okay, please stop."

"I know what you've done to her, Nathan—I just need to know where?"

"Did you know when you first appeared what would happen to me?"

"I knew what you'd done."

"In the beginning, you wanted to ask me a question. What was it?"

"Do you want me here for the rest of your days, Nathan?"

He sighed, then shook his head. Nathan felt a sudden and terrifying fear of this woman's otherworldly presence. He thought back to when she had first appeared to him. *Why wasn't I afraid then?*

"Because of guilt," she whispered.

"Did you read my mind again?"

"Do you have something for me?"

"It's always been about her, hasn't it?"

"She'll never rest until I know where."

Nathan turned on the reading light next to his bed. He pulled out a piece of paper from a notebook, and on it, wrote down a location. He held it out for Julie. Nathan refused to say out loud where his girlfriend's body was buried. *To say it was to admit it.* He wondered if Julie had her otherworldly hooks into another loser like himself, a guy that would see the headless ghost of Julie Willington, former murder victim of Joel Rifkin.

Nathan shut off his table lamp, then ate the paper with the location he'd given Julie. If twenty-five more years were coming his way, he wanted the cops and lawyers to work for it.

"Julie? Are you still here, Julie?"

BRUISED AND BATTERED NEVERMORE

AMY GRECH

Something strange about the decrepit apartment in Brooklyn where Jackie Crawford lived for the past year unnerved her. The lack of heat and hot water didn't set her on edge. No, it was something more ominous...

Her boyfriend, Jeff Dutton, had a hunch one night while they snuggled on the couch and watched *The Exorcist*. She leaned on his chest, and he wrapped his strong arms around her to keep her warm, both inside and out.

When the movie ended, they heard a loud click that caused Jackie to flinch and set Jeff on edge.

"What was that noise?" Cringing, Jackie clung to Jeff.

"Beats me." He shrugged. "Maybe your creepy neighbor Al snuck in while we were watching the movie to poke around your lingerie drawer." Jeff snickered. "He looks like a pervert to me."

Jackie punched his arm, a playful love-tap. "That's not funny."

He stopped laughing. "Lighten up."

She sat bolt upright on the couch. "Something's wrong. Better go see what it is."

"Sure thing." Jeff got up to look around, straining to see in the dark. He flicked the light switch and searched for intruders. There was no one in the living room besides Jackie.

Cautiously, he made his way into the bedroom with Jackie skulking nearby and turned on the light. They found the room unoccupied, but the window was open halfway despite the chill.

"Why did you open the window?" he asked, teeth chattering as he shut it.

She frowned. "I didn't. I thought *you* did."

"Nope, I didn't touch it." Jeff shook his head.

"I probably opened it last night for some fresh air…" Jackie bit her lip, unable to remember touching the window.

"Why would you do that? It's a bit nippy out this time of year." He folded his arms and rubbed them to keep warm.

"Sheesh. I forgot to shut it. Cut me some slack." She frowned. "Why don't you keep me company in the kitchen while I whip up some hot chocolate."

"Roger that." Jeff followed her into the kitchen and sat down at the table while Jackie puttered around near the stove.

Five minutes later, they brought their steaming mugs of hot chocolate with marshmallows back into the living room and set them down on the cluttered coffee table crammed full of books about ghosts and other atrocities.

Jeff picked up a dog-eared paperback, *The Complete Tales and Poems of Edgar Allan Poe*, and thumbed through it. "Where did you get all of these books?"

"My Super, Sy Mann, gave them to me when I told him I'm an author. He's a spiritualist who believes in the paranormal, in all its guises. That's why there are so many."

He nodded and set the book back atop a shaky stack. "How thoughtful. Looks like you've got lots of inspiration to draw from here."

"Definitely — a genuine wellspring of inspiration." Jackie smiled and sat next to him on the couch. "This is guaranteed to warm you up."

"Not like you do." Jeff kissed her deeply, making her blush.

She took a sip of her hot chocolate.

He hoisted his mug and took a long drink. "Halloween's right around the corner."

"Should I be scared?" Jackie rested her head on his shoulder.

"Yeah. I think you've got ghosts." Jeff leered at her.

She laughed. "What gives you that idea?"

"You've got a window that opened all by itself, and, seeing as how you don't remember doing it, what else could it be?" He set his empty mug in his lap.

Jackie finished her hot chocolate and brought their mugs into the kitchen. "I don't know. That noise we heard could have been anything."

"Like what?" Jeff followed her.

Her eyes lit up. "A stray cat knocking over a garbage pail."

"It sounded much worse than that. Didn't it?" He scratched his head.

"Definitely. And look—that picture in the living room that came with the apartment fell again." Jackie pointed to the wall adjacent to the window where the picture that depicted a murder of crows, mid-flight on a dark stormy night, lay on the ground.

Her boyfriend frowned. "Does that happen a lot?"

"All the time," she replied, rolling her eyes. "Let's go see if Sy is home. Maybe he can get to the bottom of this."

"Right. Since Sy is a soothsayer, he can raise the dead." Jeff wiggled his fingers in the air for effect, as if conjuring spirits.

"Not quite. If we know why the spirit is unhappy, we can hold a séance to help right the wrong, and hopefully put an end to these strange happenings," she said, sighing.

"What's with all this spirit mumbo-jumbo? I didn't know you were into that." Jeff folded his arms.

"You don't believe in ghosts, do you?" Jackie grabbed her keys off the kitchen table.

"Not unless I can see them. You know, like Casper the Friendly Ghost?"

"There are no 'friendly' ghosts. Besides, Casper is just a cartoon character," she countered.

He slammed the door shut and followed her to the Super's apartment on the first floor. "What makes you such an expert?" Jeff frowned.

"That picture of the crows doesn't spend a lot of time hanging on the living room wall—it's constantly falling—that's why the glass is cracked." She cringed.

"Or it might be a weird coincidence."

"Let Sy be the judge," Jackie quipped.

They walked down three flights of sagging stairs to Sy's apartment.

Jackie knocked once and waited. As usual, Sy had the TV blaring, so she knew he was home.

They heard him shuffle over to the door and fumble with three deadbolts. "Don't get your panties in a knot. I'm comin'," Sy's stern voice declared.

She cleared her throat and blushed, caught off guard by the old man's crass words. Jeff snickered.

The door creaked open, and Sy, a tall, slight man with fluffy tufts of white hair sticking up every which way, appeared in the doorway. The Super smiled when he saw Jackie but looked confused when he realized she wasn't alone.

"Hello, Jackie. I had a feeling it was you." He grinned, revealing toothless gums, and waved.

"Really?" Jackie winked.

"Oh, just a hunch. Who's that young fella?" He pointed a crooked, trembling finger at Jeff.

She sighed, embarrassed that he forgot so soon. "This is my boyfriend, Jeff. I introduced you to him a few weeks ago."

Jeff extended his hand, and Sy shook it.

"Ah, of course. Now I remember. He looks like a fine young man." Sy grimaced, looking confused. After hesitating for a moment, he opened the door wide and led them inside.

Jackie and Jeff stepped carefully to avoid slipping on the worn linoleum and old newspapers with yellow stains strewn about.

"You're wondering why my hands shake, aren't you, boy? I saw you staring." The Super scowled at Jeff.

He nodded slowly, tilting his head.

"My nerves are shot from the war, but you don't want to hear about that—it's an *awful* story for another time." Sy shook his head.

Jeff admired his own strong, steady hands. "Fair enough."

The Super petted the ancient orange tabby with rheumy, green eyes sprawled out next to him on the unmade bed. He sat on the edge and motioned for Jackie and Jeff to take a seat. They sat on the rickety, wooden chairs facing the bed that creaked under their weight.

"What can I do for you?" He scratched Tiger's chin.

Jackie leaned forward so the Super could hear her clearly. "Do you remember how the previous tenant who lived in my apartment died?"

"Who died?" Sy scowled.

Tiger purred, too content to realize the conversation did not match his mood.

Jeff groaned. "The tenant who lived in the apartment before Jackie moved in. What happened to him? Did he commit suicide, or did he die of natural causes?"

"The guy who used to live in Jackie's apartment? Oh, you must mean Marty Leary… odd fellow. Always came and went at weird hours, usually in the dead of night. Never did figure out what he did for a living. I just know the rent was always paid on time. That's all the landlord really cared about, so I didn't stick my nose where it didn't belong." He scratched his head. "Why do you want to know how he died? Marty's dead and gone—so long."

"Strange things have been happening in my apartment lately. There's a spooky picture of crows in the living room. It seems like every time I turn around, it's on the floor — it really takes a beating. If we can pinpoint his cause of death, that might shed light on these strange occurrences." Jackie gave them a thumbs-up.

Sy rubbed his pointy chin. "You don't say."

Jeff folded his arms. "Yeah, not to mention strange noises and windows opening by themselves."

"Sounds like you've got a spook. Maybe even a couple of 'em." Sy chuckled.

"I think knowing how the last tenant died might help solve the problem." Jackie took Jeff's hand in hers and squeezed.

Sy studied Jackie. "Let's see... he'd been dead for a couple of weeks last summer when the tenants complained about the terrible stench coming from the place; smelled like rancid meat, they said. So, I dug up the spare key I had for 4-D and went to investigate. I found poor Marty in bed, rotting; his blue eyes glazed over, wide with fright. Poor guy's mouth was wide open, frozen in a perpetual, silent scream. The covers pulled up to his chin, and his rigid fingers curled up into claws."

The old man fished a cat treat out of his shirt pocket and fed it to Tiger. "The coroner removed the body late at night, so the chances of someone seeing were less likely. According to the autopsy, a heart attack did him in. But from the look on his face, I'd say he was scared to death by someone he didn't expect to see, and that's what killed him! Al Ash's wife, Emily, fled soon after. He lived across the way from Marty. They weren't exactly bosom buddies. Al probably did Marty in — he got wise to him being more than neighborly with his wife — might have scared him to death. I caught Marty looking her up and down more than once when they passed each other in the hall, undressing her with his eyes. Sometimes Emily was with her husband, coming home from work, but she was usually alone when he turned on the charm. Al probably got wise to Marty's romantic overtures. If I had to guess, I would say all of that hate boiled over, and one day he just flipped his lid."

Deep in thought, Jeff shuddered, glancing at the hand-carved crucifix hanging on the wall above the Super's bed. "So much for your theory, Jackie." He glared at her.

"What theory would that be?" Sy shifted his weight on the bed.

She lowered her head, feeling dejected. "I told Jeff if we contacted the spirit of the deceased, we could find out what made it unhappy; we could right the wrong so the strange occurrences would stop and the spirit could find peace."

"A séance might just do the trick. How long have these 'strange occurrences' been going on?" Sy frowned.

Tiger made himself comfortable on the Super's lap and settled down for a nap.

Jackie crossed her legs. "About a month."

"I see. Is it unusually cold in your apartment?"

"Yeah, why?" Jeff folded his arms. "I think the radiator's busted."

Sy's green eyes twinkled. "No, it isn't the radiator — the spirit's presence is making your apartment so cold. I can prove it."

Jeff stood and started to pace. "I've heard just about enough of this nonsense! If you're so sure it's Mr. Leary's ghost, show us how to drive it out."

"I lent Jackie several books about ghosts and haunted buildings — they're fascinating — I never get tired of hauntings or uncovering the mysteries that come with them."

She nodded. "Thank you, Sy. I keep them on my coffee table. I've always got my nose in a book. Jeff isn't much of a reader, so he could use a primer."

"Don't show anger or try to chase it. That will only make things worse. Take it from someone who knows." Sy stroked Tiger.

Jeff rolled his eyes. "How do you chase a ghost? You can't see it."

"There are ways, son, but I don't think you'd understand." Sy stared at Jeff.

Jackie sat forward in her chair. "I think holding a séance might guide Marty's tormented spirit to finally go to the light."

"Anything is possible." Sy nodded.

She breathed a sigh of relief. "Would you do the honors, Sy?"

"Why me?" He set a frail hand on his chest.

Jackie smiled, putting him at ease. "You know all about the occult and knew the dearly departed."

"Once in a while, I would have a beer with Marty at Sunny's Bar. I guess we were pals, but I didn't know his life story. I don't think I'll be useful." The Super shrugged.

She leaned back in her chair, feeling more relaxed. "Close enough. A familiar voice might help draw out his spirit."

"Oh, I suppose. It's worth a try." Sy nodded at Jackie.

"I'll bet he had an unresolved gripe; that might explain why his ghost lingers in Jackie's apartment, looking for closure. Isn't that right?" Jeff smirked.

"Could be, but I think Marty wants revenge." Sy grinned.

"What makes you think Marty wants payback?" Jackie's boyfriend mused.

"Well, the poor schlub keeled over just like that." The Super snapped his wrinkled fingers. "No one dies like that without leaving behind unfinished business."

Tiger twitched in his sleep as if he were chasing something.

"Will you help us?" Jackie clasped her hands together, practically begging.

Gingerly, Sy lifted Tiger up and set him down on the bed. "You betcha. I'm sure this hasn't been easy." He got to his feet slowly, with a little help from Jackie.

She smiled, obviously relieved. "You have no idea how much I appreciate this."

"Yeah, things that go bump in the night are downright scary when they aren't on the big screen." Jeff shivered.

She led them back to her apartment. On the way out, the Super grabbed a white pillar candle and a book of matches.

When they got upstairs, Jackie unlocked the door and switched on the light. "Jeff, go check and see if the heat is on while Sy prepares the kitchen table."

"No problem." When he walked over to the radiator and cautiously reached out to touch it, hot metal scalded his left hand. Jeff screamed, ran into the kitchen, and grabbed some ice cubes from the freezer to soothe his throbbing fingers.

Sy groaned. "I *told* you the heater wasn't broken. Now, do you believe me?"

"I do now!" Jeff licked his swollen fingers.

Jackie rushed him over to the sink and had him run cold water over the burn while she grabbed a washcloth from the bathroom, wrapped the ice in it, and handed it to Jeff. "Oh my God! Are you alright?!"

"No, my hand is *killing* me." He pressed the cold, damp cloth over his swollen hand.

The Super placed a plate under the candle and lit it in the middle of the kitchen table. He shut off the light, bathing them in its eerie glow. "Both of you sit down. It's time."

Jackie and Jeff reluctantly followed.

"Now, take my hands. Bow your heads and be quiet." He took a deep breath before he began.

They each took a wrinkled, liver-spotted hand. Jeff used his uninjured right hand, focused on the candle's flickering flame and waited.

"Marty, if you're here, give us a sign. This is Sy Mann, the superintendent of the building you died in. I need to ask you a very important question." He scanned the room.

A minute later, all the books in the bookcase near the kitchen came tumbling down. Jeff yelped. "Maybe this wasn't such a good idea after all."

"It's too late to stop now." Sy shook his head and pursed his lips.

Startled, Jackie tried to bolt from the table, but Jeff reassured her.

"Hey now, Jackie. This séance was your idea. Stay put, and we'll see this through together. There's safety in numbers."

"You're absolutely right. Sorry, I'm feeling overwhelmed." She took a deep breath and tried to get comfortable.

The dictionary landed at Sy's feet. He leaned over for a closer look. Coincidentally, it opened to the M's. A minute later, a raven flew into the room through the closed window. Glass shattered, leaving a trail of jagged shards in its wake. The reckless black bird landed between the pages, and its beady black eyes twinkled knowingly.

The Super addressed the raven. "Marty, tell us how you died."

In answer, the bird rested its beak on the word murder for a moment and pecked a hole in the page.

"Do you know who killed you? Caw twice for yes, once for no."

They all looked on in awe as the raven cocked its head to one side as if to ponder the question for a moment before cawing twice.

Sy smiled expectantly.

Jackie and Jeff gawked at the raven, unable to believe their luck. They leaned in for a better look at the mysterious messenger.

The Super followed his hunch. "Did your neighbor Al Ash kill you?"

The raven cawed twice more and flapped its wings.

"Do you know why?" Sy smiled.

This time, a single caw was the reply.

"Will you rest in peace if we get Al to confess?"

The raven cawed twice more before flying off.

The candle went out, casting them in darkness.

Al Ash lived on the fourth floor, in the apartment directly across from Jackie; Sy had to stop several times to catch his breath to walk across the hall.

Jeff whispered in Jackie's ear: "I can feel myself growing older."

"Shut up, Jeff." She jabbed him in the ribs. "You'll be old too, someday."

He gritted his teeth. "Not if I can help it."

Jackie sighed. When they reached the other apartment, Sy knocked on the door and waited.

A gruff voice answered: "Who is it?!"

"Sy. Can I come in?" He smiled broadly.

"Why? Is there a problem? I value my privacy."

"Could be. Open up so we can talk."

Al peered through the peephole. "Is that Jackie and her boyfriend?" He undid two deadbolts and cracked the door for a closer look. "What do they want? I'm not in the mood for visitors."

Sy shook his head. "They just want to ask you some questions about Marty's death. Some strange things have been happening in their apartment lately, and they're trying to find out why."

"So, is that my fault? I *despise* drama." He laid a hand on his chest.

"Maybe." Mr. Mann wedged his foot in the doorjamb before Al could slam it shut. "Maybe not. It depends. We aim to find out."

Reluctantly, Al stepped aside, ogling his uninvited guests as they went in. Unlike Sy's place, this apartment was immaculate—not a speck of dust anywhere. Copies of *The New York Times* and *The Rifle Rack* were neatly stacked on the antique coffee table, and from the glimpse they caught of the bedroom, they noticed a bedspread pulled so taut you could bounce a quarter off it.

Sy sat between Jackie and Jeff on the couch. Al made himself comfortable in his worn recliner and stretched his long legs.

Mr. Mann clasped his hands together so tightly his knuckles turned white. "Al, did you kill Marty?"

"Are you accusing me of murder? What makes you think I'd stoop so low?" Al laced his fingers and rested them behind his head.

Sy pointed an accusing finger at Al. "You're the meanest man I know, seething with resentment."

"Since when is being a curmudgeon a crime," Al demanded to know.

"It's not against the law, but it goes against common human decency. I saw Marty undressing Emily with his eyes whenever they ran into each other in the hall. You had good reason to do him in."

"Why should I dredge up the past. What's in it for me?"

"All of this guilt has made you miserable. Confess, and the truth shall set you free," the Super said, goading his unruly tenant.

He gnashed his teeth for a few minutes before answering. "Marty stole my sweet Emily right from under my nose! I did my best to turn a blind eye to his sunny disposition. He carried my wife's groceries up to our door. At the time, I thought, *fantastic, one less thing for her to nag me about.* Then I spotted Emily with Marty at the corner coffee shop a few times, laughing and practically sitting in his lap. When I confronted her, she shrugged it off as harmless, playful banter. And I wanted to believe her. Though I had a sinking suspicion..." When he spoke, his voice was icily calm.

"Care to elaborate?" Jeff inquired.

"When I came home early from work and Emily wasn't there, that confirmed my suspicion. I ran across the hall and pounded on Marty's door. Then I heard him pounding my wife. Squeaking bedsprings were a dead giveaway. I caught them in bed together. Emily wriggled around beneath him, and I told her to get out of my sight while the getting was good. She struggled to break free from Marty's embrace, scooped her clothes up off the floor, and hightailed it out of there. I snapped—I wanted to end it, quick and dirty. Plenty of muss, no fuss." Al rubbed his sweaty palms together and shot a side-eye at his firing squad.

Jackie's jaw dropped. "You can't be serious."

A raven flew into the room and landed on Sy's bony shoulder to listen.

"When Marty saw me coming with my hands balled up into fists, he pulled the sheets up to his nose as if he were bracing himself for the worst beating of his life. Just when I leaned over to strangle him, half expecting him to beg for forgiveness, he got dead quiet, even though his mouth was wide open. I thought he'd be screaming or trying to run away, so I leaned in close to see if he was breathing. Imagine my frustration when I checked his wrist for a pulse and discovered he had none. I guess he had a heart attack. What a cop-out."

Sy shook his head. "You sound disappointed, Al."

"You bet I am! I wanted to wring his scrawny neck!" Al did a double-take when he saw the raven perched on Mr. Mann's shoulder. "Hey! How'd that damn raven get in here?"

"Karma can be a bitch." Jeff snickered.

Jackie nodded. "You never know who might drop in, especially in New York."

"Sy, what the *hell* are they talking about?" His eyes locked on the raven, and he spat on the bird.

Sy cleared his throat. "Al, that raven has an important message."

The raven cawed twice in agreement.

Al stood up and walked over to Sy for a closer look. "I *hate* ravens. They're evil!"

"That's Marty Leary's ghost, Al. His spirit has been lingering in my apartment ever since the day you scared the life out of him. He's got a score to settle with you before he can cross over." Jackie stared at him, eyes full of contempt.

"Give me a break. That's no ghost! It's just a damn bird!" He reached out to grab the raven and missed. "Prove that's Marty's ghost."

In response, the raven swooped down and let something shiny slip from its sharp talons. The object landed on Al's lap with a distinct *click!* He picked it up and stared; it was a key with Apt. 4-D scrawled on a scrap of paper taped to the top.

"That's pretty wild!" Jeff grinned.

Jackie patted Sy on the back. "Nice work."

"Boy, that Marty sure is clever! I have a feeling he's just getting warmed up." The Super's eyes twinkled.

Al let the key dangle between slender fingers. "4-D. Isn't that Jackie's place, Marty's old apartment?"

The Super clapped his hands softly. "Bingo!"

"What am I supposed to do with this damn key?" Al waved it in the air.

Jackie shook her head. "That raven is headed straight for you."

"Think fast, or you'll miss it!" Jeff pointed to the black bird.

Al shifted his gaze at the exact moment the raven made a beeline for his face. He swatted blindly when the black bird plucked his eyes out swiftly and devoured them. Still clutching the key, overturning the coffee table while crimson tears flowed freely from the new holes in his dense head, Al shrieked and stumbled, scattering the neat piles of magazines and newspapers everywhere.

Sy winced.

Jackie screamed and buried her face in her hands, shocked by the raven's gruesome act.

Unable to tear his gaze away, Jeff looked on, lost in morbid fascination.

Al's massive hands continued to grab and swipe, missing the crafty raven by a mile; it landed on his broad shoulder and pecked his meaty neck with its pointy beak, going for the jugular. He howled as his hand found his attacker, seizing the raven in a death grip and squeezing until all the life flowed out of the brave, black bird.

Bruised and battered... nevermore.

THE SOURCE OF FR. SANTIAGO DE GUERRA DE VARGAS' MONSTROUS CRIMES

ROBERT MASTERSON

They rode, those who had horses, and they walked, those who did not, south from Mexico, south from the Aztec capital, Tenochtitlan, brought low. Led by el Caballero Pedro de Alvarado under orders from His Most Catholic Commander Hernán Cortés, the expedition bore letters of marque to explore, locate, and conquer every pagan country to be found. Under the flags of His Holiness Pope Pius IV and His Majesty King Phillip II, every devil, demon, and dybbuk berobed in the drifting ash of that once floating empirical city rode with them and, in particular, with the priest de Vargas. Armor and arms glittering in the New World's sun, banners and streamers afloat from pike and pole, soldiered ranks and mounted gentlemen of adventure, trains of mules and two-wheeled carts baggage laden, the mass of native fighters conscripted, chained slaves and women, and with the religious processioned holding Holy Cross and icon before them, a slow clot of dust loosed into the air to rise and mark their journey. The corridor they laid upon the ground was both deep and broad, ignored the native highways leading who knew where, and would remain after their passing to become *nueva carretera* for any to follow. The enterprise moved south from the marshy, high plano surrounding the Mexican capital to climb the pass between the Sierra Madre Oriental and the Sierra Madre del Sur skirting the snow-capped Pico de Orizaba, the dormant volcano of "pleasing waters," and down, down into the green maelstrom of Yucatán with only two directives: find gold and save souls.

Santiago de Guerra de Vargas returned to his wooden hut after bearing witness to the day's mass baptisms/executions. He had duly recorded, as was his wont and duty, the number of converted and the number of those propelled to the welcoming arms of their new Savior. Though watching so many people die upset his scholarly tendencies (today's total was 783 bound heathens washed with the Holy Water that would cleanse their blackened souls before they were hung and then sent straight to Paradise before the opportunity to sin tempted them from the true path of Righteousness), he was compelled to silently rejoice at the bounty of new adherents to the One True Faith, how God the Father and Jesus Christ His Son would smile upon their efforts to induce the growth of the Holy Mother Church in this New World. The voices that droned in his ears were his and his alone, their constant tintination a familiar commentary on all to which he was witness, a devilish, native criticism of all the expedition accomplished. He waved his hand around his head as if to banish flies, but the voices persisted in their Nahuatl interpretation of events.

Unlike other expeditions franchised by His Majesty Charles V, Lord over the Holy Roman Empire, Austria, the Burgundian Low Countries, Naples, Sicily, Sardinia, and the wonderous New World, this expedition followed the True Cross. They were intent on finding not merely riches, but souls, human souls, to feed the always hungry Church. His Excellency, the Most Revered Bishop Diego de Landa rode his black gelding on the right hand of el Señor Alvarado to lead them all in service to God with plunder a most secondary consideration. To Santiago, the entire troop seemed to glow with the holiness of its mission, to become the beacon of light that would guide these monstrous pagan idolaters to salvation, death, and Glory. And it appeared to be working.

Pedro de Alvarado, there to take the heathen enclave of Q'umarkaj, moved forward with 180 armored cavalry, 300 men-at-arms in infantry, four barking cannons, and five hundred allied native warriors from the conquered north. Three and twenty friars, priests, and the bishop himself observed the battle from a nearby hill, and they blessed and prayed for the fighting contingent and its victory in this New World's Valley of Elah. The assembled force did there meet in the field more than five thousand Mayan warriors in full war display. The profane horde carried mahogany macahuitl glittering with knapped obsidian shards, and they voiced Nahuatl chants while costumed in feather cloaks and headdresses and masks of remarkable beauty and form. There followed slaughter as Spanish steel and crazed war-horses engaged the massed pagan horde with cries of "a Dios!" and "Jesucristo!" that overwhelmed the skirling whistles and flutes shaped from human bone and played as Mayan war cry. The befeathered warriors, all from noble Mayan families, fell like ripe wheat under a new scythe. Smoke from the cannon, harquebus, and matchlock drifted heavy over the battle. Slavering dogs of war, horses mad and flailing spiked shoes, Spanish footmen gone blood-mad collapsed the Mayan line, folded in the Mayan flanks. The northern native warriors, all newly converts, exerted and concluded ancient vendetta. Short and brutal, the conflict ended in prolonged massacre. Above the field did fly the banners of Church, its Saints, and God.

Santiago entered his cubicle and prepared to create the day's document. He enjoyed his work and, with the seemingly limitless supply of blank Mayan paper the expedition had confiscated, Santiago could indulge his propensity toward expansive narrative. He was in love with details, the small sights and sounds and odors and textures, which supported the veracity of his chronicle. Santiago understood the importance of numbers, the exact counts of objects and entities that proved the expedition's importance and worth. So many miles from Mexico, so many casks of wine in baggage, so many men-at-arms, so much gunpowder and so much shot, so many priests and prisoners and converts. Numbers were the *logos* of the mission. But the *pathos* and the *ethos* lived in the details, and Santiago was dedicated to ensuring the legacy of their endeavors there in the jungle rot and pagan ruin would resonate with readers yet unborn.

The drops of blessed water shimmered in the afternoon sun as they flew from the aspergillum. There in the thick and weighty air of Yucatan, they seemed to pause for a moment as if to savor their freedom before splashing down upon the brows, thick and heavy, of the assembled savages. Their cleansing and blessing were inspiration to every assembled Christian, and the miracle of Holy Communion uplifted even the heaviest heart.

Santiago stopped his pen to reread his writing.

Every Christ-loving soul was swollen with awe when the brothers sang the Auroras for salvation at the end of a rope when the reborn creatures were prodded to the gallows for their triumphant convention at the Throne of God. Many a soldier drew his sword to thrust into the soft earth and knelt to pray before a holy warrior's cross. Three and eighty and seven hundred cleansed and perfect souls were sent to the outstretched arms of our Lord and Savior, Jesus Christ. Our miracles are daily and magnificent to behold.

Santiago was moved by his own words. He actually ached toward poetry to fulfill the lover's quest of expression, to capture the blinding instant in perfect prose. The Mayan paper, pounded out from the bark of certain trees, seemed to not just take his strokes upon its surface but to absorb the meaning of his words beyond their definition. The voices buzzed angrily in counterpoint to his enraptured prose.

Still, there were details Santiago would not record. How could he write the truth of what he'd seen to then offend His Excellency? The reluctance of the newly baptized to discard their mortality and embrace the Savior. The thin lines of urine that outlined the contours of their legs when they dangled there in the Yucatán sun. The gasping, the gagging, the choking, the struggles both earnest and sincere for even one last gasp of humid air. These were secret images.

The box and the hut, he both had fashioned himself from lumber torn from idolatrous structures. Planks of tropical wood he'd pounded into a frame, some still fragrant with perfumed sap, and a roof of fronds all pointing downward to direct the rain away from the interior, formed his crude abode on the outskirts of the camp away from the bonfires and tents and huts of both church and army. From lighter planking had he fashioned the box, the casket, the repository of his history most secret. A door, no windows, a rope bed, a writing table, a stool, his garments and linens, and the box were his dwelling's only contents. A stark carven crucifix and a single, fat candle stub adhered to the edge of the table provided the only illumination, day or night, to enter his monastic cell.

He was afraid to devise a lock for his rough door, assuming that someone of the party would venture into his chamber. There were, indeed, thieves and brigands among the company and, espying a bolted door, such men would be tempted to think it treasure inside and such men would take the box to a secret place, an unseen place there to open it by force to reveal not gold nor jade but the priceless record of their true adventure. He was afraid to leave it unlocked, and upon this dilemma, he fretted almost constantly. Santiago was afraid his words would send him gallows-wise and to there dangle among the newly Christianized, the newly deceased Mayan. Instead, he left it on the pounded dirt floor, but he threw a coverlet upon it. He prayed every night and every morning and, in those prayers, offered with humility and fearful love, he asked the Lord to protect his secret history enclosed in pagan carpentry. He found himself unwilling to venture too far or for too long away from its sight.

They whisper among themselves, these foul and bloodied miscreants, during the ceremonies of redemption, their horrid language all clicks and throaty exhalation. They seem deliberately ignorant of the gift of eternal life, and, instead, accept our blessings as they accept their meals without thanks or recognition.

Their jungle empire is broken, shattered under Spanish steel and cleansing fire, and so, they, too, are broken. They speak of devilish prophecy, a forewarning from their demonic gods, and bow their heads to annihilation. They are disgusting and more deserving of Satan than of Saints, but His Excellency proclaims them bounty for the Church, and so we force the Body of Christ into their clacking maws, pour the Holy Blood across their clenched lips, anoint them, bless them, and kill them all in one stroke.

I think it, though, a kind of madness that justifies murder with Christ's limitless bounty, and each evening the soldier-hangmen confess their sins and receive absolution to go and sin tomorrow. But the Inquisition is ever zealous. Every commandment is shattered hourly in drunken, licentious abandon, and every soul is whitened through Confession and Communion by sunset. The piles of gold and jade and skillfully worked flints are made small by the mounds of dead converts that smolder constantly to foul the air with the stink of human grease.

And the books. All of them. Satanic by His Excellency's decree, and every book plundered is thrown upon the pyre to be consumed with their authors. Only God will know what they contain — laundry lists or tallies of maize, unholy curses to breach the gates of Hell, or songs of love and courage. The flare of their ignition gives brief outline to the skulls upon which they burn. From the gallows and the libraries, we have made another kind of Inferno for ourselves, one that will burn long after these fires have burned away.

But my voices keep the Great Library alive and describe to me the secrets and the spells where once therein they lay. Yum Kaax, the lord of the forest, Chaac, the bringer and the withholder of rain, Yumil Kaxob, who lives in flowers, and great Itzamna, who rules the heavens themselves in splendor and fearsome beauty all are known to me through them, and I feel their torment in my Christian soul. I long to and cannot bear to desire the warmth of human blood and the joy of a beating human heart in my hands as benefaction of dark faith older and more powerful than that of Jesus Christ, our Lord and Beloved Savior.

I am lost.

Santiago returned the paper to the casket, and he returned the casket to its hidden-in-plain-sight corner. He knelt in silent, futile prayer. He lay himself down upon his rope bed, pulled a thin blanket up across his chest, and closed his eyes. His dreams, if dreams came to him, were dark and full of confusing, disturbing turns. The tick-tock, click-clack of Mayan whispers insinuated his heated torpor, the meaning of the hellish syllables dancing just outside his consciousness. He moaned his heresy while his eyes jittered beneath their lids.

There is spectacle in the rise and fall of empire. Around such calamity lives the drama of all things human and the struggle to become and remain human in the grand gesture of civilization. But, so, too, there is marvel in the crossing of rivers, in the weaving of cloth from cotton fiber, in the simmer of beans in a kettle suspended over fire.

This army, if such a name can be rightly applied to such a gathering, quavers in near-constant state of mutiny and drunken rebellion. His Excellency chooses to blind-eye the egregious nature of the assembled felons and sodomites and brigands that form his company. He speaks of them as children, reprobate children, in need of firm guidance and massive lashings of pulque and bacanora, daily confession and communion, and the leadership of true warriors of the Cross. His most considered opinion on the expedition is that of Crusade, that his crusaders are therefore divinely attributed, and that which is guided by Providence cannot be sinful. Our passage through the forest left the imprint of misdeed upon our trail, but His Excellency is manifestly incapable of looking back.

They are still here, these horribles with their feathers and with their drums, though we have slain them in multitudes. The essence of their being, their refusal to become past tense and "has been," remains to pollute our souls, and I alone can hear the doom to which we plunge.

Santiago drew his daily rations of corn, beans, and goat to deliver to the mute Sacniete, his designated and personal Mayan slave, for her to cook. She was a pretty girl with a smear of small pimples across her cheeks. While she labored over grindstone and hearth outside the hut, he removed his secret casket and placed it upon the table that was his.

So small a thing, he measured. So small a thing to be the largest thing left of the city from which it was fashioned. So many buildings, so much wilderness labored into angled form and structure, with this the largest unburnt fragment. That the whole of the city Nojpetén, burnt now with only its stone shell survived, should be reduced to this small box…

He removed the sheaf of bark-paper and began to write.

When we burned the library at Zaculeu, the priests and monks and friars rejoiced. They chanted the Prayer to St. Michael the Archangel [Eph., 6:12].

In the Name of the Father,
and of the Son,
and of the Holy Ghost.
Amen.

Most glorious Prince of the Heavenly Armies,
Saint Michael the Archangel,
defend us in our battle against principalities and powers,
against the rulers of this world of darkness,
against the spirits of wickedness in the high places.

The flames of the bonfire created a new kind of Inferno, and I turned to weep alone at such treasure incinerated. Oh! The Alexandrian Calamity and now this. The tongues of flame reached into my heart and burned my faith away. The language and the voice of murdered authors invaded me. I stood alone in the light of wisdom lost forever and prayed to nothing, felt no Divinity remained in this shattered world, as drunken caballeros sang barroom filth and danced intoxicated fandango in the light of Armageddon. I became the Keeper of Hosts, the Guardian of Forbidden and Forgotten Learning, the man to whom the ghosts and spirits spoke.

Impoverished Santiago lay himself down upon the thin pallet that served as his mattress, the secret box behind his head, and there he fell asleep again to dream confused betrayal and benighted landscapes. He twitched and groaned in desperate lethargy.

And the box moaned back.

The faithless priest jolted upright, unsure what pulled him back to consciousness. The box made its presence known.

"Tick tock. Click clack," it said in Nahuatl.

Santiago, somehow now fluent in the language of the boxed specters of ruined countries, the language of ten times ten thousand murdered souls, could understand each rattle issued from the box.

"Kenin chiua teuatl continue? Tlein propels teuatl axkan ikamo neltokokayotl ipan amoyolotl? Kenin uehka s teuatl ya nik kuepiltia mo sacred Christ?" the box asked with blood-sodden gloom. "How do you continue? What propels you now without Faith in your heart? How far will you go to avenge your sacred Christ?"

Santiago could not answer. He looked for Christ in his heart, looked for the shape of the Holy Cross, and found only emptiness where it had once been.

"I am bereft," he told the box. "I have nothing in my heart, my soul, my hands."

"Will you avenge your lost Faith? Will you avenge the murder of our civilization? Will you take up arms to stop the slaughter?" the box sang.

"I was a man of Divine Peace," he replied. "I came to carry the Holy Word to those souls doomed by ignorance. I watched the library burn, and it burned my soul to nothing."

The box moaned.

"You have the power. You can free the souls you trapped between your Paradise and our Thirteen Heavens. You must spill the blood of Papist hypocrites to release us. You must carry forward with your task and free the souls you've enslaved in darkness between worlds. You must murder the murderers.

"*Break in hispantlahtolli teposmekameh teuatl forged nik tekipanoa tehuantin ueika iuikpa teotl. Kaua tehuantin ualtepotstoka se trail iuik estli toward melauak freedom,*" the box continued. "Break the Spanish chains you forged to keep us away from our Gods. Let us follow a trail of blood toward true freedom."

Santiago sat with his consternation, his dilemma, his last true test of Faith. Could he break all vows and assertions to become a new kind of Christian, an assassin for the Lamb?

The box grew and changed its form before him. Santiago was witness to wonder as the box became something entirely else, something that contained more than it could, a moving, shimmering tesseract of Divine Intervention, the Deus ex Machina, which would define the end of his story. He held the world in his trembling hands; he felt the movement of multitudes, the cry of slain races for mercy and revenge, the music from broken drums and shattered flutes throbbing and shimmering the very atmosphere surrounding him.

"Call forth, then, his Terrible Holiness, the emperor Yum Cimil, the God of Death, and let him guide your hand to our retribution. Take a knife of shining metal and let it drink its fill," the box intoned.

Leaving his worn sandals upon the hard-packed dirt floor of the hut, Santiago insinuated himself into the camp. It was an easy matter to find a displaced *falcata* amidst the tumble of baggage and gear. The hand that had never filled itself with aught but Crucifix and Communion and Holy Text marveled at the dead iron weight of the thing, at its loathsome hunger to kill. Santiago licked the blade.

A Mighty Ghost followed him, a spirit composed of spirits, the multitude made one. It stalked him on his mission and wore the sacred raiment of befeathered divinity. For each step the Ghost took, it carried the weight of the hundreds, the thousands, the millions of murdered *indios*, and deep were the prints it left in the tamped soil of the camp. The Ghost sang, it chanted, it murmured, it howled in all the tongues of the slain, but only Santiago could hear its damned voices. He continued as barefoot as that which trailed him, the fallen thorns and sharp pebbles a path of penance before him. He feared to look back, could feel the Ghost and its hot exhalation on his nape, but was compelled to stealth as he moved about the camp.

The first *soldado* that Santiago the priest approached was nodding in fermented stupor at the flames of a dying fire. His name, the priest remembered, was Pedro Alacard.

"*Oye*, Pedro," Santiago said for greeting. "Still awake this lonely night?"

The drunken Pedro roused himself to see it was the good Father, the one with the pen who remarked the company's adventure.

"*Oye*, Padre," he slurred. "Awake and dreaming. Yes. Awake and dreaming both, I think."

He looked around and behind the priest to better ascertain the figure at the edge of firelight, the disturbance of the atmosphere with the glittering blackstone eyes.

"Who's that with you there?" Pedro asked. "Who have you brought with you?"

"This is my friend," Santiago replied. "This is my friend and my tormentor, my shadow and my Ghost. This is my devil and my redeemer."

"Huh?" Pedro grunted as he turned his slitted, bloodshot eyes up to glean Santiago's face.

And just that quickly, the priest's war-knife found and buried itself in poor Pedro's throat. The warm gush of blood washed hot and thick over Santiago's hand, the cry of surprise and outrage Pedro attempted reduced to gurgle and gasp as the priest drove him down into the Yucatán soil, the ashy margin of the firepit, there to choke and sputter his sinner's life-breath away.

"*Por Jesús y maldita sea tu alma*," Santiago whispered and made the sign of the cross upon the fresh corpse. "For Jesus and damn your soul."

The Ghost upon his heels raised spectral baying of hard delight. The priest wrenched the falcata free with some trouble. He would need a soldier's practice to handle the weapon with more skill.

With slow stealth and Mayan glamour encloaked, Santiago moved deeper into the camp. He walked a ring around the next smoldering fire, three men-at-arms asleep in their clothes with armor heaped behind them. The first, the priest dispatched by, again, ruining the man's throat with his blade. The two others stirred but did not awaken. Pulque dulled their wits and senses. Their dreams were too loud to properly hear the world around them, their doom approaching. The second, a large man who kept a beard and known to the camp as El Oso, clawed his way to consciousness and wrapped his weighty hands around Santiago's slender wrists and there to struggle against the thick blade. The priest recoiled in mortal terror, having lost any sense of spiritual fear. Their push-pull enraged the Ghost, who stamped its feet and shrieked its impatience.

"*Tepopololiztli! Tepopololiztli!*" it shouted a whirlwind into the priest's ears. "Kill! Kill the thing!"

The third soldier was awake and staring at the blood-soaked cleric with eyes wide open.

"Padre?" he said softly. "What are you doing, Padre?"

Santiago propelled himself in a lurching crawl to the man's side. His name was Porfirio.

"I have come to give you peace, my son," he told the drowsy, drunken, confused soldier. "I have come to send you home."

Porfirio did not understand, was troubled by the blood spatters the priest wore on his face and cassock. Santiago laid his palm against the man's wet mouth, and he slipped the blade under his ribs. When the tip touched Porfirio's beating heart, he could feel the vibration in the handle.

The Ghost was sniggering tick-tock click-clack glottal laughter.

"*Yollo Tetecuiquiliztili,*" it snickered. "Take the pain of the heart."

And the murderous priest began to pry and lever his way through poor Porfirio's ribcage to make known the heart of the man. He cut, he pried, he pulled until the organ snapped free, dangling vessels and webbed by pericardium. Santiago looked to the Ghost for instruction.

The Ghost, all feathers and black glass, brought its hand to its yawning chops. It repeated the gesture. And again, it pantomimed the directive.

Santiago had received and given innumerable Holy Communion, brought the Blood and the Body to lips in supplication, and received the Sacrament himself inside the eloquent cathedrals of Spain as well as along the blood-choked dust of the conquistadors' highway. How, then, his brain churned, was this so different? Weren't all men possessed of God? Did God not bestow His Holiness on all creation? Was not all Blood and all Flesh both sacred and holy?

The murderous priest brought the late Porfirio's hot heart to his mouth, stretched his mouth to receive the essence of divinity manifest in blood and flesh. But the muscle was strong and tough and resisted his effort to tear from it enough to swallow. Blood emptied from its ventricles and poured down his jawline, a thin tissue of membrane all he could wrench from its perfection. He swallowed the meat from the man and, again, tried to tear a mouthful away from the whole. He ground and sawed his teeth against its fibrous resistance, and he succeeded in pulling a slight shred of muscle free. He swallowed it as whole as any other Host he had received, blessed himself with its passing into himself, and made the sign of the Cross in blood at forehead, shoulder, and core.

The Ghost was ecstatic. It twirled in a vaporous enchantment, phantasmic feathers awhirl such as the columns of dust that rose from the northern plains. It barked its wonderous approval. It grinned a terrible grin.

The assassinations followed quick, one upon the other, with each that much more uncomplicated than the last. He moved from rough fire to greasy tent to lonely picket, in each case propelled and guided by the spectral dervish whose grunts and yowls only Santiago could hear, the exhortations high-pitched and cadenced ceremonial.

"Yes," the priest would whisper at each blade thrust. "Yes. Yes."

The blood filled him, it covered him, it glistened on his face and hands even as it dried to be layered upon with blood anew. His cassock soaked in blood, it gathered the ground's particulates along the hem and at the knees where he genuflected to dispatch more souls. His holy costume grew heavy and made a new kind of sound, a rattle that would be his undoing.

Diego del Esparanza heard the murderous priest's approach and, springing to his feet, drew his long sword in challenge and in terrified awe at the apparition of the foul creature he'd only known in passing as Fr. Santiago. When the cleric refused to halt or acknowledge Diego's challenge, the miserable soldier ran his blade into the flesh of Santiago's left thigh. And still, while falling to the earth, the priest stretched out his killing hand as if to stab Diego despite his incapacitation. The Ghost was enraged at Santiago's failure and kicked him there in the dust. Diego saw the priest curl as if in pain, unknowing of the ghostly blows that drove the breath from his body.

"Alarm!" Diego cried, keeping the point of his sword upon the felled priest. "Alarm!"

As the camp aroused itself in reply, men ran, stumbled, shambled, and some even crawled to the spot still besotted with native alcohol. There was much shouting, calls of confusion and despair as torchlight revealed the desecrated bodies of their compañeros. They could not position the evidence of foul deeds and the man of the cloth writhing before them in the same place. It was beyond their ken to imagine the man and those deeds conjoined. They called for the captain. They called for His Excellency himself.

The caballero and the bishop considered the men, the events, and the evidence before them. Santiago's hut was searched, and his precious box uncovered. The bishop read the manuscript therein. The captain himself could not read but accepted the clergyman's summation of the blasphemous narrative. The bleeding priest lay before them, the testimony of his very state of being the harshest of evidence for his conviction. The representative of the Spanish throne and the representative of the Crown of Thorns conferred swiftly. Their conclusion and their verdict were both precipitate, unanimous, and terminal. Santiago's brief rampage ended in the mud at his superiors' feet. Whatever consternation he had brought to the camp would be expelled with his summary execution. The verdict pronounced, his tonsured head pulled back, his heretical throat exposed and gashed open by firelight, the mad priest's blood contributed nothing so much as more thick liquid for the expedition's thirsty and already muddied camp.

They threw Santiago de Guerra de Vargas' body, his box, and his heretical scribblings on the same bonfire that consumed the corpses of the converted and the books that held their heathen history. Beyond the light of the conflagration, before the Maya and long after the Spaniards, green Yucatán chittered, whistled, ticked, and roared. As the poor, lost priest oxidized to lacy ash, the Ghost in the flames danced a glimmering dance of welcome for his soul.

INSUBSTANTIAL

OLIVER BAER

Greene considered the message the Living Darkness had sent him to deliver. It wasn't the message that unnerved him. It was something he had done countless times before. As a matter of fact, he liked doing it. Or perhaps he liked the mayhem it caused. The reason never seemed to matter so much to him. It was the place. He didn't like being summoned to The Witch House, the unofficial name of the Institute. He felt haunted when there. As if he was a component of the diseases that were treated. That's why he always went with Redd and Blackman. Together not even the grave had been able to contain them. They helped him focus. The place was filled with fear. It was everywhere. The Witch House was built with it and on it. It was in the walls, the floors, the ceiling, and the land it stood on. Without Redd and Blackman, he would always be Greene.

Insubstantials were mere whispers made form. Wraiths of verbal contagion collected from the dead and conscripted into messengers. Poltergeists not tethered to place or emotion. As insubstantials, Greene, Redd, and Blackman were the best. They knew this because an insubstantial's ability to affect corporeals or to become some measure of corporeal was based on how well they did what they were sent to do. An insubstantial didn't even have a name until they were able to become somewhat corporeal. Their names were symbolic of emotions they specialized in manipulating. Emotions that were gateways to possibility. Other states of being, as the corporeals' limited thinking would put it. The highest level of this was demonstrated by Blackman, whose abilities now mimicked the Living Darkness. Some even said that he was a direct vessel of the Living Darkness, for he seemed able to do things outside of the confines of the mission. But their names weren't important. Greene didn't really understand the corporeals' fascination with identity. It seemed more like a disease to them, even their own, confused and confounded. It was the message.

There were insubstantials who became fully corporeal and fully vested in their new identity. They forgot their purpose and had to be reminded by other insubstantials of who and what they actually were: insubstantials. They were stripped of their corporeality in stages until they remembered what they must do. The insubstantial who called himself Dr. Dominic Vox knew he was failing the Living Darkness. The transformation of Arnold Brown-Jenkins, or whatever he wanted to call himself, was behind schedule. They were all Brown-Jenkins to Greene. Whether or not they were stricken with the disease of identity, the Living Darkness still needed Brown-Jenkins to establish a more permanent conduit to the corporeal world. What better choice than one with a fractured identity could there be?

To get inside The Witch House, Greene, Redd, and Blackman thinned themselves. Greene wasn't sure how they did it. They just thought about not being seen, and it happened. Blackman had tried to explain to them how it worked. Something about rats in a box being both alive and dead, something they called the fear particle wave theory, dimensional travel, and their arcane connection to the Living Darkness. "Feel the particles of fear within you. Now send them back to the ocean of Living Darkness. Feel them leaving you in waves," Blackman told them. It was all noise to them. The one thing they did understand is that they were only visible to those for whom the message was meant. They envied Blackman their understanding. They couldn't seem to grasp the concepts. Not that they wanted to, really. Making sure the message was received seemed a much higher priority considering the consequences. They liked having an identity and not being some nameless shadow mannikin. This, of course, confused them more. Perhaps they were diseased. Once the Living Darkness established its foothold, perhaps Arnold Brown-Jenkins would be the antibody they needed.

They watched Arnold Brown-Jenkins skitter down the hallway to Dr. Vox's office. The attendants flanked him with ease despite his erratic movements. His need to get to the office was intriguing. Could they have been wrong? Could the process have been further along than they thought? Could Arnold have caught a glimpse of their reality? Greene dismissed the questions. If the shadows had been effective, they wouldn't need to be here. The conduit would have been prepared.

Dominic Vox hasn't been sleeping well, his eyes ringed with shadows, not unlike the ones Arnold spoke about in his sessions with him. "They're coming," Arnold has told him in session after session, "the shadow people."

"If they do, how will they know where we are?" Dominic has asked each time.

"I don't know, but they do," is the answer he has received every time.

Now he wakes up at night seeing them in the dark corners of his room, beckoning him to follow. He tries to dismiss them by going back to sleep. Only to find himself in Arnold's dream, a spectral spectator witnessing the carnage. He watches Arnold walk home from high school. He's not sure what he's doing here or why Arnold is so young. He didn't know him then. Or did he? This all seems way too familiar to Dominic. Arnold walks down a long curving hill leading to his house. As he approaches a sharp bend in the road, which crosses a bridge over a little brook, a hearse comes racing down the road. It appears to be after Arnold, who starts running feverishly, but the hearse is too fast. It is almost on top of him. He looks back for a brief second, only to notice the driver of the hearse is a clown, holding in his left hand a bunch of multicolored balloons; his passenger is an executioner, complete with black raiment hood and giant double axe. Dominic rushes forward to help Arnold. He screams as he runs. Only he's running through a jello mold. His legs wobble with the effort of pushing through the air. His scream is a soundless breeze blowing the balloons apart. The hearse springs forward, a window opens, the axe is raised to strike. At this point, Arnold stops, turns around, and seems to look at the guard rail of the bridge. The guard rail flies into the swinging axe. The hearse stops. Arnold's wife, Lynne, in a dominatrix outfit of a leather hood, bikini, and thigh-high boots, steps out swinging an axe at Arnold, who's now wearing the clown outfit. Somehow seeing his wife here like this doesn't seem as weird as it should to Dominic. Her presence does make him realize why he's here. They sent him. The messengers did. Things are not proceeding fast enough. So they're showing him. He wishes they wouldn't do that. His whole being feels disjointed after this. Not to mention being in the black presence of the Living Darkness makes him feel like pieces of him are being eaten away. Arnold blocks the axe, grabs it, and chops up Lynne. He hands the pieces to the smiling shadow man who appears in front of him. The shadows lead to a vacant blackness of the man's eyes, which engulfs the pieces. Dominic gasps. A cold sweat runs through him; he falls through the eyes, tumbling down. Then he's back.

The second stage has begun. He feels physically diminished by the thought. Not made smaller but stretched thin as if his body were losing substance.

When Vox wakes up this morning, before he gets out of bed, he turns to his wife and tells her his dreams. She seems too nonplussed by the whole thing. *Have they already gotten to her? Has she been one of them the whole time?* He decides this is just the fear talking. He pushes these questions into the basement storage closet of his mind and padlocks the door. He stumbles into the office. His clothes are disheveled. The office has been made a mess. His furniture has definitely been thrown around. He doesn't remember his desk and chair being so close to the door, almost blocking it. He's not sure how they were moved, given their size. These questions become secondary as he sees Arnold there, moving erratically, shadows of color guiding his movement and within them a shape all too familiar to Dominic. *They're just playing with my mind,* he thinks. *That shape can't be my wife.* He shakes his head and slaps his face. The shadows dissipate some. *Time to be a professional.* He steels himself. *Arnold needs you to finish what you started. Even crazed murderers no one is going to miss should be prepared if they are going to be used as pawns by the Living Darkness.*

Arnold is pacing back and forth around and through everything in the room. Various voices and other noises come from him. As if called by his seance, Greene, Redd, and Blackman appear, willing themselves into partial substance. They approach Arnold. They push and pull him in various crazy directions, some of which seem impossible in terms of Newtonian physics. Blackman has even cleverly recruited one of the shadows to take female form and help throw him around like a rag doll. It's all fun and games until the eminent "doctor" starts to speak. Blackman reaches into the female shadow and wipes it away. Then he points to the four corners of the room, points to Redd and Greene, moves to a corner, thins himself, and waits. Greene follows suit after Redd moves to a corner, annoyed they had to end so soon.

"I see you are angry at me," Dr. Vox starts. *This is not a good sign*, he thinks. Anger is a sign that Arnold is fighting the regression therapy.

"Angry is not the word," Arnold says tightly. "That's an understatement."

"Well, what's wrong?" Vox asks, concerned.

"I'll tell you what's wrong," Arnold snaps back. "This office makes me feel claustrophobic. The couch is uninviting, the desk is ominous, and the bookshelf taunts me with its organization. I'm failing my tests, getting ready to study for finals, writing dozens of papers, going to meetings, it doesn't seem to end. The ghosts are real, and no one is safe." Arnold's eyes dart to the photo on Vox's desk. "My dead wife, Lynne, is still in your photograph."

"Well, how about if we play a game?" Vox offers, thinking a distraction will be the best way for them both to get back on track. At least Arnold still thinks he's a student. There are only so many false memories he can be fed. Vox had thought the family photograph on his desk had helped him plant memories. Now he himself cannot shake the uncanny similarity between the woman Arnold killed and his wife.

"Yeah, sure." Arnold tries to cut the doctor with his voice. "It will probably be one of your stupid word associations again, right?"

"No," Dr. Vox parries. "This time, we are going to look at some pictures." He reaches for a stack of cards. As he peels one off the top, a green door opens, and there's a fluttering sound. *Just the cards shifting*, he thinks. Then he sees Greene holding up tatters of a bloodstained ball gown. Grotesque wings dancing their way toward him. He blinks, shakes his head, suddenly unsure of what he's doing. He's sure he has to show the cards to Arnold in order to help him, but why eludes him. He hopes Arnold doesn't notice his growing apprehension. He pushes the waves of fear out. He turns the card toward Arnold. "So, what does this look like to you?"

"A butterfly." Arnold's voice flutters with the cards.

Vox pulls another card from the deck. The air rips, a red door opens, and a putrid smell fills the room. Redd steps through the rip with two plates in his hands. A head on each plate. They are Dominic's children. A hallucinatory threat to keep him motivated. He tries not to gag or look as shocked as he feels as he holds the card up for Arnold. "And this?" He lapses into a paroxysm of coughs. The fear, an ocean threatening to drown him. *Got to get it out of me.* He concentrates on pushing it to the corners of the room. *Don't they understand how long it takes to get someone's mind ready to deal with the power of the Living Darkness?* He needs more time.

"*Devil?!*" Arnold screams his inquiry, but his throat has been scraped raw. Only a guttural rasp pronounces the syllables.

Vox's hand hesitates above the deck. He's not sure he's ready for the next card. Or its effects. *This has to be done*, he sighs inwardly to himself. He grabs the card, his hand and arm feeling as if they are moving of their own accord, and shows it to Arnold. "And this?" The lights dim, and the knocking starts. It's not really a knocking so much as a punching.

"People surrounding me while I'm on a couch... going to attack me?" The guttural rasp is gone. Now replaced by a plaintive quaver.

The cards jump from the doctor's hand, fly around the room, each one revealing its face to Arnold, their movement a Rorschach projection itself. Arnold flails at them. Then is still. The lights come back. There is a peculiar cold brightness about Dr. Vox. A noticeable shadow hovering over and around Arnold.

"You know there has to be an end to everything, Arnold," Vox states, in a tone that he hopes doesn't reflect how rattled he is.

"Yeah, even life." Arnold's downcast tone has a measure of resignation to it as he furtively looks around the room. His nose twitching. His lips quivering.

"Now, Arnold, don't be so depressing," Vox admonishes, then wonders why he did so. The cards must have jangled his nerves more than he expected.

"You would be depressed too if you were in my state," Arnold retorts.

"What state is that, Arnold?" Dr. Vox tries to get back to his professional exploration of the problem. He's lost again. He sees the black door opening. Blackman steps out. This is it. They can wait no longer.

"I can't sit still anymore. I am constantly pacing back and forth and talking to myself now. Imagine the idea of talking to oneself. Let's see, the last time I did that..." Arnold's voice walks itself back, unwinding to that time. "Oh my god, look at me, ex-sergeant of the police sitting in an unemployment office for the fourth time, but I wouldn't be there if it wasn't for that lousy Jake Mcruff. Looks like everyone was right. No matter what I do, something goes wrong. I was on my way to a promotion too...

"…until the Malone incident. *God!* I wish I wasn't such a chicken!" The words just run out of Arnold's mouth. "They laughed me out of the station. They believed I killed Malone during questioning when it wasn't me at all. It was *Mcruff!* But I'm too much of a coward to tell anyone so I just took the blame for it rather than deal with Mcruff. After that, jobs were hard to come by. Nobody wanted to hire an ex-cop who was involved in a police brutality case. Then there was Weiss' drugstore where they blamed me for emptying the till because they couldn't count correctly, and I was in the line of fire again. It was my fault 'cause I always dropped money when I was giving change to customers. Then at Feinman's deli I was there two days, and they blamed me for almost killing a customer. I can't help it if the knife kept slipping out of my hand! The last job I had was at Stop 'N Shop stocking shelves, and I got caught on a drug bust." On a full sprint, the sentences race to the finish. "It wouldn't have happened if I didn't drop that bag and see five pounds of cocaine instead of flour. But of course, I didn't tell anyone and tried to literally sweep it all under the rug. I think this is it. If I don't get another job I'll crack."

During this tirade, Arnold gets up from his chair, interacts with Vox, and interacts with the people who seem to have formed them-selves from the cards. Or rather, the faces of the cards have changed and grown bodies. An inkblot representation of people acting out the charade of his tirade?

Blackman moves his hand as if painting a picture. The fear parti-cles move themselves into an office scene. Dark waves condensing themselves into chairs outside an open door. A shadow man sitting at a desk inside. The door manifests in front of Vox's desk. Arnold's chair is one of the chairs "outside." Arnold's sitting in the unemployment office waiting, berating himself for letting Jake Mcruff get the better of him. He and Jake were partners for years. Turns out he was just the chump of the department.

"*What!* You will not even give me the courtesy of seeing me! I see you're jealous of me, aren't you?" Arnold yells angrily. "It wasn't my fault. It was Mcruff."

A manikin person with an inkblot body in a suit walks out of the manifested door and approaches Arnold.

"Mr. Brown-Jenkins, I'm sorry to say that I just looked at your folder, and I don't think that meeting with you would help your situation. Maybe you should take a nice long rest." As he talks,

Blackman's face can be seen behind the manikin person whispering in his ear.

"I feel sorry for you, but I cannot give you a job," the manikin person/Blackman states unequivocally.

"No, you don't understand!" Arnold pleads. "If I don't work for a living, my father will cut me off from the family. It wasn't my fault." Arnold tries to explain to the manikin person/Blackman's head as he turns around to walk back into the office. Arnold grabs manikin person/Blackman's shoulder and wrenches him around. "Hey, you're not listening!" Arnold's anger was losing to fear, but now this. He can't have it. They won't ignore him.

"I'm sorry, this agency will not be responsible for an irresponsible person. That's all I have to say now. Good day, Mr. Brown-Jenkins."

With that, manikin person/Blackman walks away. Arnold follows and bludgeons him. Dominic presses the button on his desk to call the attendants to restrain Arnold. "*Arnold, stop!*" he yells commandingly, but his voice sounds like a whisper. The guards won't get here in time. Perhaps they are not even coming. He jumps from his desk to intervene but just like in the dream, his movement is through gelatinous mud. He's too slow to get to Arnold, and when he does, his hand passes through him. Manikin person/Blackman's gore is all over. Arnold begins screaming in hysterics.

"Oh god! What did I do?" Arnold wails.

Blackman reappears. This time Arnold's face is on his body. He looks at Arnold and smiles. He turns, his hand washing the air of the office scene, and it's gone.

Arnold implores, "I can't hide this! What do I do? Mommy, I can't do this!"

"I can't, Mommy!" Blackman/Arnold's fear-stricken cries echo.

"Well, Arnold, why don't you try using a broom," Dr. Vox says in a voice that is not his own.

"Well, they say there is no better person to talk to." Arnold's cries have stopped. His voice starts on the edge of mania but seems to back away.

"Who are they?" Vox asks, trying to get answers for the both of them. Dominic is barely holding it together, hoping that outwardly he's maintaining his professionalism and that Arnold hasn't noticed how close to the edge he is.

"People to talk to..." Arnold trails off only to switch thoughts in midstream. "But why would anyone want to talk to me... *Because you're a failure!*" Arnold's voice trails off again then changes in tone. It's deeper, angrier.

The family sits in the living room. The father stands and points at Arnold. "You're a failure, Arnold!" Father's anger fills the room.

"No, Father, give him one more chance," Mother pleads, falling to the ground. "PLEASE!!"

Blackman reaches through the black door he initially stepped through and beckons. Shadow people walk through. Manikin friends appear with manikin versions of Arnold's past friends and roommates. All point at Arnold.

"Don't be so depressing," advises Friend 1.

"Grow Up!" admonishes Friend 2.

"Don't be so pessimistic," is Friend 3's two cents.

"So, Arnold, you have to stop being such a big hit with the girls," teases Friend 4.

"Stop failing school," Roommate 1 commands.

"You create your own problems," Roommate 2 suggests.

"This agency doesn't accept irresponsible people," Manikin person/Blackman states firmly.

"See, I told you! They're all coming to get me—help! Someone help me!" Arnold is back in panic mode.

"There is nothing there, Arnold," Dr. Vox says, trying to be re-assuring. At this point, Dominic knows his reassurance is for both of them. *If they had only given me more time, Arnold. I could have done something for you. Now we're down to only one option*, Dominic thinks.

"Oh yeah, what do you call this?" Arnold's hand describes an arc around him. A show of recognition for them all that somehow Dr. Vox is not reacting to. How does he not see?

"Nothing, Arnold. It's all your imagination. I'll send someone to take care of you." Vox keeps up the reassurance as his finger presses a button on the underside of his desk.

Two attendants appear, put Arnold in a straitjacket, and then take him to bed.

"Why doesn't anybody listen!? Why don't the pressures stop? Where is everybody? I want my mommy... where is she... hello... somebody... please..." Arnold's voice trails off as a sedative starts its work.

A light pierces the darkness; it grows into a blinding flash. Lynne appears in a sheer gown and begins walking toward Arnold. The costumes change to very formal ballroom dress. The two begin to dance. They dance all over... to a merry-go-round and then to the outdoors. As they dance along the cliffs, Arnold is too fast and reckless. Lynne tries to keep up but slips. Arnold catches her by her dress, but it tears. She plunges to her death. Arnold's back at the sparkling pond with the bizarre mixture of colors. Once again, a campfire illuminates the water while Arnold sits warming his hands. He rubs his wrists to get the blood flowing and rolls up his sleeves. He takes a razor to his arms and cuts another coiled line into them. The red pool in the bowl bubbles as it lays in the fire.

The bubbles jostle each other violently. The bowl flips out of the fire, splattering the dark crimson soup on the ground. Each puddle shapes itself to form limbs. Limbs scattered upon the ground crawling back to the bowl, attaching themselves to its bottom and sides. The bowl now seems to have features. A face that was not noticeable before. The face is very much like Lynne's. She is looking at the leftover wood for the fire. She waddle-limps over to a branch in the pile, her legs starting to remember how they used to work. She runs her hand over the top of the stick; sticky redness hardens into an edge, becomes an axe. Lifting it over her head, her arms know the motions to use. The arc veers toward Arnold. It stops in midair. A hand has stopped it. Dominic's hand has grabbed the axe, but Lynne keeps pushing. Arnold is frozen in place. Dominic is not sure why Arnold is not reacting. He yells at him to run. Arnold just stares into the fire where the bowl was. Dominic's grip is slipping so he pushes back. The axe's trajectory changes. Now it swings back toward Lynne, whose legs grasp for the muscle memory as to how to sidestep. The blade misses, but she falls with the momentum, axe blade buried in the ground. She tries to get up, but somehow her limbs no longer know what to do. Dominic reaches down to help her. The air crackles with starlight. A flash and the night seems to form itself into the shape of a human. Holding Dominic's hand in place, the dark thing's face clarifies into Dominic's as it reaches into the void in what would be a hip and pulls out a scalpel. It turns toward Lynne. The night thing with Dominic's face falls upon Lynne with the scalpel. Pinning her to the ground, it reaches into its hip void again. Another scalpel appears, the face shifts, Arnold's now. The scalpel cuts surgical slices in the form of a coiled spiral across her pelvis. The screams echo in Dominic's ears. He is unable to move. Once done, the being gets up. Now with the long gaunt face of the shadow man from his dreams. The man looks at Dominic, smiles, then jumps at him. Dominic tries to put his arms out to stop the onslaught. Nothing but blackness engulfs him. It's in his eyes and his mouth. He feels it moving within him.

Greene and Redd watch Blackman envelope Vox and finish what they had come to do. Greene never got tired of watching Blackman work. They were an artist. Stitching fear together into a message for each individual. Stealing parts of them little by little. This was why Greene loved working with these two. The creations they fashioned, or unfashioned in many cases, were something to be admired. A piece that would not exist had only one of them taken their hand to it. Blackman reached up and opened the black door. They walked through. The door closed.

The end can now begin. The grave provides no rest.

RAWHIDE REX

RICK POLDARK

Earl stood over the pile of gore that was once a cow. Joe and Boss stood next to him. The sun breached the horizon, and it was a cool morning.

"Goddammit," was all Boss could manage. He appeared pained beyond speech.

"Damned wolf pack," said Joe, removing his filthy cap and scratching the top of his head with the visor, yawning luxuriously. "Has to be."

Boss shook his head, never taking his eyes off the bright green tag on a disembodied ear. "That girl from the university said there aren't any dens around here."

"Maybe it's one they haven't tagged."

Boss flicked his toothpick between his teeth. "Nah. Besides, wolves usually go after the calves. All the young'uns are accounted for."

Earl stroked the gray stubble on his weather-beaten face. "How many dogs have you lost?"

Boss glanced up at the lanky ranch hand. "A few."

"Security?"

Boss chuckled, but it was a hollow, bitter sound. "Found one's boots, standin' in the dirt, empty. His wife called, wonderin' why he never came home. Had to call the sheriff. This ain't good for business. No sir, not good at all."

"Who was it?" asked Joe.

"Big Ed," said Boss.

"Aw, hell, Big Ed probably had a damned heart attack out here. He weighed three hundred pounds."

Boss frowned. "Then where's the body, smart guy?"

Earl scratched the back of his neck. "Just doesn't add up."

Boss squinted. "Then there's the other one, Larry Wilkins. Somethin' spooked him real good. Most've what he said didn't make a damned lick o' sense."

"What did he say?" asked Earl.

"Something about a monster coming out of the fog. Took Big Ed. Ate the dogs."

"Monster?" Joe looked amused. "What, like a sasquatch?"

Earl elbowed him in the ribs. "Ain't no such thing as sasquatch, you damned fool. Besides, sasquatch is up in the woods, not here."

Boss shook his head. "Four cows missing. I need you two to find the carcasses and document them. Hell, return what's left if you can. At least I'll get reimbursed by the government. Earl, bring that dog of yours."

Earl winced. "I don't know if that's such a good idea."

Boss narrowed his eyes. "What do you mean?"

"I mean, I don't want Dolly getting snatched up by some fog monster."

Joe feigned confusion. "I thought you said there was no such thing as monsters, Earl."

Earl arched a bushy, gray eyebrow. "I said there wasn't no such thing as sasquatch. Not down here."

Boss put his hands on his hips. "Bring the dog. That's all there is to it." Before Earl could summon a retort, Boss strode off.

They returned to the main house, where they parked their trucks.

Joe smirked. "You ain't goin' sentimental on me, are you?"

"What?"

"I thought you said dogs were tools, like a reliable pump shotgun."

"They are," said Earl, "but I'd be depressed if I lost my old Remy."

"Rifles on this one?" asked Joe.

Earl shook his head. "This ain't a hunt. Shotguns for any close encounters."

"That works."

Earl shot him a look. "You're not going to bring that plastic space gun, are you?"

"What? It's Italian, it's polymer, and it happens to be a damned good pump."

"Looks like something out of a damned sci-fi movie."

Joe puffed his chest up. "Hell, I could drag that sombitch through mud and run it over with my truck, and it'd still go bang."

At last, they reached their trucks, parked side-by-side. Earl snickered at the sight of Joe's truck. "Italian scatterguns and Japanese trucks. You're all mixed up."

"Both are incredibly reliable," said Joe. He approached the passenger side of Earl's truck. The window was rolled down, and Dolly greeted him, licking his face. He scratched her behind the ears the way she liked. "Let's take my truck."

"No, thank you. We'll take mine. It's an American classic."

"It's a fossil, and so are you."

Earl ignored the remark. Joe grabbed his pump shotgun and ammo bag out of the bed of his truck, leaving the bolt-action rifle behind. He tossed the bag and shotgun into the bed of Earl's truck. He opened the passenger door and slid in. Earl put the truck in gear and drove out onto the range. The truck's suspension squeaked and creaked.

"Earl, this ol' fossil might be older than you." Joe reveled in Dolly's kisses on his face.

Earl looked disgusted. "You know she licks her ass with that tongue."

Joe hugged the mutt. "Aw, you're just jealous."

"You love her so much? Help make sure no harm comes to her today."

"Boss's story got you spooked, huh?"

"Well, I don't think I believe in fog monsters, but something took the cows, dogs, and maybe Big Ed."

"You think it was a person?" offered Joe.

"That looks like a fog monster?" Earl chortled. "I wish I could ask Larry Wilkins about what he saw last night."

"That man's a drunk. Probably crawled inside a bottle and never came out."

Earl scowled. "You know whose fault this is? Those damned conservationists. Should've never reintroduced wolves into this area. And to add insult to injury, they're protected. Who do you think pays for all these reimbursements? The taxpayers, that's who."

"Come on, Earl. We're all God's creatures. Even you. Besides, it's good for the ecosystem."

Earl gawked at Joe as if he had three heads. "Well, it ain't good for Boss's ecosystem, which means it ain't good for our paychecks."

Joe's eyes widened. "Earl, stop the truck."

"I see it." Earl slowed to a stop.

They exited the truck, each looking around. Earl thought better of it and reached inside the cab to grab his shotgun. "Come on," he prompted Dolly. She hopped out and sniffed the air.

Joe squatted over some blood on the grass. Dolly sniffed the bloody grass, and Earl scanned their perimeter.

Joe touched the blood with his fingertips and examined it. "It's from last night." He looked around. "But no sign of a carcass."

"Do you think it's human or bovine?" asked Earl. Dolly remained close by, ears pricked.

Joe stood up, wiping the blood off on the thighs of his blue jeans. "You mean, do I think it's Big Ed's or a cow's?"

"Yeah."

Joe shrugged. "Not sure. Did you know scientists are working on using cow blood extract for a human blood substitute? I read that in a magazine."

Earl's eyes narrowed. "You know what bothers me?"

"I don't know... everything?"

"If the cows were slaughtered way back where we were talking with Boss, how did we make it this far without seeing a carcass?"

"You mean, how did the *wolves* make it this far without leaving a carcass?"

"Exactly."

Joe sniffled, looking around. "Maybe Boss was right. Maybe it wasn't wolves."

"What the hell could've dragged four cow carcasses out here?" asked Earl.

"Somethin' big," said Joe.

Earl took a knee next to Dolly and scratched her head. He pointed at the bloody grass. She shifted her feet, excited, sniffing the blood again. "Dolly, go find it."

She picked up the trail and followed it.

Earl nodded at Joe, and they returned to the truck. Earl turned the ignition, threw the truck into gear, and followed behind Dolly. Both men were silent now, watching her and searching for any signs of the missing cows. As they drove, a fog rolled in, thick as pea soup, swallowing the dog whole.

Earl squinted. "A little late in the day for fog."

Joe grabbed Earl's arm. "Stop!"

Earl slammed on the brakes as Dolly suddenly emerged into view, circling and sniffing a carcass.

"Jesus H. Christ," gasped Earl. "Thanks, Joe."

Joe was out first. "You okay, Dolly?"

She jumped up on him and returned to the carcass, probing it with her nose.

Joe squatted on his haunches, examining the remains. "Body number one."

"Do you see a green ear tag?" asked Earl.

Joe let out a low moan.

"What is it?"

Joe stood, his face green. He looked as if he was going to vomit.

Earl looked down at the remains. "No way."

"That there's Big Ed," said Joe, through gritted teeth. He produced a hanky from his back pocket and covered his nose and mouth.

"Take a picture and toss him in the truck."

Joe took out his cell phone and took a few pictures, the flash bouncing off the fog.

"No flash," said Earl. "It won't come out."

Joe deactivated the flash and took a few more. He grabbed his work gloves out of his left back pocket and slipped them on. He knelt down in the dirt and grabbed Big Ed by the ribcage. There wasn't much left of him. "Christ, what a mess."

"Hurry," pushed Earl. "I don't like this fog."

Joe rounded the truck to the bed, holding the human remains out in front of him. "I don't see you helping with this mess."

"That's Big Ed you've got there," snapped Earl. "Show some respect." He looked down and saw an impression in the dirt. He crouched and probed it with his fingers, assessing its outline and depth. Earl cocked his head sideways.

When Joe returned, Earl had stood and backed away, his eyes darting around the ground. "Joe, come look at this."

"What is it?" When he saw Earl's expression, he looked down at the ground in front of them. "That's a big track. It's got to be a meter long."

Earl glared at him. "Really? The metric system? Do you do anything normal?"

Joe pointed up ahead. "There's another one. What kind of animal leaves tracks like that?"

Earl stepped inside the large footprint.

Amused, Joe snapped a pic with his cell. "Wait till Boss gets a load of this."

Earl's eyes widened in panic. "Where's Dolly?"

Joe looked around. "She was just here. What's with this fog? It's getting thicker."

They heard barking up ahead.

Earl placed his calloused thumb and forefinger inside his mouth and let out an ear-splitting whistle. "Dolly, come!"

Dolly's barking grew more frantic, and then it stopped.

Joe slapped the side of his thigh with his hand. "Come on, girl!"

Earl's stomach knotted. "Dolly."

"I'm sure she's okay," said Joe. "Let's get in the truck and see if we can find her. She couldn't have gone far." He looked down at the ground and scratched his head. "That's funny."

"What's funny?" snapped Earl.

"Where'd the tracks go? They were right there, weren't they?"

Earl didn't bother to look. He turned and headed toward the truck. "Let's go."

Joe turned heel and slid into the passenger side of the rusty old truck as the engine turned over.

"This is wrong," said Earl, putting the truck in gear. "This is all wrong." The little hairs on the back of his neck stood up. "I knew it was a bad idea to bring her."

"Maybe we should tell Boss to call the County in on this," said Joe. "Or the State."

"Not without Dolly. We find her first."

"You really *do* love that dog."

Earl shot him a look.

Joe chuckled. "I didn't think you loved anything."

Earl set his jaw. "I'd have traded any of my three ex-wives for a good mutt like Dolly. She's my best friend."

"Hey, what about me?"

Joe's quip went unanswered. They drove for a while, and the rock canyon came into view. Earl stopped the truck at the edge of a dirt road that led down into the canyon. They exited the truck, scanning the ground.

"I've got large drag marks over here," said Joe, touching the dirt, rubbing it between his fingertips.

Earl bent over and picked something up off the ground. It was small and bright green. He looked at it and held it up for Joe to see. "One of Boss's ear tags." He looked around. "Dolly! Here, girl!"

"The tracks lead down into the canyon," said Joe.

Earl leveled his gaze at Joe. "Maybe we should go back and get more men."

"For what? We haven't seen anything yet. What about Dolly?"

"I'm tellin' you, Joe. Something ain't right. We found Big Ed, half of him missing. We haven't found a single cow yet. Somethin' dragged them all the way out here. Anything that could do that and leave tracks like we saw I don't want no part of."

Joe frowned. "What about Boss?"

"He can find the cows his damned self."

"Earl, he'll fire us. You're not tellin' me you believe in fog monsters now, are you?"

Earl hesitated.

Joe placed hands on his hips. "Oh my God!"

Earl pointed a bony finger at Joe. "Now hold on a minute…"

A big, shit-eating grin crept across Joe's face. "You *do* believe it."

"I—I… I didn't say that exactly."

Joe shook his head. "Okay, listen. We don't even know what we're dealing with here."

"Those tracks, Joe."

"What tracks? We don't even know if we really even saw those tracks. One minute we thought they were there, and the next minute they were gone."

"You took a picture of the tracks. I was standing in one, remember?"

Joe pulled his cell phone out and toggled to the picture, but he looked disappointed and then confused.

"What is it?" Earl snatched the phone out of Joe's hand and looked at the screen. "There I am… but where's the track?" He looked up at Joe. "All I see is a glob of light at my feet. I told you to turn the damned flash off in this fog."

"Earl, listen. If there really was something that big—and it'd have to be about fifteen feet or so tall…"

"Thank you for using the Imperial system of measurement."

Joe rolled his eyes, "… we'd see something like that coming a mile away, right?"

Earl shrugged. "I suppose so."

"So, if we see something that big coming at us, we hop in the truck and get the hell out of Dodge. Like you said before, this ain't no hunt."

"Yeah, I guess..."

"In the meantime, let's see if we can photographically document Boss's losses, collect our pay, and turn what's left of Big Ed over to the sheriff. We'll be heroes, we'll be paid, and you'll have your dog back. Happy ending for everyone."

Earl nodded, looking dubious. They both got back in the truck, and Earl drove them along the path descending into the rock canyon.

"Maybe Larry Wilkins was right," said Earl, driving slowly and cautiously through the soupy fog, searching for cow carcasses.

"He's crazy."

"We both saw those tracks. Are we crazy too?"

"One of us might be," Joe muttered.

"What did you say?"

"You heard me. Slow down. I see something on the ground."

"I go any slower, and I'll be going backward." Earl strained his eyes. "I can't see shit in this fog."

"Stop the truck."

Joe hopped out of the truck before Earl had even come to a complete stop. This time he grabbed his shotgun out of the truck bed and ran ahead. Earl put the truck in park as he saw Joe standing over a heap in the road. He grabbed his shotgun and got out, leaving the truck running.

Joe had laid his shotgun on the ground at his feet and snapped pics on his phone. "It's a carcass. Mostly bones."

Earl looked around. The canyon looked ethereal bathed in mist. It was quiet and still and lonely. He crouched next to the remains and ran his fingertips along the broken edges of what was left of a bovine ribcage. "These bones were snapped. Wasn't no wolves that done this."

"I don't care if it was Jack the Ripper," said Joe, snapping more pics. "As long as we can document it and get paid."

Earl pointed to somewhere ahead of them. "Well, we're in luck. I think I see another one."

Joe winked. "See, our luck is improving by the minute."

Earl waded through the haze, stopping in front of a heap of crushed bones picked clean. He looked ahead, and there was yet another. They seemed to materialize out of the mist, forming a trail. "Whatever took these cows must've did most of the eating here. Quick, snap a pic of these bones. There's more."

"You think it's all the missing cows?" Now Joe looked spooked. "Jesus, Earl. Let's get this done and get the hell out of here."

One by one, they accounted for all the missing cows. They even discovered the partial remains of what must've been Boss's dogs. At least Earl hoped they were *only* Boss's dogs. Poor Dolly. Bless her heart, wherever she was.

Another bunch of shapes emerged in the heavy mist as they walked, slowly revealing themselves. Earl pointed. "Look, Joe." Earl was shoulder-to-shoulder with Joe, careful to stay close to his friend. "Those are tents. Two large ones."

"What are those tents doing down here?" Joe kicked something. He looked down and picked it up, holding it out in front of him. It was a square yellow marker of some kind. "What's this?"

Earl nodded. "This here is that archaeological dig Boss was talkin' about. The university found some dinosaur bones."

Joe frowned at Earl. "Paleontological."

"That's what I said."

"No, you said…" Joe thought twice about it and waved a dismissive hand. "Never mind."

"Where do you reckon everyone is?" asked Earl. "The place looks deserted."

Joe cried out in excitement, causing Earl's old heart to skip a beat, and dashed over to the canyon wall. "Earl, come here! Look!"

Earl followed the silhouette until Joe became fully visible again. "Ho-ly shit." His young friend stood in front of bones embedded in the rock canyon wall. They were large, and Earl thought he made out a skull with foot-long, razor-sharp teeth.

"I think it's a T. rex, Earl!" Joe looked like a kid on Christmas morning. He leaned his shotgun against the rock wall and took out his phone. He started taking pics.

"Yeah, well, Boss ain't gonna get paid for *those* bones," said Earl. His eyes darted around the campsite and the canyon. "Let's wrap this up and get out of here."

As if in answer, a low, deep-throated growl emanated from somewhere in the fog, closer than Earl would've liked. A chill shot down his spine that had nothing to do with the brisk morning air. "Joe, grab your gun."

The ground shook once, then twice, then again.

"What is that?" asked Joe, snatching up his shotgun. "I can't see a thing." He flipped off the safety in front of the trigger. He didn't have to rack the slide because he already had a shell loaded in the chamber. "Earthquake?"

Earl's eyes bugged out of his head. "Footsteps. Big 'uns."

Two eyes glowing like hot coals cut through the murk. They faced the parked truck, and then they turned on Joe and Earl. A massive figure lumbered out of the mist, translucent, as if it was made of smoke. It hunched over, angling its massive jaws straight ahead of it. It ambled on muscular legs ending in clawed feet big enough to make the tracks Joe and Earl swore they saw a-ways back. Small arms dangled in front of its body, and a thick tail swept behind it.

"Earl?"

"Yes, Joe."

"I think I see a T. rex, but that's impossible."

"No, I see it, too."

For a moment, the cowpokes and the thunder lizard eyed each other. The T. rex glared at them, its fierce eyes sunken under sharp cranial ridges, lending it a sinister look. It emitted a low sound that made Earl's bones vibrate and sent his mind into a panic. Suddenly, the massive dinosaur lunged at them. Joe and Earl each ran in opposite directions as the towering beast collided with the skeleton embedded in the rock wall, disapparating.

Joe trained his shotgun at the skeleton. "Did you see that?"

Earl swallowed hard, adrenaline coursing through his body. "I seen it, but I don't believe it."

"It wasn't real," said Joe, creeping closer to the T. rex skeleton.

"It sure looked real to me," croaked Earl. "Get back before you get yourself killed."

A growl came from behind them, opposite the canyon wall. Both men wheeled around to find the giant lizard standing behind them. It stood straight up, opened its jaws, and let out a mighty roar that sounded like a cross between a freight train and a twister up close.

"Get to the truck!" cried Earl, his ears ringing. He fired double aught buck at the lizard, but he saw the pellets and wad pass right through it as if it were merely a projection cast onto the fog. He racked the slide and fired again with the same result. It lurched forward, head lowered, mouth open. Earl pumped his old legs as fast as they could carry him, ducking as jaws snapped closed where his head was but a second ago. He dashed in the direction of where he left the truck, and at last, it appeared out of the murk. He saw Joe reach the truck first.

With the dinosaur's massive stride, Earl knew he didn't stand a chance in a straight run. He juked left as sharp teeth gnashed to his right.

Joe had already slid into the driver seat of the truck, rolled up his window, and was gesticulating wildly for Earl to hurry up. Earl made it to the passenger side door, but because of his momentum, he overshot. Cursing himself, he skidded in the dirt and climbed headfirst into the truck bed. "Punch it, Joe!"

The T. rex stomped toward the truck, building speed. With Earl's legs still dangling in the air, Joe threw the truck in reverse and floored it. The truck's tires spun, kicking up dust before they found traction. This was enough time for the massive beast to catch the truck, even as it retreated. The tyrannosaur grabbed the hood with its clawed, diminutive arms and leaned forward, snapping its jaws at Earl.

Earl threw himself on his back, kicking away from the back of the cab, narrowly avoiding being snatched up but finding himself next to Big Ed's sorry carcass. He racked the slide of his old Remy and fired at the beast as the truck took off. Earl saw the creature still clutching the dented hood of his truck as they pulled away.

"Hold on, Earl!" Joe spun the wheel, causing the truck to turn abruptly, and threw the truck into drive. Earl bounced off the inside flank of the bed and then slid into the tailgate as the truck sped forward. He gasped in terror as the T. rex dropped the truck hood and took off in full pursuit.

An older model built more for utility than speed, the truck struggled as the ghastly predator gained on it. Earl felt naked out in the open, and his scattergun didn't appear to do anything helpful. The T. rex snapped at the truck bed, catching the tailgate in its teeth and ripping it clear off. This caused the truck to buckle. When the tailgate tore off, the truck pitched forward, causing Earl to slide toward the open back and certain death. He threw his arms and legs out, dropping his shotgun, and caught the sides of the truck bed. He barely remained inside, but his scattergun and the remains of Big Ed slid out into the dirt, trampled under clawed feet.

"Aw hell." Earl was almost as upset about losing the Remy as nearly being trampled or eaten.

The truck fishtailed in the dirt as Joe took a turn at high speed, but the T. rex flickered and glitched past it, changing direction with ease. "Hold on!" cried Joe from inside the cab as the ground rose under the truck.

Earl hung on for dear life as he slid around the back of the truck bed on his back. The beast, made of mist and shadow, flickered as it pumped its muscular legs, appearing and vanishing closer and closer.

Joe jerked his head around, praying his buddy was all right. His skin went cold and his mouth bone dry when he saw the empty truck bed covered in what must've been Earl's blood. As if in confirmation of his worst fears, a booming roar erupted from the fog behind him. It appeared Earl had joined Dolly. "Shit! Dammit, Earl."

Joe looked at the rearview mirror, waiting for the massive specter to emerge as he gunned the engine, driving faster than his headlights. There was only one thing to do, and that was to return to the ranch and explain to Boss what had happened. What was he going to tell Boss exactly? That his cattle, security guard, and now one of his best ranch hands and his dog had been eaten by the ghost of a damned T. rex?

The fog was thick as Earl's gumbo that reminded Joe of his childhood in Louisiana. He remembered when he believed there was a monster that had taken residence in his closet, resulting in countless sleepless nights. He also remembered what his father told him. 'Joe, there ain't nothin' in the dark except what your mind puts there.' Had he gone bonkers? Was this spectral dinosaur real, or was it a figment of his imagination? Was he going to wake up in his bed in a cold sweat, and Earl would still be alive, berating him for his taste in trucks and guns like usual?

Something emerged in the thick mist, but it wasn't what he expected. He hit the brakes, bringing the truck to a stop. Two shadows drifted toward the truck, one smaller than the other, both too small to be the T. rex. Joe squinted to try and make out what was coming his way. His mind reeled as it processed what he saw in the headlights.

Earl stood in front of the truck, Dolly by his side, but they looked different. Their images flickered on the fog like projections. Joe sat there, a mess of conflicting emotions. That little voice in the back of his mind telling him to run grew louder as his pulse pounded in his ears. His breath materialized in a fleeting cloud in front of him like it did on a frigid winter day, only it was late September. Something was very wrong about all this.

Earl extended his right arm and pointed his long, bony index finger at Joe. After a heartbeat, Joe realized that Earl was pointing behind the truck. He checked the rearview mirror and saw it. The spectral T. rex stood behind the truck, hunched over, looking into the back of the truck cab.

Before Joe could hit the gas, the T. rex rolled the truck upside down. Having neglected to fasten his seatbelt, Joe rolled around inside until he lay on the ceiling of the cab. With the groaning of metal, the truck cabin began to compress under great pressure. He managed to crawl out of the open passenger window as glass exploded all around him.

Joe found himself facedown in the dirt. The ground shook with heavy footfalls. He scurried along the earth on all fours until he pushed himself to standing, and then he ran. He ran as fast as his legs would carry him. He ran through the fog, never daring to look over his shoulder.

Boss stood in the moonlight behind the ranch house regarding Joe with a pained expression, the kind he wore when his back was killing him. Behind him, the windows were all dark except the kitchen, where Boss's wife made a pot of tea, shaking her head at the late call in disapproval. "Let me get this straight. You walked all the way back from the rock canyon, woke me and the missus up — and you know how Betsy gets when she don't get her beauty sleep — dragged me out into the cold, foggy night because the ghost of a goddanged T. rex ate Earl, Big Ed, *and* my cattle?"

Joe nodded. "That's right, Boss. Crazy as it sounds, it's the truth."

Boss narrowed his eyes. "You been drinkin', boy? I told you to lay off the sauce."

"It's the truth, Boss. I swear."

"*And,* the only documentation you have of this spectral thunder lizard is a pic of a huge footprint that didn't come out because it's a ghost footprint?"

"Well, Boss, I… I actually did get some pics."

Boss placed his hands on his hips. "Of the ghost T. rex?"

"Yessir."

"Oh, this I've got to see."

Joe produced his cell phone and opened an image. Boss went to snatch the phone, but Joe held it up to Boss's face so he could view it.

Boss squinted. He produced his reading glasses from his robe pocket and slipped them on. For a moment, he was silent, examining the image. "That's it? I see a tall figure and some eyes. It's a damned bear, not a T. Rex, son."

Joe swiped right, revealing the next photo. Boss leaned in, studying it. He shot Joe a quizzical look, and Joe swiped right one last time. Boss's mouth hung open like he was catching flies. "That's... not a bear."

Joe's eyes lit up. "That's what I'm saying."

Boss staggered on his feet, overcome. Joe reached out to steady him, but Boss yanked his arm away, defiant. "This is what killed my cattle?"

Joe nodded. "And Earl and Big Ed."

"Send me those pictures. We're definitely going to have to bring the university in on this. The state, too. I'm gonna get reimbursed."

Joe pressed a few buttons and slipped his cell back into his pocket. "Sent. I'm exhausted, Boss. I'm gonna go."

"Nice work. Now go get some rest."

Joe nodded, turned, and walked away. The fog swallowed him whole.

"Oh, I'm sorry about Earl," said Boss as an afterthought, but Joe was gone. Shivering, Boss went back inside, joining his wife in the kitchen. She sat at the table, sipping her tea. A second mug sat on the table next to her. Boss lowered himself into a wooden chair, which creaked almost as much as his old joints. "Well, we found out what's been eating the cattle."

"Oh, really?" said Betsy. "Who called you at this ungodly hour?"

"Joe walked all the way back from the rock canyon. You'll never believe what he found out there... a damned ghost... of a T. rex, no less."

His wife arched an eyebrow. "That boy been drinkin' again?"

Boss frowned and shook his head. "I didn't believe it neither. It may not, in fact, be the ghost of a damned T. rex, but that boy found something out there that's been eating my cattle, and it's damned big. It ate Big Ed and Earl, too."

Betsy grimaced. "That's terrible."

"The good news is, he sent me pictures." Boss pulled his cell phone out of his other pocket. "I may get reimbursed after all." Wearing a triumphant grin, he opened Joe's text and then the attached pics. "Wait a minute." He pulled his reading glasses on again and squinted at his phone's screen, crinkling his nose. He swiped right, then left, and then right again.

Betsy leaned in for a gander. "What is it?"

Boss scratched his head. "The pictures... there's something wrong... there's nothing there. That damned moron! I'm gonna wring his neck. He just told me..." He stood up. "Maybe I can still catch him."

Betsy tilted her head. "Catch who?"

"Joe! Who do you think I was talking to outside?"

"I didn't see Joe," said Betsy.

"What do you mean? You were looking at us through the kitchen window!"

Betsy pursed her lips. "Archibald Tiberius Abernathy, you've been wearing your hatband too tight. All I saw was you ranting and raving outside, by your lonesome, like a damned fool. I think the pressure's finally gotten to you."

Boss stamped his foot. "Now listen, woman..."

Betsy rose, pointing her finger at his chest. "No, you listen, mister. I'm going to bed. I suggest you do the same." Before he could answer back, she turned and walked away, switching off the light on her way out, leaving Boss alone in the dark to wrestle with his confusion.

A distant roar rolled over the plains.

ABOUT THE AUTHORS

Marc L. Abbott is the author of the YA novel *The Hooky Party* and the children's book *Etienne and the Stardust Express*. He is the co-author, with Steven Van Patten, of *Hell at Brooklyn Tea* and *Hell at the Way Station*, winner of two African American Literary Awards. His horror short stories are featured in the anthologies *Hells Heart*, *Hells Mall*, and the Bram Stoker Award®-nominated horror anthologies *Under Twin Suns: Alternate Histories of the Yellow Sign* and *A New York State of Fright*. He is the writer and director of the short horror films *SNAP* and *Being Followed* and was twice nominated for best actor for his role in the science fiction film, *Impervia*, and won a best actor award for his role in the film *Identity Check*. A 2015 Moth Story Slam and Grand Slam Storyteller winner, he's the writer and performer of the storytelling solo shows *Love African American Style* and *Of Cats and Men: A Storytellers Journey*. He is the host of the monthly storytelling show Maaan, You've Got to Hear This! in Bushwick, Brooklyn. In addition to being an active member of the HWA New York Chapter, Gamma Xi Phi Fraternity, and co-host of the Beef, Wine and Shenanigans podcast, he also heads the Beyond the Tropes reading series with the Center of Fiction in Brooklyn, NY. Find out more about him at www.whoismarclabbott.com.

Meghan Arcuri is a Bram Stoker Award®-nominated author. Her work can be found in various anthologies, including *Borderlands 7* (Borderlands Press), *Madhouse* (Dark Regions Press), *Chiral Mad*, and *Chiral Mad 3* (Written Backwards). She is currently the Vice President of the Horror Writers Association. Prior to writing, she taught high school math, having earned her B.A. from Colgate University with a double major in mathematics and English and her masters from Rensselaer Polytechnic Institute. She lives with her family in New York's Hudson Valley. Please visit her at meghanarcuri.com, facebook.com/meg.arcuri, or on Twitter, @MeghanArcuri.

Oliver Baer was the editor of *Cthulhu Sex Magazine* and Two Backed Books. His epistolary novel, *Letters to the Editor of Cthulhu Sex Magazine*, was published in October 2019. His essays have been on blogs as well as books. His poetry has appeared in *Goodreads Best Poems 2020*, *Paper Teller Diorama*, *Hell's Mall: Sinister Shops, Cursed Items and Maddening Crowds*, *Birds Fall Silent in the Mechanical Sea*, *Cthulhu Sex Magazine*, *Horror Between the Sheets*, *Horror Writers Association Poetry Showcase, Vol. II*, and other publications. His book of poetry and photographs, *Baer Soul*, came out in 2011. His CD of poetry set to music, *Gathering Souls*, which came out in 2013, spawned the show "A Conclave of Baer." Lucky Witch and the Righteous Ghost released an EP, *Dreams in the Witch House*, inspired by HP Lovecraft and Oliver's poems. He has appeared as an indescribable horror from the depths, sometimes with a light saber. He is visible using the virtual spectrum of social media by following him on Twitter https://twitter.com/obaer or Facebook https://www.facebook.com/obaer3. Much of his work can be found at http://tentacularity.wordpress.com

Alp Beck lives in New York City. She writes in all genres but prefers horror. Her essays have been featured in the *New York Times* and the *New York Blade*. She is a big fan of the short story format and believes "only when you master the art of the short story, are you ready to tackle novels." Therefore, she will continue to write in the format until "she gets it right." You can find her story, "To Thine Self Be True," in *Hell's Grannies: Kickass Tales of the Crone*, "Deadmall," in the anthology, *Hell's Mall* (Lafcadio Press), and "Heels," in *A New York State of Fright* (Hippocampus Press).

Allan Burd is a science fiction author hailing from Long Island, New York. He loves penning exciting stories about the supernatural and aliens. He also occasionally dabbles in children's books and short stories. His first novel, *The Roswell Protocols*, about a second UFO that crashed at Roswell, New Mexico, published in 2009, got the ball rolling. He's been writing ever since and published the YA novel *Hellion* in 2020. For more information visit www.allanburd.com

Randee Dawn is an author, journalist, and lucky denizen of Brooklyn. Her first novel, the humorous pop-culture fantasy *Tune in*

Tomorrow, will be published in 2022 (Solaris). Her short fiction has appeared in publications and podcasts including *3AM Magazine*, *Well-Told Tales*, *Where We May Wag*, *Children of a Different Sky*, *Magic for Beginners*, *Dim Shores Presents*, *Another World: Stories of Portal Fantasy*, *Dim Shores*, *Horror for the Throne*, and *Stories We Tell After Midnight 3*. She has a short collection of dark speculative fiction short stories, *Home for the Holidays*, and co-authored *The Law & Order: SVU Unofficial Companion*. She co-edited the speculative fiction anthology of "what if" stories about The Beatles, *Across the Universe: Tales of Alternative Beatles*. When not making stuff up, Randee publishes entertainment profiles, reviews, and think pieces regularly in outlets including *Variety*, *The Los Angeles Times*, Today.com, and *Emmy Magazine*, and writes trivia for BigBrain. She can be found at RandeeDawn.com and @RandeeDawn (on Twitter).

Trevor Firetog writes out of Long Island, New York. He is the author of the horror-thriller novella, *Usual Monsters*. His short fiction has appeared in various magazines and anthologies. Aside from writing, Trevor collects and restores vintage typewriters. When he's not reading on the beaches of LI, or scavenging used bookstores, he's usually holed up in his office, working on his next project. Find him on Twitter and Instagram @TrevorFiretog.

John P. Collins has been telling stories since he was a child. He loves the feeling of uncomfortable creepiness that comes from dark basements and staring at abandoned houses. When not watching horror films or reading 80's splatterpunk, he's haunting used book stores.

Caroline Flarity is a freelance writer living in New York City. Her fascination with fringe topics and scary movies led her to begin her writing journey penning creepy screenplays. Her debut novel *The Ghost Hunter's Daughter* began its life as a feature script, placing in the finals of the StoryPros Awards and as a semifinalist in Slamdance Film Festival's writing competition. *The Ghost Hunter's Daughter* was named a "Best YA of 2019" listee by Ginger Nuts of Horror and won Crossroad Reviews' 2019 Indie Book Award. Caroline is a proud member of the Horror Writers Association.

Patrick Freivald is the four-time Bram Stoker Award-nominated author of nine novels, including *Black Tide, Jade Sky, Special Dead,* and *Twice Shy,* and dozens of short stories, many of which are collected in *In the Garden of the Rusting Gods*. A physics teacher and beekeeper, he lives in Western New York with his wife, cats, parrots, dogs, and millions of stinging insects.

Teel James Glenn's poetry and short stories have been printed in over two hundred magazines including *Weird Tales, Mystery Weekly, Pulp Adventures, Space & Time, Mad, Cirsova, Silverblade,* and *Sherlock Holmes Mystery.* His novel *A Cowboy in Carpathia: A Bob Howard Adventure* won best novel 2021 in the Pulp Factory Award. He is also the winner of the 2012 Pulp Ark Award for Best Author. His website is: TheUrbanSwashbuckler.com He can be found on Facebook as Teeljamesglenn, and Twitter, @teeljamesglenn.

Amy Grech has sold more than 100 stories and poems to various anthologies and magazines including: *A New York State of Fright, Apex Magazine, Dead Harvest, Flashes of Hope, Gorefest, Hell's Heart, Hells Highway, Hell's Mall, Needle Magazine, Punk Noir Magazine, Scare You To Sleep, Tales from the Canyons of the Damned, Tales from The Lake Vol. 3, The One That Got Away, Thriller Magazine,* and many others. She has a poem forthcoming in the *Under Her Skin* anthology. Amy is an Active Member of the Horror Writers Association and the International Thriller Writers who lives in New York. You can connect with her on Twitter: @amy_grech or visit her website: https://www.crimsonscreams.com.

April Grey's short stories are collected in *The Fairy Cake Bakeshop* and in *I'll Love You Forever.* She is also the author of urban fantasy novels *Finding Perdita, Chasing the Trickster,* and its sequel, *St. Nick's Favor.* She edited the anthologies: *Hell's Heart: Tales of Love Run Amok; Hell's Bells: Wicked Tunes, Mad Musicians and Cursed Instruments; Hell's Garden: Mad, Bad and Ghostly Gardeners, Hell's Grannies: Kickass Tales of the Crone* and last year's, *Hell's Kitties and Other Beastly Beasts.* She is a co-editor on the Bram Stoker Award®-nominated *A New York State of Fright.* She and her family live in Hell's Kitchen, NYC in a building next to a bedeviled garden. Gremlins, sprites, or pixies, something mischievous, lurks therein. Someday she'll find out.

Jonathan Lees has spent over a decade creating strategies and video series for outlets ranging from Complex Media to TIDAL and twenty years championing filmmakers through his programming work with the New York Underground Film Festival, Anthology Film Archives, TromaDance, and now, Final Frame hosted by StokerCon™. His first published story, "The Ritual Remains," debuted in the NECON anthology, *Now I Lay Me Down To Sleep*, and he is looking forward to ruining your dreams for years to come.

Gordon Linzner is founder and former editor of *Space and Time Magazine*, and author of three published novels and scores of short stories in *Fantasy & Science Fiction*, *Twilight Zone*, *Sherlock Holmes Mystery Magazine*, and numerous other magazines and anthologies. He is a member of the Horror Writers Association and a lifetime member of the Science Fiction & Fantasy Writers of America.

Robert Masterson is an English Professor at CUNY-BMCC in Manhattan. His publication record stretches back to the 1970s. His first real job while still in high school in Los Alamos, New Mexico, was in a print shop and, in some form or another, he has worked in the literary arts as a printer, writer, editor, teacher, and investigative reporter ever since. Masterson's work as a student, a professor, and a reporter has taken him all over the United States, Japan (to seek out and interview writers and artists who'd survived the atomic bombing in 1945), China (to study Chinese and work as an English Instructor at Shaanxi Normal University, Xi'an, Shaanxi, PRC), Ukraine (for a visit to the Chernobyl reactor and a six-week tour of pediatric hospitals to observe the long-term health effects of catastrophic radiation exposure), to India (for literary conferences and presentations), and inside maximum security penal institutions in Colorado, New Mexico, and New York to lead creative writing workshops. He is the author of *Trial by Water*, *Garnish Trouble*, and *Artificial Rats & Electric Cats*.

Robert P. Ottone is an author, teacher, and cigar enthusiast from East Islip, NY. He delights in the creepy. He can be found online at SpookyHousePress.com, or on Twitter & Instagram (@RobertOttone). His collections *Her Infernal Name & Other Nightmares* and *People: A Horror Anthology about Love, Loss, Life & Things That Go Bump in the Night* are available now wherever books are sold.

Rick Poldark is a member of the Horror Writers Association and the Science Fiction & Fantasy Writers of America. He writes science fiction, fantasy, and horror. He is an amateur archer, loves to travel, brews his own ale, and loves to play D&D whenever possible.

Lou Rera writes horror, supernatural crime, and subjects that delve into the darker side of humanity. He is the author of *Sign*, a supernatural thriller of deception and murder. His collection titled, *Awake: Tales of Terror*, features 13 stories of horror, supernatural crime, and murder. He is a professional designer, media producer, writer, and musician. He is an experienced music producer, working in studios in Western New York and Los Angeles. He is a member of the Horror Writers Association, New York Chapter, Just Buffalo Literary Center, and IMDB. His short stories have appeared in the Canadian anthologies, *Group Hex*, Vol 1 and Vol 2. His collection of flash fiction, *There are no doors on a cocoon*, is a caustic look at the seedier side of existence. His flash fiction has won awards in *Art Voice Magazine*. His fiction has been published in *Queen City Flash, The Writer's Eye, Twisted Dreams*, and *The Flash Fiction Magazine*. Lou writes occasional reviews for Horror Novel Reviews. Lou holds an M.A.H. in Information Design from the University at Buffalo. He lives in New York State with his wife MaryRuth, a personal chef, and their wire-hair fox terrier.

Steven Van Patten is the author of the celebrated Brookwater's Curse vampire trilogy, and the Killer Genius serial killer series. He's also co-author of *Hell at The Way Station*, which won Best Anthology and Best in Science Fiction at the 2019 African-American Literary Awards. Numerous short stories have been published in over a dozen anthologies and he's a contributing writer/consultant for the YouTube channel Extra History as well as the Viral Vignettes series. He's a member of the New York Chapter of the Horror Writer's Association, the Director's Guild of America, and professional arts fraternity Gamma Xi Phi Incorporated. He's also the publisher of *Growth: The Basics of Our Gardens*, a how-to guide for anyone interested in growing medicinal marijuana. A fourth of the Brookwater's Curse series and a final Killer Genius installment are in the works now that *Hell at Brooklyn Tea* dropped in early 2021. His website is www.laughingblackvampire.com. When he is not writing scary or salacious tales, Steven can be found stage managing a plethora of TV shows and events across the tri-state area.

ABOUT THE EDITORS

James Chambers received the Bram Stoker Award® for the graphic novel, *Kolchak the Night Stalker: The Forgotten Lore of Edgar Allan Poe* and is a four-time Bram Stoker Award nominee. He is the author of the collections *On the Night Border; On the Hierophant Road*, which received a starred review from *Booklist*, which called it "satisfyingly unsettling, with tones ranging from existential terror to an uneasy sense of awe"; and *The Engines of Sacrifice*, described as "chillingly evocative" in a starred review by *Publisher's Weekly*. He has written several novellas, such as the dark urban fantasy novella, *Three Chords of Chaos* and *Kolchak and the Night Stalkers: The Faceless God*. He edited the Bram Stoker Award-nominated anthology, *Under Twin Suns: Alternate Histories of the Yellow Sign* and co-edited the Bram Stoker Award-nominated anthology, *A New York State of Fright*. His website is: www.jameschambersonline.com.

Carol Gyzander was nominated for the Bram Stoker Award® for Superior Achievement in Short Fiction for her story, "The Yellow Crown," which appeared in the Bram Stoker Award-nominated anthology, *Under Twin Suns: Alternate Histories of the Yellow Sign*, from Hippocampus Press. She writes and edits horror, dark fiction, and science fiction. Her stories are in over a dozen anthologies, including a dark fantasy story, "Deal with the Devil," in the alternative Beatles anthology, *Across the Universe: Tales of Alternative Beatles*, edited by Michael Ventrella and Randee Dawn. She's edited four anthologies from Writerpunk Press of punk stories inspired by classics, including Edgar Allan Poe and classic horror tales. Find her at www.CarolGyzander.com or on Twitter @CarolGyzander.

ABOUT THE ARTISTS

Lynne Hansen (cover) is a horror artist who specializes in book covers. She loves creating art that tells a story and that helps connect publishers, authors and readers. Her art has appeared on the cover of the legendary *Weird Tales Magazine*, and her clients include Cemetery Dance Publications, Thunderstorm Books and Raw Dog Screaming Press. She has illustrated works by New York Times bestselling authors including Jonathan Maberry, George Romero, and Christopher Golden. Her art has been commissioned and collected throughout the United States and overseas. For more information, visit LynneHansenArt.com.

Jason Whitley (interior) is the illustrator and co-creator of *The Midnight Hour*. Jason's work as a newspaper illustrator has appeared across the country and won many awards. His portrait of civil rights leader Charlotte Hawkins Brown is in the Charlotte Hawkins Brown Museum.

With writer Scott Eckelaert, he co-created and illustrated the classic comic-strip, *Sea Urchins*, which has been collected into four volumes. The fourth volume, *So Long, Frozen Ocean* is forthcoming. Jason leads a Hermes and Telly Award-winning multimedia team of five in North Carolina. He's working on a crime-noir graphic novel with no set release date and looking forward to the complete *The Midnight Hour* collection from eSpec Books in 2023.

SOUL SUPPORTERS

ABD
Agnomaly
Amy Grech
Angela Yuriko Smith
Anna Taborska
Annelise Pichardo
Anonymous Reader
April Grey
Arthur Kinsman
Aven Lumi
Avis Crane
Becky Wood
Bill Ginger
Brian W. Matthews
Carl W Bishop
Carlos Valcarcel
Carol Mammano
Chandler Klang Smith
Charles E. Wood
Cheri Kannarr
Chris Ryan
Christopher J. Burke
Cori Paige
Craig Hackl
Curtis Steinhour
Dale A. Russell
Damon Griffin
Dan Dalal
Danielle Ackley-McPhail
David Swisher
Diane Raimonde
Drew Biehl
Drew Cucuzza

Dusk Zer0
Ef Deal
Fiona A. Elder
Frieda Schultz
Gail trotter
Gary Phillips
Giusy Rippa
Hank Blumenthal
Howard Blakeslee
Isaac 'Will It Work' Dansicker
J.R. Murdock
Janet Lees
Janito V. F. Filho
Jeff
Jenn Whitworth
Jennifer L. Pierce
Jessica Sarchet
John L. French
Jonathan Lees
Jp
Karen M
Karl Markovich
Kierin Fox
Kirk Larson
KJSP
L. E. Daniels
L.E. Custodio
Lakota Lara
Lara Frater
Lark Cunningham
Laurel Anne Hill
Laurie Jones
Lisa Kruse

Lisa Morton
Liz
Lorraine J. Anderson
Lou Rera
Lynne Hansen
Mallory N Pate
Mandi
Marc "mad" W.
Marc L Abbott
Maria T
Martha Huggins
Maya G Goldstein
Meghan Arcuri
Michele Clemente
Michele Kutner
Nathan Toby
Nicholas Diak
Nicholas Stephenson
Rachel & Jim Larson
Rachel Brune

Randee Dawn
Rebecca E. Hoffman
Reckless Pantalones
Robert Claney
Robert P. Ottone
Sarah
Sasquatch N
Scott Schaper
Scout McLoud
Sherry
Steph Parker
Stephen Ballentine
Steven Van Patten
Tasha Turner
The Creative Fund by BackerKit
Thomas Alan Horne
Timothy DuBois
Venessa Giunta
Victoria Navarra
WD Stancil

CPSIA information can be obtained
at www.ICGtesting.com
Printed in the USA
BVHW091944050422
633362BV00001B/20